I0724199

THE MADNESS OF MOLL DYER

HEART *of* ST. MARY'S COUNTY

BOOK FOUR

CHRISTINE TRENT

In Loving Memory of

Lynn Joyce Buonviri
June 21, 1946—May 2, 2024
Author of *Moll Dyer and Other Witch Tales of
Southern Maryland*

The Madness of Youth

Devon, England

CHAPTER 1

Kenn, Devon,
February 1634

"WELL, NOW, LIZZY, isn't she as pretty as a primrose? Just as bald as I am, but those eyes!" The elderly man reached into the rough-hewn wood cradle and gently tapped the nose of its occupant. "Green like emeralds already. Such an unusual babe. What will your hair be, I wonder?"

The woman lying on a pallet next to the cradle rose up to one elbow. "Hard to know whether she'll take after her father's side or mine, Callum. William was certain she'd be a boy, wasn't he, so when he says she'll be fair-haired to go with her deep eyes, it's a mite hard to trust it." She sat up completely, her own fair hair tousled.

Callum laughed his usual low rumble. "Well now, your Thomas is middling dark, then Agnes and Dorothy following him reflect their mother's beauty with their fair skin and blue eyes. My guess is that this wee one and her green orbs will finally take on her Irish ancestors and show you hair of fire. Like mine once was." He patted the side of his head.

He looked back down at the infant girl, who lay nestled in cloths and blankets that had been handed down from her own siblings and before. "Little

Mary, little Moll," he sang softly in his gravelly voice. "Precious as a little doll."

Elizabeth Dyer lumbered up to her feet. Callum refrained from observing aloud that it was apparent she wasn't recovering as quickly from this childbirth as she had the previous three. He hoped his daughter-in-law would fare well through any future childbirths. His son had quickened Elizabeth four times in nine years, and she was still relatively young and strong, so there would no doubt be more.

Not that Callum minded having the little ones around. Gave him a sense of purpose, they did, what with him living on William's charity these days. Callum was glad to live under a roof—no matter how leaky and in need of re-thatching—but it didn't do a man's soul any favors to be beholden to his son.

Best to forget the past, though. Dwelling on it wouldn't bring Fiona back. It wouldn't rebuild their cottage that had been burned down in county Roscommon by Protestant colonizers, authorized by the crown to replace Catholic landowners with those so-called "reformers."

Dwelling on the past also wouldn't ease the pain of fleeing to his son in Devon for whatever it was that passed for peace in England.

No, it was the present day that required his full attention. And the future, which included this precious little *cailin* and her two sisters and brother.

As if reading their grandfather's thoughts, three children came bursting into the cottage's door, each carrying a dead rabbit by its ears. Even Dorothy, just two years old, had a young hare dangling from her tiny fist.

"Shut the door, you imps!" Elizabeth exclaimed.

"Is it not bitter enough in here without you leaving the door hanging open?"

Back home, in County Donegal, Callum's home had several windows with glass panes in them. Here, though, there wasn't enough money for that. This cottage had two window openings with patched-together clothing forming a covering for the openings. Now, in the winter, the holes were stuffed with bags of straw, which prevented most light from getting in and provided little in the way of protection from the cold.

Spotting Callum, Thomas dashed over, ignoring his mother. "Granda, look, we have dinner." The boy held up his prize. "Agnes and Dorothy each found one, but I had to get the rabbits out of their hiding places."

The boy's expression told Callum that naturally the silly girls required assistance from their older brother.

"The ground must have been nearly frozen, eh?" Callum asked.

Thomas nodded.

"Well done, then, digging them out of their warren."

Callum smiled at the way Thomas beamed from the praise.

A flash of ebony fur streaked into the cottage at that moment, running up to Dorothy and snatching her baby hare with a menacing snarl and a strike of the paw. Seconds later, both thief and hare were gone.

"Granda, a black cat!" Thomas said. Callum's grandson remained stock still, seemingly terrorized by an animal no one had ever seen prowling about before.

At the same time, Dorothy started crying, holding up her now empty hand.

This would not do. This would not do at all.

"Now, Thomas, we must be men when we see signs of bad luck." The boy must not be allowed to be frightened. "Make your mam proud by showing her your hare." He nodded toward Lizzy, which directed all three children's attention to her.

Thomas nodded and led his siblings away.

While the other children chattered noisily to their mother, Callum looked down into the cradle again at the child, whose gaze seemed to be absorbing everything her grandfather did.

The old man was disquieted by the unnerving omens of both the child's unusual looks and the cat's ominous materialization from nowhere.

But little Moll had already invaded his heart, flooding him with an overwhelming affection. He wasn't about to allow anything to intimidate or menace this cherished new member of the Dyer home.

Callum spoke quietly so that no one could hear besides the new child. "Margaret Mary Dyer, you're a blessing to me and this family. But I'll wager to say that not only will you sprout flaming locks of hair, but that there is an evil sprite out there, determined to plague you with terrible luck for all your days. But don't you worry. I'll protect you, I promise."

CHAPTER 2

May 1641

MOLL'S MOTHER SIGHED loudly again. To Moll's mind, her mother sighed frequently and did so mostly when she was near Moll.

"Come now, you little angletwitch," Mama said. "Quit squirming so I can get your hair under your cap. Won't do for all those red locks to be tumbling out while in town. I want to return before your father gets home from Exeter."

Dada was the smartest father in all of England. He made physicks inside a little shed behind their cottage and then rode to various towns to sell them. "To cure any ailment," he had said to Moll. "Whether someone knows they have one or not."

How brave and generous of Dada to try to cure people in distant towns.

Moll attempted to sit still as her mother stuffed her unruly hair under a plain linen coif that was to sit over a matching linen cloth strip that was wrapped around Moll's forehead.

But the stool was rickety on its legs, and soon she was swaying back mand forth, trying to find her balance.

"There! Enough!" Mama said, throwing up her hands in exasperation. "I think you'll do."

Moll reached up to touch the cloth covering her

hair. She couldn't feel any of her natural hair, so Mama must have hidden it all.

"What's wrong with my hair?" she asked. "And can I have a cheddar cake from Mrs. Bunting when we go to town?"

Her mother stood before her and gently cupped Moll's chin in one hand. "Truthfully, child, there is nothing wrong with your hair or any other part of you. But there are others who will see those flaming locks and not be pleased one bit. Not with what's going on in Ireland."

She released Moll. "If the cheese monger is offering her cheese at a good price, I'll get you one. I don't know why you like those things so much."

Moll loved the irregularly shaped pieces of cheddar cheese that Mrs. Bunting would hack off a block and let sit over the fire in a heavy pan. As the pieces melted, the edges would become brown and crispy. Mrs. Bunting would then set the pieces on a table to set. When dry, they were delightfully crispy, sweet, and savory.

"Mama!" she admonished her mother. "How do you not like them? Cheddar cakes are the best thing in the world."

Moll's anticipation of a delectable treat made the two mile walk to the city center for the Friday market seem like an instant. She loved these moments, when her three younger, squalling siblings were left in the care of her grandfather, while her older siblings were otherwise distracted with chores, and she could have private time with her mother, even if it was just to walk down a muddy lane into Kenn.

It didn't even matter that her mother, a basket over one arm and a furrow in her brow, always seemed preoccupied with other matters. When Mama was far away like that, Moll could sing and skip without her mother chastising her for annoying behavior.

There was a farmer's son,
Kept sheep all on the hill;
And he walk'ed out one May morning
To see what he could kill.
And sing blow away the morning dew
The dew, and the dew.
Blow away the morning dew,
How sweet the winds do blow.

Yes, these were the best days.

At the market's gated entrance, a boy around Moll's age was standing next to a post with a large broad sheet nailed to it. "Come read about this opportunity," he called out. "Father Andrew White writes of the successful beginnings of Lord Baltimore's plantation in Maryland. Settlers needed for this colony. Indentured servant contracts being let by farms, ale house keepers, grocers, coopers, and barber-surgeons. No charge for your transportation there. 'Tis a free way to start a new life in a new place filled with riches."

Moll's mother stopped in front of the parchment and its large lettering. Moll knew that her mother couldn't read well, but she had an amazing memory and had no doubt absorbed everything the boy had said.

"If I hadn't chosen William so quickly and set my life on its course…" Mama's expression was pensive. Moll felt a prickle of unease over it.

But her mother's face quickly cleared, and they marched on to the various stalls inside the crowded market, the boy's voice fading into the background as he continued hawking the colony to all the passers-by.

As always, Mama haggled with vendors over the prices of tomatoes and other vegetables—"These tiny things, so early in the season? I'll pay you half!"—and housewares like a new deep pot—"This wouldn't hold enough to feed a dog, much less my family. Your price is robbery!"

Today, though, there was tension in the air among the sellers. Moll caught snippets of conversation that she didn't understand.

"Earl of Strafford executed for what he did, wasn't he? Like a lowly criminal. Though they say his trial was a spectacle."

"But the Irish had to be brought to heel, din' they? Not civilized, they aren't, what with their popery and refusal to conform to our good Church of England. What else could the Lord Deputy of Ireland do?" There was much nodding at that statement.

"He had a heavy hand, though. His death won't be enough. They's planning for rebellion up there, you mark my words. And then where will we be?" More nodding.

"Scotland and Ireland will be King Charles's undoing." Doleful tsking accompanied this statement.

Bored, Moll wandered off to let her mother conduct her business and gossip. There were so many interesting things to see and do at the weekly market. The constant hum of voices, periodically interrupted by an argument between seller and buyer, was a backdrop to the stalls draped in colorful cloths and pennants.

Every type of food, cloth, metalware, and animal could be found at the market. The Dyer family could afford little of it, she knew, but it was so much fun to go from stall to stall and touch it all. Which usually earned Moll a rap on the knuckles from the seller, but she didn't mind. It was worth it.

She often had to dance around piles of manure dropped by dogs, fowl, lambs, and other animals, and that was part of the fun, too. Moll had even invented her own version of Scotch-Hopper that enabled her to make a game of jumping over the odorous heaps.

The dung competed with the aromas of baked breads, fresh pies, and salted meats, creating a blended fragrance that could be found nowhere but at the market.

Sometimes there were even wandering minstrels hoping for a coin or two for playing their songs. Moll couldn't offer them coins, but she did attempt to sing along with them, mostly to their amusement.

Today, there was a hurdy-gurdy player, rattling off a ditty about a lost cow who went from town to town asking residents where its home was. None of the residents seemed to find it silly that the cow talked.

Moll loved the amusing story and pranced about before the troubadour, swinging her drab, patched skirt back and forth as she danced to the music the stringed instrument produced. The musician picked up the tempo as she continued her movements. Soon, Moll was jumping about furiously. She hoped her mother wasn't noticing her, for she would be made to stop instantly. She was heady with the joy of simply *being*, twirling and cavorting until—

"Look at 'er!" came a shout from a tanner selling leather goods, an old man who always stank of the urine used in his trade.

Moll paid no mind to him. She was happy that he had noticed her joyful abandon.

Suddenly, though, she was on the ground. Her

front teeth had bitten painfully into her lower lip, and she tasted blood in her mouth. She rolled over slowly, a shadow looming over her and blocking the sun.

"Look at 'er!" the tanner said again, his reeking odor floating down and covering her like an unpleasant blanket. Moll realized that his previous tone had not been the friendly one she thought it was.

He knelt and peered into her face. His smell was almost unbearable as he stared at her with intense dark eyes set inside a fleshy face.

"Thought you were hiding from us, did you?" He held up a fist, in which he grasped her head covering. "Are you part of that rebellious lot up north?"

Moll was confused. What was the awful man talking about?

"Bah!" he said, his breath almost worse than the rest of him, if that were possible. "They're sending little brats to sneak in their popish ways."

She heard a shriek from some yards away, then she was being pulled to her feet. "How dare you molest my daughter, James Burney?" Mama shouted at the tanner, shoving Moll behind her as she grabbed the coif and forehead cloth from him. "You're nothing but a brute, casting an innocent girl to the ground. Come, Moll."

A few of the other marketgoers were gathering around, murmuring among themselves.

"*No mistaking the Irish in that one.*" There were nods all around at this.

"*She's just a wee mite. She doesn't know the pope from James's piss pot.*"

"*James Burney has spent too much time drinking his own piss, if you ask me.*" People began laughing.

Mama grabbed Moll roughly by the arm and walked quickly away from the market, her full basket crooked in her free arm. Moll had to run to keep up. Once they were out of view, Moll's mother stopped, knelt, laid aside the basket, and reattached Moll's head covering. "This is why I had to do it, sweets. There are bad doings back in the home country, and people here are scared. Your red hair shouts your heritage to everyone, so it's best if we keep it covered whenever you go out. For now. Understand?"

Moll didn't resist as her mother quickly stuffed all her hair back under the coif. "No, Mama, I don't understand. I didn't do anything to anyone, and I can't help what my hair looks like."

There went another one of Mama's sighs. "No, you didn't do anything, and you can't help that bright red mass. You'll have to trust that I'm keeping you safe. One day you will understand why your mere presence makes others angry."

CHAPTER 3

October 1641

MOLL REFRAINED FROM venturing into town for several months. But by October, she had nearly forgotten how frightened she had been at the market. Not only that, she missed the private days spent with her mother.

So, when Mama stated that she planned to attend the Friday market in Kenn to purchase some chicks for the youngest children to care for, Moll stated her intent to go. "I won't let my coif fall away this time, I promise."

Mama arched an eyebrow. "That means you will have to refrain from dancing like a wild beast."

Granda interjected. "Ah, let her be, Lizzy. She's a good child."

Moll went to her grandfather and threw her arms around his waist. He wasn't as solid and trim as he used to be, and her arms could no longer go completely around him, but he was still comfortable. She gazed up at him. "Thank you, Granda."

He patted her head and smiled indulgently down at her. "You remind me of your grandmother. Just as pretty and the same sweetness in you."

Mama wasn't impressed. "You're spoiling her, Callum. We're not a family that can afford any member thinking she is special."

He shook his head. "Ah, Lizzy, you're a hard woman

sometimes. Life is difficult enough, especially now. We must appreciate that which brings us joy. Like little Moll, here." He touched Moll's nose with his thumb.

Moll's mother shook her head and called on Thomas, the eldest, giving him instructions for chores to be done that day. Now sixteen, Thomas had shot up and was nearly as tall as Granda. Thomas was also handsome…and he knew it. As did many of the girls in their tiny village.

He nodded in agreement at Mama's instructions, which included scrubbing out some pans, cleaning out ashes from the fireplace, and spreading the ashes in the garden. Moll knew that Thomas would give them an hour's start, then be at the cistern in the nearby village square, practicing his charms on the maidens who were there to draw pails of water.

Moll wrinkled her nose at the thought. When she married, it wouldn't be to a clay-brained boy like Thomas. No, she would marry someone kind and strong, who loved her without reserve. Like Granda.

But who gave a fig for wasting thoughts on Thomas? Moll was to have a day with her mother.

However, they hadn't made it past the village center when a man galloped in on horseback, stirring up a cloud of dust as he brought his mount to a sudden halt next to the tall oak post that stood near the village well. Riddled with nail holes, the post served as a convenient place for people to tack notices about market fairs, wares for sale, lost animals, runaway servants, and the like.

The rider seemed to be a man of some importance, so everyone stopped their movements to observe him as he jumped down effortlessly from his horse.

"I come on behalf of His Majesty, King Charles," the man said in a tone that was not just commanding but held an ease that suggested he had said this many times before.

"His Majesty wants his people to know of great events in the kingdom." He unlatched a satchel strapped to the horse and withdrew a rolled-up scroll. There appeared to be many of them stuffed together in the bag.

Moll crept closer with her mother, as did everyone else, until they made a half circle around the man and his horse. Unrolling the scroll, the man said loudly, "A great rebellion in Ulster, County Donegal, in the north of Ireland, has been quelled by His Majesty. These miscreants, who sought to undermine the king's benevolent rule by demanding a return to popery and away from our true Reformed faith in their land, have been justly punished. Do not weep for them, for they committed treason by taking up arms against the king."

Moll noticed that the man's clothing was very dusty and rumpled, although it was made in what Mama would call "a fine manner." The man also rocked back and forth, favoring one leg and then the other.

He had surely been traveling for quite some time with this news he was announcing. Moll tried to focus once more on his loud pronouncement.

"As our Lord Jesus Christ once told His disciples, you will hear of wars and rumors of wars, but our good king assures you that he has prevented a war and has done so without the assistance of a treacherous and ineffective Parliament. In fact, he has done so despite those wretched creatures."

Murmurs of shock rumbled through the townspeople.

Moll vaguely understood Parliament to be a body of men who helped ensure the king's absolute, divine rule. So, it made sense that the king compared himself to the Lord. But why were the men who helped him so terrible?

"I have here the names of the traitors who were captured in their attack on innocent Christian subjects of the realm. Butchers, they all were, massacring more than a hundred fifty thousand, stealing livestock, and plundering property. It was an offense against God, king, and the Church of England. They were all duly hanged for their trouble. This—" he held up the sheet. "—is a list of those who were executed."

Thus finished, with one hand, he pulled a tiny sack and a hammer from the satchel full of scrolls. Withdrawing a thick iron nail from the sack, he proceeded to nail the scroll to the post.

That done, he said looked around at the assembly. "I could use some refreshment."

One of the girls there to retrieve water from the well went ahead and did so, then offered her pail to the crier, who drank deeply from it and then rinsed his hands in it.

The girl was very comely, which the rider appeared to appreciate with his long gaze at her. Moll thought that Thomas would most certainly not appreciate the competition had he been here.

The crier walked his horse to a nearby mounting block, stepped onto it, placed a foot in the stirrup, and heaved himself onto the saddle, quickly urging the horse back the way they had come.

With his departure, the townspeople shrugged and returned to what they were doing. Moll's mother pulled her along as she walked over the post and stared at the sheet tacked to it.

Moll became impatient, waiting. "What does it say, Mama? Are there names on it?"

Mama frowned. "Yes, but I can't read most of it. I recognize the name 'Dyer' in several places, though. Your grandfather will…"

Glancing both ways as if to ensure she wasn't being watched, Mama tore the sheet down from its nail. She quickly folded it into as small a square as she could fashion and tucked it into one of her sleeves.

"Come," she said to Moll. The market completely forgotten, they hurried home to share the news.

⚬≈⚬

Arriving home not an hour after they had left, Moll watched as her grandfather knelt before a smoothly cut old tree stump, a goose held firmly by its neck in his hand. On the stump lay a knife, its blade rusted from years of hacking through animal flesh and bone. The goose stared wildly, flapping its wings.

Around Granda stood Moll's three younger siblings, William, Elizabeth, and toddler Christian, watching as their grandfather instructed them on how to swiftly grab the goose and twist its neck with both hands, instantly killing it. The goose's orange-billed, brown-grey head flopped over Granda's closed wrist, while its brown and white body with pink feet dangled below that fist.

Just as swiftly, Granda laid the bird down on the stump, picked up the rusted knife, and removed the goose's head from its body. Very little blood spilled.

"Now I'll show you how to fix it for cooking," he was saying, but looked up at Moll's approach with her mother. He frowned at Mama's expression. "What's the matter? Is they's trouble at the market?"

"Never made it to the city market, Callum. There was a rider come into the village. Announced some trouble in Ireland." Mama pulled the folded sheet from her sleeve and held it up.

Granda rose, tossing the limp goose near the cottage door. "Inside, all of you little imps." He put an arm around Moll's shoulder as they all entered the dark cottage.

"Can we afford to burn a candle?" he asked, sitting on a bench at the table.

Mama nodded wordlessly. From the lone table, she took a tallow candle, set in a tiny tin holder, and tipped it toward the ever-burning hearth flame. She set it on the table, and it offered a faint glow to the room.

Their cottage consisted of one room with two makeshift bed chambers. The family's main living space had a hearth on one end that reached up through the ceiling. Their furniture consisted of a table and two long benches, one on either side of it. The two small bed chambers, each just a compartment made by a curtain draped across it, were reserved for the adults, one for Moll's parents and one for Granda.

A vertical ladder reached up to a loft, where all seven Dyer children slept on an array of straw-stuffed pallets.

She knew her grandfather had given up everything when he had come to live with them, but he at least had a chamber all to himself. That seemed very luxurious. Maybe he didn't miss his wife so much now that he had a private space.

Sensing dread but unable to understand what it was, Moll felt an urge to crawl into her grandfather's lap, but at seven years old, she was far too mature for it.

She sat next to him, instead. Her siblings were

already involved in a game that was evolving into an argument.

"That'll be enough from you," Mama said sternly. The worry was clearly etched in her face, despite the shadows in the room. The other children lowered their quarrel to a furious whisper.

Before Granda could start to read the messenger's poster, Dada also arrived home, dropping his healing case with a thud as he entered. His jovial entrance was a stark contrast to Mama's and Granda's somber expressions.

"What have we here?" he asked, putting an arm around Mama and kissing her forehead.

Mama quickly told him what had happened when she and Moll had been in the village center.

Now Dada was quiet, too. He sat on Moll's other side while Granda started to read. It was comforting to have the most important men in her life flanking her. She felt secure, as if whatever that sheet of paper said couldn't harm her now that her father and grandfather were protecting her.

Mama stood by the hearth, supervising the other children and worrying her fingers around the bottoms of her sleeves.

With the paper close to the candle's glow, Moll's grandfather said, "It opens with, 'King Charles of England, Scotland, and Ireland, the first of that name, hereby declares that the following persons in Ireland have been executed for their part in unnecessary bloodshed, cruelty, and treason. They were responsible for butchering more than one hundred fifty thousand English newcomers to their lands, in addition to pilfering livestock and crops, and taking over homes.'" Moll's grandfather lowered the paper for a moment.

"'English newcomers'?" Granda said. "Does

he mean the slaughtering Reformers? I think it highly unlikely that there were that many people in County Donegal to be killed, but I'm sure this claim is better for gaining sympathy from his subjects." He grunted in disgust and continued. "'This insurrection by Irish insurgents was quickly quelled, resulting in the removal from life of the following individuals.'"

He sighed and began reading through names. "'Conor Brannon of Ballyshannon. Fergal Delaney of Ardara. Seamus Kilpatrick of Ulster. Oisin Dyer of Ramelton. Lorcan Dyer of Ramelton.'"

Granda dropped the sheet. "No, it cannot be. Oisin and Lorcan are cousins of mine. Have not seen them in many years, but still..." He breathed heavily several times but remained stoic. Moll loved her grandfather deeply in that moment, but didn't completely understand why she was so filled with emotion for him.

Granda read on. There were at least three more Dyer names inside a very long list, and each one caused her grandfather to stumble in reading them. Yet he finished the entire list, then touched the document to the candle's flame. The resulting torch lit the room brightly. Moll's father took it from her grandfather and walked it to the hearth, tossing it in where it extinguished itself into the merest ashes.

"We need to discuss this," Moll's mother said. "But not with young ears around. Moll, take your brothers and sister outside. They need to know how to prepare the goose your grandfather just killed."

Why did it always have to be Moll watching the ones younger than her? Why couldn't Agnes or Dorothy do it? They were older. Agnes was practically a woman now at thirteen. Where were Thomas, Agnes, and Dorothy, anyway? Moll was disappointed but knew better than to protest. It was never fruitful to cross Mama.

Once outside, she picked up the goose's body from where it lay motionless outside the door and carried it back to the stump where Granda had killed it. She began instructing her siblings on proper goose dressage. "After you've killed the goose, you need to pluck it. This is the longest part of it all. Watch me. Elizabeth, pay attention, and don't worry about that mouse. Now, first, you pick the largest feathers off the goose. Pull them toward the bottom of the animal. See? Then make your way up around the body."

She handed the goose to William, who practically attacked the bird.

"No, you dolt, don't just rip them out," she said to her brother, smacking his hand away. "You'll tear the skin. Do it like this." She demonstrated again.

This time, her six-year-old brother did much better. Leaving her three siblings to finish pulling the large feathers, Moll quietly crept back into the house. Her parents and grandfather had retreated into Granda's compartment and were talking in low voices.

Knowing she shouldn't, she quickly untied the leather thongs on her square-toed leather shoes—handed down from Agnes, then Dorothy—and slipped out of the worn foot coverings. She walked silently across the compacted dirt floor to Granda's compartment and turned an ear to listen to what was being discussed.

Her father was speaking. "First, King Charles began tampering with Scottish land titles, unnerving landowners. Then he and that idiot Laud, Archbishop of Canterbury, tried to force the Scots away from the true faith and to the English style of worship. No doubt Laud believed the king had the power to quell any rebellion of the Scots, not understanding the steely backbone of that people. No surprise that the king's instructions on worship were hastily withdrawn, but the damage had been done. The king had become too accustomed to ruling without Parliament until the Scots forced him to call Parliament back two years ago. Now this horror with Ireland."

Moll had no idea what Papa's words meant.

There was murmuring between her mother and father that Moll couldn't understand, then her grandfather spoke up. "I s'pose the king doesn't recall that it wasn't so long ago that the Protestants were slaughtering Catholics in Ireland, taking our lands and property. No tamping down of that uprising, eh? But now the king is officially murdering his own subjects. Our friends and relatives. The execution of Strafford last year has now emboldened our relatives to the north into action, I'm afraid."

There was a rustling sound, as if someone were standing up. Or sitting down. Granda spoke again, his voice low. Moll had to put her ear close to the curtain to listen.

"They's be many like us, with kin up north though we make our home here. We must remain quiet until this storm passes."

Dada made a snorting noise. "'T'will be civil war, mark my words, and across three kingdoms."

"Oh, William, you don't really think so, do you?" Her mother's voice was tinged with fear.

Her father must have not replied, for Moll's grandfather's voice was the next one she heard. "I'd say as not you'd be wise to avoid having any more little ones. You'll be hard-pressed to care for the lot you already have if there's war here."

"War here? In Devon?" Mama's voice was now incredulous, and Moll could feel her mother's worry permeating through the walls.

Granda grunted. "The king's reach is everywhere. And we may find that an angry Parliament also has long tentacles. Tentacles that will intertwine with the king's. And we will be forced by both sides to choose one side."

So, was Parliament bad because it had tentacles? What exactly were "tentacles"?

"Moll..." her mother murmured.

"No more market days for her," Dada said. "And she *must* remember to keep her hair covered whenever she is outside. We have good neighbors now, but troubled times can make the finest people suspicious, and that suspicion can turn ugly. No need to remind them of our ancestry. Plenty of English called Dyer, so at least our name isn't a problem."

"I don't know that it isn't a problem." Mama was still hesitant. "I've seen notices whenever I've gone to the Friday markets. There is a need for settlers in the new colonies. One can go by paying his own passage or by agreeing to an indentured servant's contract. It's a possibility..."

"It could even be an opportunity for success," Dada said. "Although I don't know how we could have the youngest signed on to contracts."

"Perhaps we could start sending the older children to either Maryland or Virginia, and join them later, once the youngest are a little older," Mama offered.

Moll's grandfather huffed. "No one would ever sign me as an indentured servant, I'm too old. I have to live out my days here in Kenn. And I'll not see all of these children taken away from me. We will weather through this. Promise me, both of you, that you won't entertain such a ridiculous idea."

Moll slipped away, unwilling to hear any more. It almost sounded as if she were causing a problem for her family. A problem that might have everyone sailing to some strange place.

She shook her head. It couldn't be. Moll would talk to Granda later. He would comfort her and make it right.

⚬⚬⚬

Moll dashed back outside, barefoot, and rejoined her siblings. They were done with the large feathers, so she showed them how to work on the down feathers. Picking up the blood-stained knife from the tree stump, she knelt and ran the knife against the skin, scraping upward as if scraping paint flakes off an old piece of wood.

Her brother and sisters made squealing noises over the grating sound it made.

"Now you try. Not Christian, though, she's too young."

The other two began fighting over the sharp knife, so Moll had to assign time with it to each of them. She wondered briefly if she should let them use the knife at all. Mama had said to teach them to pluck the goose, and scraping the skin for the down feathers was part of plucking, so surely this was what Mama meant.

As William and Elizabeth taunted one another over how poorly a job the other was doing, Christian began wailing over being left out of the activity.

It wasn't fair. It should be Agnes having to endure all this fuss and crying.

Elizabeth had the knife now and was pushing

down too hard, breaking the goose's skin. Moll took the knife away. "Honestly, Lizbet, I could do this when I was a little girl of four."

Moll's sister glowered at her.

Moll quickly finished scraping the goose herself. No one had come out of their cottage yet. Should she continue preparing the goose?

She shrugged. May as well. As with the ever-burning hearth inside the house that was never permitted to go out, so too did they have a small outdoor hearth made of small rocks that Moll and her older siblings had collected. She picked up the goose's body and the knife. "Come on, you three."

She led them over to the hearth. The fire here was mostly embers. "Go find me some sticks," she instructed Christian. That was something a toddler could do. Christian wandered off and soon came back with several in her tiny fist.

Moll added them to the glowing base using one to poke the others until a small flame emerged.

"Now you have to singe off the rest of the down," she said. The others watched, entranced, as she held the goose's body close to the flame without allowing it to actually touch the skin. Soon, what down remained was curling up and dissipating into the air.

"The fire takes care of the rest, you see," Moll said, proud of herself in this moment as her siblings seemed to admire their elder sister.

Perhaps Agnes probably wouldn't have been able to do as good a job.

Granda would be so proud of her when he learned what she had taught the others. Mama, too, would tell her she was growing up fast.

So lost in her thoughts was she that when a scream split the air, it felt as though she had been blinded by lightning. Moll reeled backward, falling onto her rump.

She shook her head back to recognition of her surroundings, which was when she realized that William, his face redder than her own cap-covered hair, was squalling as he held up his hands. They were swollen, scarlet, peeling in places, and streaked with black ash.

"What did you do?" Moll shrieked, jumping up to tend to her younger brother. Elizabeth, ever attuned to the brother who was only three years older than she, also began crying.

"I wanted to help…help…" William was breathing in deep gulps. "…to help build the fire so you could get the feathers off faster."

Moll immediately understood what had happened. The smell of his burnt flesh was terrible.

"Foolish brother, why did you—"

Before she could finish, her parents and grandfather came rushing out of the cottage. All three appeared shocked, but Mama was wild-eyed.

Mama's sparrowhawk gaze surveyed the scene in an instant. That gaze ended up on Moll. "Mary Margaret Dyer! You let your brother burn himself? I told you to show him how to pluck the goose, not cook himself in its place."

Mama was making her way to Moll, and Moll knew that a severe punishment was coming.

But Dada caught Mama up in his arms. "Wife, be calmed. It was an accident. I'll fix the boy." Dada flashed a glance at Granda, who came and picked Moll up, hugging her close. She was too old to be picked up like this, but it was comforting, just like sitting next to him on the bench was.

In a fit of emotion, she threw her arms around her grandfather's neck and buried her face against his aged, leathery skin that smelled like potatoes fresh from the ground.

"There, there, my little Moll. All will be well. Look, your dada is off to fetch his case of remedies."

Moll ventured a glance up from her hiding spot in her grandfather's neck. Mama had William folded up in her skirts, although he was holding his hands outward. Moll's brother was still sniffling but had calmed down.

Elizabeth stood nearby, seemingly still in shock, while little Christian was obliviously back to gathering sticks.

Dada returned, holding his large wooden box by its handle, setting it down next to William and Mama, and crooking a finger at Moll.

Granda slowly put her on the ground. "Off with you, Moll. And don't you worry about your mother. Your Granda will always protect you, isn't that right?"

He offered her a conspiratorial wink, which made Moll feel immensely better. She dashed over to her father.

"You can help heal William," Dada said as she approached. "Lizzy, why don't you, Callum, and the children occupy yourselves otherwise?"

Mama frowned. "I need to stay with William. He needs his mother right now."

"He doesn't." Moll was surprised at Dada's firm tone. "I want Moll to learn how to dress the burns she caused. It should be done without you hovering."

"But—" Mama began.

Dada picked up the goose, which was covered in dirt and bits of leaves but still in good shape. "Take this to the cottage and finish the job so we can have it for supper."

Mama must have understood that there were

times you didn't argue with Dada, for she flashed him an annoyed look before doing his bidding. He might be quiet most of the time, but if he raised his voice at you, there would be nothing pleasant following his words.

Granda and Moll's siblings trailed behind Mama.

"Now, Moll, there are many remedies for a burn, but all of them involve different types of plasters. Do you know what a plaster is?"

She shook her head no.

"Well, now, my plaster is a covering made with either beef fat or some oil, mixed together with water and a bit of ground hyssop to make it coat whatever wound you want to heal. Run and get some water from the well. Quickly, my girl. Your brother won't be able to remain brave much longer."

Moll ran to the front of their cottage and retrieved an empty bucket that was sitting near the door. With as much speed as she could muster, she ran to the village square cistern and dipped the bucket in. She filled it halfway, the most weight she could carry. The return to her father was slower, what with her effort to carry the heavy bucket in her arms without sloshing much out.

By the time she had returned, her father had an array of pouches on top of his medical case, in addition to an irregularly shaped wood bowl. William stood next to him, clearly controlling tears of pain.

"Ah," Dada said, looking up. "Now we can produce our plaster."

Moll placed the half-full bucket next to her father. He tipped the bowl into it, partially filling it.

"See this?" he asked, putting the bowl on top of the case and holding up one of the larger pouches. "This is some old beef fat. This helps form the basis of our plaster." With that, he squeezed the contents of the sheepskin pouch out into the water, put the pouch down, and stirred the contents into a slurry with his hand.

Dada held up the bowl. "Feel it?"

Moll reached out and dipped two fingers into it. It was like a thin gruel. She sniffed her fingers. The old fat smelled rancid.

"Not thick enough, right? This will do naught but run off your brother's hands, and we need it to adhere and stay there awhile." Her father added more fat and stirred again with his fingers.

"Now touch this." He offered the bowl to her again.

It was much harder to run her fingers through it. She understood that this would lie on the skin much better.

"That's the plaster. But we need to add something to it for the boy's pain." Father held up another pouch. "This is ground hyssop and lavender." He tipped the pouch into the bowl, adding a small amount, then stirring again. Even at a distance, Moll could tell that it smelled much more fragrant than the beef fat alone. "It will get into William's skin and make him feel better in addition to healing the burn."

Dada turned his attention to her brother. "You've been a brave boy. Now show me your hands."

William eagerly cupped his hands together and put them forward, palms up. Dada poured some of the plaster into the well her brother's hands had created, then put down the bowl and began gently massaging the plaster into the boy's hands.

The relief on William's face was palpable.

Dada smiled at William, which in turn made Moll's heart swell. Dada was usually very serious, but when he smiled, it was as if the sun had forced its rays through storm clouds. His green eyes, paler than Moll's, sparkled, and his lanky frame relaxed.

Moll was fascinated by what Dada was doing. "How do you know what brings relief from the pain?"

Her father shrugged. "It's just wisdom handed down through the ages. Some say that healing is women's work, some say it's men's work, but I believe it to be everyone's work."

He turned his attention back to William. "Go sit by the house in the shade, now," Dada said to him. "You mustn't move for a while."

William went to do his father's bidding, leaving Moll alone with her father.

"Now, Moll, it was careless what you did, letting your brother burn himself," he said as he began cleaning up his medical spread.

"But I didn't—" she started.

"No," he said, tipping the contents of the bowl into the fire. "It was careless, and that is that. But if you know how to correct mistakes, it will serve you well. If you can correct others' mistakes, even better. I believe you would be well served in going out with me and learning how I sell my physicks."

She frowned. Her father had turned serious again. His eyes dimmed, and he was tense once more.

"Did Thomas, Agnes, or Dorothy ever do this with you?" she asked.

"They did not. But I suspect you have a greater need to know how to correct mistakes."

That didn't sound flattering. But the thought of traveling with her father was appealing, especially now that she was apparently no longer in her mother's good graces.

"I'll be sure to wear my cap tightly," she promised.

Her father smiled gently. That was much better. "I know you will. And, Moll, your grandfather is right. You *are* a good girl. There is just much you don't understand yet about life."

———— ✖ ————

"Nothing I give him is working." Dada's tone was frantic. Moll had never heard her father sound this agitated, even when she overheard him discussing the bad events occurring up north.

Granda lay on a pallet next to the hearth, sweating mightily and speaking to invisible persons, predominantly Moll's grandmother, Fiona, whom she had never met.

Moll was terrified.

Her grandfather had suddenly taken ill several days ago. After a couple of days of violent vomiting outside in the cesspit, followed by wretched diarrhea—during which her grandfather had screamed that his bowels were on fire—he had ended up here on the pallet.

The stench of her grandfather's emissions had floated into the house, and Moll had taken it as a sacred duty to dig holes and bury it all in service to her beloved Granda.

No one understood what had happened to cause him such wretchedness.

Her father had scratched his head. "Was it that cursed goose?"

"But we all ate it," Mama said. "How could it affect only him?"

Moll's heart sank. Had she been responsible for this, as well as for her brother's burned hands?

William had been recovering well after several applications of Dada's plaster, the third of which Moll had applied herself. It was already obvious, though, that William would have permanent scarring.

But her brother was now inconsequential as compared to Granda lying there, alternately muttering and raving, while the entire family stood around helplessly.

The best her father seemed able to do was to give him a liquid—containing crushed wintergreen, Dada said—that seemed to calm the worst of the symptoms.

After a week of witnessing her grandfather's agony, she climbed down the sleeping ladder before dawn one morning to check on him, only to find him motionless, his head to one side and his mouth agape.

No! It just couldn't be.

Moll retreated to her sleeping pallet, scampering quickly up the vertical oak ladder to the loft she shared with her six siblings. She flopped belly-down onto the straw mattress, burying her face into the crook of her right arm. She knew she shouldn't weep aloud and act like a baby, but she didn't care.

Her noise awoke the rest of the family, who ran to tend to her grandfather, each expressing grief with either their own noisy sobs or hushed murmurings.

Without Granda, Moll's world was destroyed. She would never recover. No one could ever take his place.

CHAPTER 4

Kenn, Devon,
September 1643

MOLL SAT ON a low stool next to the hearth, trying to stay warm while waiting for her father. A splash of water fell on her from above, so she scooted the stool over and huddled her arms around herself again.

The fall had been unseasonably damp and cold, and the Dyer cottage had been unable to fend off the onslaught of constant dripping rain. There were multiple leaks in the thatched roof.

With Granda gone almost a full year now, on top of war that had broken out in the country, the family was suffering more than could be imagined. Both Mama and Dada worked themselves to the point where they had gray circles under their eyes that never went away.

Thomas and Agnes didn't seem to notice that their parents were each as tired as a dog in a turnspit wheel, but Moll did.

What if something happened to either Mama or Dada? It would be unbearable.

Also concerning to Moll was that Mama and Dada had whispered together at all hours about the rebellion that continued in Ireland, something else to which her siblings paid no attention, but it disturbed Moll. Granda had been very upset about it, so knowing that it was still a problem made her sad.

It also made her miss him dreadfully.

But over the past couple of weeks, her parents had either stopped talking about it altogether or weren't talking about it in the house. It was curious.

"Ready, Moll?" Her father stepped out of his compartment.

Moll rose and pushed the stool into a corner. *Splat.* She quickly rubbed the drop of moisture into her hair through her tightly affixed cap.

Dada was taking her with him to Powderham. He hadn't been there in several months to sell his cures, so he figured there were villagers there who could use them. This was her third outing like this with her father, and she enjoyed them more than she thought she would.

He had even found an old leather satchel that someone had thrown out a window as trash and had given it to Moll to use as her own carry bag for powders and herbs. Carrying it while making rounds with her father made her feel very much like an adult, even though she was just nine years old.

They walked the four miles to Powderham. Sometimes Dada would offer money to a passing cart and driver to take them at least part of the way, but only when he'd had good success in his most recent outing.

Today would be a walking day, Moll was sure, but she didn't mind. As with the outings she used to take with her mother on Friday market days, this was special time alone with her father.

She ignored how chilled she felt in her thin dress and tattered, laced leather shoes. Moll took extra care to avoid any puddles, which would have soaked her feet, leaving them frozen and numb the rest of the day.

"How are you getting on with your older brother and sisters?" her father asked.

What a strange question. Why did Dada care?

She shrugged. "I stay out of their way. They don't notice me much."

"Hmm. And the younger ones?"

Now Moll smiled, feeling a glow from inside. "Elizabeth and Christian don't bother me at all. But William is such a love, Dada. Only a year younger than me, so it's like we're twins. I wish we *were* twins. He means more to me than even Grand—"

She stopped. Was she about to insult her father by implying that he wasn't as important to her as her brother and grandfather? And did she really mean that William had supplanted Granda in her affections?

"He is my favorite sibling," she finished, shifting her bag from one fist to the other as she picked up her steps to keep up with her father. She didn't carry nearly the supplies that her father did, but her bag grew heavy with time just the same.

She caught her father's lips quirking up in a smile. "Well done, Moll, well done."

Speaking of Granda…

"I know it was wicked of me to listen, but I've heard you and Mama talk about the fighting in Ulster that took away some of our family members."

"Oh, Moll, you shouldn't—"

She continued in a rush to avoid being chastised. "But I haven't heard you talk about it lately. Have you—did you—forget about Granda's worries over it?"

"What? Of course not, little one. You see, the

rebellion, as the king calls it, seems to be petering out."

Moll frowned. "Does petering mean it's over?"

"Yes. It's only those who don't realize they've lost who are continuing to fight."

"And…is it our relatives in Ulster who continue to fight?"

"I'm afraid so. King and Parliament will make a quick end to them now."

Moll had a good idea what a "quick end" meant. Her stomach roiled at the thought that her relatives—distant and unknown as they might be—would be killed like that. Maybe their heads put on pikes. She shuddered.

"Still cold?" Dada asked.

She shook her head no.

A herder with around a dozen sheep passed them in the other direction, stepping slightly off the path so that the sheep would follow him and get out of Moll's and Dada's way. Moll envied the sheep their heavy wool coats, even if they did stink from the manure stuck to the hair at their bottoms.

One of the larger sheep glared at her balefully and emitted an angry "baaaa" as he trotted past her, as if he had read her thoughts about her distaste of his odor. Or perhaps he had noticed her wrinkling her nose.

Dada glanced at her thoughtfully as they continued walking. "You're wise beyond your years. Your mother might not agree, but I think it's time you knew certain things."

Moll stopped, the cold and damp forgotten. "What things?"

Her father pointed to a sign. "We're entering Powderham now. Let's head to the village center so that we can meet as many people as possible. Praise the Virgin Mother that the rain has stopped. If we make enough money today, I'll take you to an inn for a meat pie and then tell you things. Have we a bargain?"

Meat pies were almost as good as cheddar cakes. The offer of one would make Moll agree to nearly anything. She nodded.

CHAPTER 5

THE CENTER OF Powderham was like most larger, prosperous villages. There was a towering castle, also called Powderham, overlooking it from a distance. Buildings—some brick, some wood, some barely shanties—with thatched roofs were haphazardly placed along a muddy lane. Many of them had signs depicting what trade lay behind the front door—a shoe for a cobbler, a coffin for a cabinet maker, a flagon for a tavern. At the far end, away from the castle, was the telltale steeple of the local parish church. All manner of people bustled in and around loose farm animals, dogs, piles of manure, and peddler stalls.

Outside a tavern along the lane, men sat drinking from a communal bowl, while shouts, laughter, and faint music emanated from inside.

Two boys, looking to be barely older than Moll, had their fists up as they danced around each other, landing ineffectual blows.

"Let's head over to that group of stalls," Dada said, inclining his head down the path past the tavern toward a crowd of women around three stalls, all of which were hawking items for females—hair combs, shawls, hats, hairbrushes, and the like.

As they walked, a woman appeared in a window opening above them and dumped out a bowl full of rotting and moldy vegetables. The contents landed at Moll's feet. She attempted to step around the mess just as two mongrels showed up to wolf down the contents of what the woman had tossed from her house. One of the dogs snapped at Moll as she moved around it.

"I don't want your supper," she said mildly, inwardly a bit frightened.

Even worse than the biting dog was a man who came down the street from the opposite direction. The man wore tattered clothes and stank terribly—worse than what the woman had thrown out the window—and he had blackened teeth surrounded by red gums.

He stopped in front of Moll, looking upon her as though her father wasn't there. She felt a prickle of fear on the back of her neck.

That prickle meant something, for the man reached into his stained breeches and pulled out his—

Next to her, Dada exploded, reaching out and cuffing the other man on the head. "Off with you before I cut it off and stuff it down your throat! This isn't London, you maggot-ridden cur."

The stinking man slunk off without a word. Moll was shaken by the encounter. "It will be all right, my girl. Sometimes men's baser instincts take over their good sense."

It all happened so fast that Moll didn't have time to continue thinking about it, for Dada pressed on to their destination.

Once they reached the stalls, Dada selected the woman who, in Moll's opinion, was the least attractive one there. Her slim figure suggested she was young enough to not be worn out by childbearing yet, but her face had been ravaged by smallpox, and her hair was faded to the color of dirty wash water. Her eyes were dull and listless, too.

"Good afternoon, milady," Dada began, dropping his case to the ground and opening it. "You surely have no need of my potions, as comely as you are, but might I interest you in a new unguent I have, one that will add vitality and rosiness to the skin?" He reached down into the case and pulled out a small tin, covered with a scrap of undyed cloth affixed to the container with string.

The woman frowned suspiciously, but then caught sight of Moll standing next to her father, which seemed to relax her considerably. "Who are you?" the woman asked, but her tone was inquisitive, not accusing.

"Milady, I am the most well-known essence seller in Devon. It is not often that I come to this town, and so very few ladies here have had the opportunity to use my elixirs that promote their natural beauty." Dada bowed and presented the tin to the woman.

She took it from him and untied the string, lifting the cloth up and sniffing the contents. "I smell roses."

"Yes. The finest rose hips to ensure the bloom of health."

"What else is in it?" She dipped two fingers into the container and pulled away some of the paste.

"Ah, dear lady. That is my secret concoction. I'll not have less talented charlatans copying me. Please, try it."

The woman handed the pot back to Moll's father and swiped her fingers across her face. She then rubbed the mixture into her skin.

"Margery, what's that you're doing?" One of the other women browsing at the stall became interested in Dada's customer.

"Try this. It feels so warm on the skin. And smells heavenly."

Dada handed the pot to the second woman, who also dipped a finger in and applied the unguent to her face.

"I'll buy it," said the second woman.

"No, Janet!" Margery snapped. "I was here first. It belongs to me."

"You know I'm to marry Ronald Malster in a fortnight's time. I must look my best," the other woman argued.

Dada let the tussle continue a few moments before intervening. "Let me check. I might have a second pot of it." He rummaged around in his bag and produced another tin. "Here we are. Each of you can enhance your natural beauty."

That seemed to satisfy both women, and coins were dropped into Dada's hand.

Janet wandered back to the stalls to examine a table of undergarments, but Margery, after glancing at Janet as if to ensure the other woman was out of earshot, said, "What else do you have?"

Dada appeared to consider her thoughtfully. "Well, I am quite sure you have no use for this, either, but I have—" he dropped his voice to a whisper, "—I have a love potion that is guaranteed to work on any man on whom you have set your sights. All you need to do is take a spoonful each morning upon arising, madam. Would you like to see it?" He reached into his bag and retrieved a capped leather pouch.

Margery glanced once more at the figure of Janet, who was purchasing a pair of honey-colored sleeves, and dropped more coins into Dada's hand without question.

For the next hour, multiple women stopped to

see what Moll's father was offering. Many made purchases, and eventually his case was empty.

"I'm sure you're hungry now," he said, clinking his leather money pouch.

Moll nodded. The pouch bulged; her father must have done well today.

They continued walking through Powderham until they came upon a building that was larger than most of them. It had a sign jutting from it that had a freshly painted spoon and knife crossed over one another. "The Great Hall," he read. "Must be named for the castle lord's rooms. Says it is 'welcoming of all respectable travelers.' That is us today, Moll." He once more jingled his pouch, which was now tucked inside his wool breeches.

Moll had never been inside an inn before, and she marveled at the interior as the owner greeted them and escorted them through it. The inn wasn't just a single room, but was broken into several spaces, each with a separate hearth and seeming to serve its own purpose.

In one room were tables at which men played cards. The centers of the tables were heaped with copper coins. Another room featured a man reading from a book, as others argued over events Moll didn't understand while smoking tobacco from clay pipes. The men were obscured by the smoke they exhaled up toward the ceiling.

Yet another, smaller room had just a few men in it, eating a meal and toasting one another with drink. There was a harp player in one corner, picking out a mournful tune quietly so as not to overpower the men's conversation. It seemed to be a private affair in here.

Moll followed her father and the owner past a staircase that wound its way up to another floor. They ended up at the rear of the inn, which contained a large room full of long tables and benches, with an enormous, merrily blazing hearth at the far end and windows with glass in them overlooking the inn's stable.

Father and daughter sat across from each other at one of the tables, and a wench served them trenchers full of the day's offering—a tantalizing rabbit stew alongside a round loaf of hot bread and cups of small beer, watered down so as not to cause a child to become drunk, but much safer than pure water.

Moll fell upon her food, tipping the trencher up to her mouth so she could down every last morsel of meat and vegetables, then tearing and dunking chunks of bread into the remaining gravy and sopping it all up.

It was even better than the meat pie for which she had been hoping.

"Careful, now, Moll, that you don't make yourself sick," Dada said.

Moll grinned, using her sleeve to swipe at a trail of gravy running down her chin.

"Dada," she said, feeling content to have a full belly and to be sitting inside such a wondrous place. "How does the love potion work? Will I need one someday?"

Her father smiled gently at her. "You are far too clever and lovely, Moll. That love potion was merely something that will freshen a woman's breath, which should make her more attractive to anyone."

Moll frowned, confused. "But if it doesn't work, why do you sell it?"

"Because darling girl, elixirs that don't work fetch a much higher price if the buyer believes it will buy her health, beauty, or love. My cures that *do* work, such as pain powders and burn salves, are viewed with suspicion that they are somehow tinged with witchcraft."

Moll was still confused. "That doesn't make sense."

He laughed. "No, it doesn't. But these are dark days, and we must be especially careful not to rouse attentions, particularly with these humorless Roundheads. Your Dada could end up imprisoned— or worse—if they thought I was messing with the Devil."

Moll didn't like that idea at all. "What is a Round—"

At that moment, Moll was distracted by motion through the large windows. A man had come barreling into the stable yard on a large white horse and was now rebuking the stable boy while staying atop the horse. The horse was lathering at the mouth. It must have run hard for quite some time to get here.

The man was dressed as fine as any lord, but his colors were muted, as if he didn't want to radiate the least bit of joy.

It caught Dada's attention, too. "Hmm. Be still, my girl."

Why did she need to be still because of some brute outside?

Everyone else in the room had grown quiet, too, as several other men on horses had arrived, attired like the brute. The new arrivals, however, remained outside, while the brute effortlessly dismounted and made his way around to the front of the inn.

The brute was soon inside, his domineering voice growing louder as he clearly stopped in every room along the way before arriving in the area where Moll and her father sat. As she had already observed, the man's clothing was odd, made of quality fabrics as befitting someone wealthy, yet a somber rust color with no ornamentation. His skin was weathered, and his hair cropped short under his hat, which was black and had no decoration except for a tawny orange feather attached to it. He did not remove his head covering as he addressed the room.

"I'm looking for Gabriel Lawrence, said to have come through here recently. What can any of you tell me about him?" the man demanded.

"Why d'ya want him?" asked a man seated further down their table.

"For crimes against Parliament that are none of your concern," the brute snapped.

The diner simply gazed wordlessly at the intruder.

"Well? Who has knowledge of Lawrence?" The brute stared around the room.

Moll felt that same prickle of fear that she'd felt outside when that awful man in the street had—

"This is a warning. If anyone here knows about him or is harboring him, I'll find out. And when I find out, you'll wish you had taken better care to be responsive to Parliament, which is now the true governing body in the land."

Moll had no idea what the man was talking about, but found herself shaking, nonetheless.

"We don't care who rules, we just care who makes our lives better," a man shouted from elsewhere in the room. "Make sure we have bread, we will follow you."

The brute was irritated by now. "Bread? You should be more concerned with whether I make sure you keep your head attached to your body." With that, he strode out. From her seated position, Moll watched as he returned to the stable yard, was assisted back onto his horse by the same boy he had yelled at earlier, then rode out at a gallop with his waiting men.

Moll could hear shouts of people in the street, complaining that the horses had nearly trampled them to death.

The room was quiet a few moments longer, then everyone returned to their conversations, although most of them were obviously about what had just happened.

"Who was that man?" Moll asked her father, as the inn's owner, a portly man clearly shaken by the intrusion into his establishment, tipped more small beer into their cups from a leather bladder. It seemed to Moll that the owner was pretending that nothing had happened.

As the owner walked away, Moll was hesitant. Was it wrong to ask about the angry man who had just threatened them?

Her father sopped up his own last bit of rich stew gravy and popped the chunk of bread into his mouth, chewing and swallowing before responding. "I suppose we're lucky it was just a Roundhead. The Puritans are worse. They would have heard laughing and music and gone mad like rabid dogs." Dada shook his head. "It's time to tell you things that will help you to take care of yourself in the future."

Dada dropped his voice, causing Moll to lean forward over her empty trencher toward him. "You see, sweetheart, the world is a difficult place," he began.

Having been assaulted at the Friday market two years ago, plus remembering that their distant family members had been killed by the king, not to mention the encounter in the street a short while ago, Moll well knew that. She nodded at her father.

"I know you believe you have seen the worst the world has to offer, but I'm afraid there's more coming.

"You remember that there was trouble up in Ulster, and that many people were killed as a result. The problem was that there had been a great deal of suffering in Ireland, not just constant lack of food and safety, but the Irish people wanted to have Mother Church restored to them. The Irish were invaded four centuries ago by the English, but had been under the thumb of the so-called Reformers since King Henry VIII's time, a hundred years ago. Do you understand me so far, Moll?"

Moll nodded, although she didn't understand completely. Four hundred years ago was back near the beginning of time. What did it have to do with anything?

"But things got intolerable, what with Reformers—Protestants they call themselves—going into Ireland and taking away lands from people who had lived there for centuries. Imagine a stranger coming up to you and snatching your satchel away because you are seen to worship God incorrectly."

Why would my satchel be taken away because of my worship of God?

"So, the Irish had been long suffering and now they were having their lands taken from them. They rose up—including some of the Dyers—and rebelled against the unfairness of it."

Moll nodded again. "So, the king had them kill—"

"Shhh." Her father put an index finger to his lips. "Speak softly, girl, lest someone—anyone—overhear you. The Irish subjects were simply trying to get their lands and their Church back. The king and Parliament argued over which of them should control the army that would be raised to stop the uprising, as King Charles and his Parliament had already been quarreling for years over many things."

"Like how Agnes and Dorothy quarrel with each other?" Moll had listened to endless arguments between her two older sisters.

"Yes. Disputes over everything, both the silly and the important. Although with your sisters, it's mostly silly. Anyway, the king decided to act on his own and raise an army to defeat the Irish, which angered Parliament, so then Parliament built an army. They are calling this the Wars of Three Kingdoms."

"Parliament," Moll repeated. "That man said that Parliament is the 'true governing body.' Does that mean they beat the king?"

Dada laughed without mirth. "Hardly. They've been skirmishing and sieging. Do you know what a skirmish is?"

Moll shook her head.

"It's a very short fight. Like those foolish boys we saw attempting to fight outside. An attempt to brawl, but without any real strength or strategy."

The innkeeper came by and asked Moll's father to settle the bill, which he did, leaving Moll with time to consider what Dada had said.

Her father dug several coins out of his pouch. The innkeeper bowed as he took the money. Dada seemed pleased by the action. It was rare that anyone would treat members of her family so respectfully.

"Then neither side is very strong, so it should be over soon, right?" Moll ventured when the inn's owner was out of earshot.

Again, the joyless laugh. "Hardly, sweetheart. Both sides are convinced of their righteousness. The king believes he is ordained by God to rule as he wishes—to include conducting an invasion of

Ireland—while Parliament believes he only rules with Parliament's consent. There is no middle ground."

Moll still wasn't sure what the king's quarrel with Parliament had to do with her and why she might need to protect herself in the future.

"If they are arguing over an invasion way up in Ireland, that won't affect us, will it?" Moll hoped she sounded mature, even if Dada's explanation was getting confusing.

"Well, we're only a few miles away from home, and you just saw a Parliamentarian—Roundheads they call them, for their strange short hairstyles—barge in here, threatening us. And last year, one of the king's men rode into our town to announce his actions in Ulster. I imagine we will see more such occurrences, one side and then the other convincing us of its right to rule. It will be dangerous for all subjects of the realm, but especially us."

The Dyers might be poor, but they were as respectable as any of their neighbors. "Why, especially us?" she asked.

"Our family hails from Ireland. I came to Devon many years ago to try and make a better living for myself than could be done back in Ireland. I met your mother, we had children, and now Devon is home. The home country became worse, and your Granda fled after he lost everything. Remember what I told you about the Irish wanting to return to Mother Church?"

"Yes, Dada."

"Many of the English don't like it. Their old King Henry convinced them—after being convinced by that witch Anne Boleyn—that the Reformers had the right of worship. Imagine stripping churches of their crucifixes and statues and everything else that makes a church a church. The English are now very suspicious of those of us who worship in the True Church. This is why we must be very careful, and it's why you must keep your hair tightly covered. If someone sees those flaming locks of Irish hair, it might call into question our nationality, and that will call into question how we worship. Assuredly, the Parliamentarians wouldn't be happy about it, and despite our good Catholic queen, we might not have safety from royal corners, either."

Moll was quiet. Was Dada saying that her mere presence within the family put them at risk. *I'll cut all of my hair off. I'll run away to the hills so no one will ever know I am a member of the Dyers. I'll—*

"Have I upset you now, Moll?" her father asked gently.

"No," she lied. This moment made her miss Granda immensely. His strong arms wrapped around her like a comforting blanket. His rich laugh and twinkling eyes that always made her feel happy inside. What Dada was telling her was so... so...scary.

"I wish Granda were here," she blurted out, feeling tears welling in her eyes.

"Ah, now, Moll, I *have* upset you. But you'll be a grown woman soon enough, and I'd rather you be prepared for what might be coming. You loved your grandfather very much, didn't you?"

Moll nodded, a lump in her throat.

"So did I, little one, so did I."

For the first time, she saw that Dada's eyes were rimmed red. Perhaps she wasn't the only one grieving her darling Granda.

Before they left the inn, Moll's father pulled the small pouch full of coins he had collected during their time in Powderham from within one of the pockets of his gray wool waistcoat, which was as worn as Moll's own dress. He slyly poured the money onto the table between them and stacked like-coins together. Dada then did some figuring, and a warm smile broke out on his face, erasing the earlier sadness over Granda.

"Despite the unpleasantness here, we did well today, Moll. I'm very pleased." He rose to leave. Moll followed him outside, where the sun was beginning its journey down the horizon.

In fact, Dada was so pleased that, despite the expense of their meal, he hired a passing cart to take them back to Kenn.

CHAPTER 6

July 1644

DESPITE DADA'S DIRE predictions, life was continuing as usual for the Dyer family. The biggest news in Moll's world was that her eldest sister, Agnes, now at the marriageable age of fifteen, had wasted no time in securing a husband, having fallen fiercely for William Martyn at the market held in Tavistock during the feast of St. Mark in April.

Martyn was seventeen and from an important cloth-working family who owned a large mill in nearby Oxton. He seemed to have fallen just as hard for Agnes, which baffled Moll. Agnes was pretty enough, but had grown even more temperamental with age, arguing not just with Dorothy, but with anyone else who disagreed with her.

Thus far, though, William Martyn could do no wrong in Agnes's eyes, the biggest sign, to Moll, that Agnes was completely smitten. She hoped that William would not one day discover Agnes's petulant side and rue his decision.

Especially since Agnes's sense of self-importance had grown immensely since meeting him. "I won't have to work at such mean things much longer," she said to Moll one morning as they scrubbed the family's few spare articles of clothing in a local stream. They always did the wash early to finish it before the sun became too high overhead.

"What do you mean?" Moll asked, sitting back on her heels to give her back a rest from the work.

"I mean that once I become a part of the Martyn family, I'll have a servant to do this work. At least a laundress, a housemaid, and a cook." Agnes's lips curved into a satisfied smile, like a stray cat who had come upon a dish of milk no other cat noticed.

"Will you be rich?" Moll asked, not believing that anyone except the finest lords and ladies could afford such things.

"Far richer than I would be staying at home. In fact, knowing that dear William will likely propose to me soon, and I will be providing so much benefit to the family through my marriage, I don't see why I'm stuck doing menial tasks like laundry with the likes of you."

Moll wasn't sure whether Agnes was upset about the laundry or working with Moll. Either way, it was insulting. After all, Moll was ten years old now and no longer a baby who couldn't hold a conversation.

Agnes had grown haughty.

Moll had one more question, one that she was sure her parents were asking. "Is he a Reformer?"

Agnes frowned at her. "Where have you heard that? And I don't know. What I do know is that making him my husband will mean I will conform my religion to his. You'll learn someday, little sister, that your husband will guide you in spiritual matters and you will worship as he worships."

Moll didn't think their parents would agree with such a notion and said so.

"As if I will give a fig about our family once I become joined to the Martyns. Mama and Dada would be best served to also conform to the Martyns."

Moll thought Agnes's plan was a poor one, but it was not up to her to convince her sister to do otherwise.

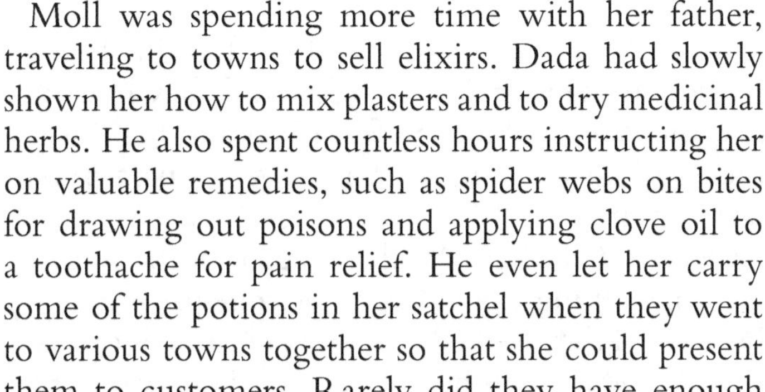

Moll was spending more time with her father, traveling to towns to sell elixirs. Dada had slowly shown her how to mix plasters and to dry medicinal herbs. He also spent countless hours instructing her on valuable remedies, such as spider webs on bites for drawing out poisons and applying clove oil to a toothache for pain relief. He even let her carry some of the potions in her satchel when they went to various towns together so that she could present them to customers. Rarely did they have enough success to relax in an inn afterward, but Moll lived each day on the hope of rabbit stew and freshly baked bread.

There had been a battle between the king and Parliament at someplace called Edgehill last October, around the time of the Goosey Fair in Tavistock, where Mama had purchased many yards of linen and lace from the Martyns. Mama had purchased even more during the Michaelmas market in December, which must have cost a great deal of money. It made Moll wonder if Mama was trying to purchase their friendship.

The Edgehill battle had occurred in faraway Warwickshire, a place Moll hardly knew existed. Neither side had won a victory, yet Dada still maintained a dour expression over the whole thing.

"If each side could not best the other, won't they eventually both make peace and go home?" Moll asked him once as they walked along the banks of River Kenn toward the town of Clapham to sell their wares.

He once more offered that cheerless laugh. "You do not yet understand men, Moll. To be both right and a hero is an overarching need for most of us. This will not end until there is a winner. I just pray to the Blessed Mother that the fighting remains to the north."

That made no sense to Moll. After all, she had witnessed many creatures fight until they got tired and then just walk away from one another. Surely men—leaders of the country—were smarter than farm animals.

Once in Clapham, Moll was agape at the number of men walking along the cobblestone paths in black hats so tall they looked like sooty chimneys on their heads. The men all had the strange hairstyle of that Parliamentary man who had burst into the inn at Powderham. But these men were not dressed quite as fine as the inn brute had been. Their clothes were much simpler and even more somber, which seemed to affect their ability to smile.

"We've run into a nest of Puritans," Dada said softly. "Best to conduct our business and be gone. Keep that hair of yours out of sight."

Moll patted around her coif to ensure no strands were falling out. They were safe, as long as green eyes, a too-long nose, a tall frame, and a coltish gait didn't suggest anything bad to others around her.

Puritan women, who wore variations of the same funny hats as the men, also wore dour clothing with little decoration.

Moll would have thought they looked sad, except they moved with such…determination.

That determination gave them a confidence Moll

had never seen before. It also made them unmovable when it came to Dada's potions. He quickly realized that none of them were interested in a beauty elixir, so he switched to pain remedies and disease cures, but they weren't very responsive to those, either.

"The Lord only gives us what we can bear."

"Pain is a reminder of our own wickedness."

Her father was able to sell a corked jar of apple bark syrup to a woman with chest pains, as well as a fuming pot stuffed with rosemary, cloves, and cinnamon to a man who complained of his wife's bodily odors from her severe case of ague, but it was clear that this town would not be profitable.

"I think we are done in Clapham," Dada said.

They walked over a bridge toward the river's path back to Kenn. At the base of the bridge was a pie seller. Moll's stomach grumbled so loudly that Dada stopped to look at her. "Child, have I neglected to feed you at all today?"

Moll didn't want to accuse her father of anything. "I'm a little hungry."

Dada stopped at the pie seller's booth, which was filled with every manner of sweets and savories wrapped up in fresh doughs.

As they looked at the seller's wares, Moll noticed that the seller, a burly man who looked to be frequently sampling his own foodstuffs, frowned at them.

"Are you a non-conformist?" the pie seller asked. It sounded like an accusation to Moll.

"Naturally, we worship in the only true way," Dada replied, not looking up from where he was examining an unbaked fish pie.

Moll marveled at her father for his ability to tell the truth yet make the questioner believe it was what he wanted to hear.

"Well said! We must stand united against any unholy reforms in our Church of England. An apple tart for the little miss?" Now that he thought Dada was of the right persuasion, he was very friendly.

Moll eyed the pastry hungrily. To her delight, Dada bought it for her, purchasing a chunk of sage cheese wrapped in bread for himself.

But sales hadn't been good enough for them to even purchase small beer to wash it down. Dada's coin pouch wasn't nearly as full as it had been on other trips.

They traipsed home to find Mama sitting next to a candle, plying needle and thread.

"Puritans in Clapham," Dada said.

Mama gazed at him sadly. "So nearby. Times will get worse, no doubt. At least Tavistock is back in Royalist hands."

Moll wondered how the dour people in Clapham would affect her family.

"We must be careful," Dada said. Her father went back outside to tend to the cleaning out of his and Moll's bags. She sat at her mother's feet to rest her own and to just be around Mama's familiar look and smell. It had been a long time since she had spent solitary time with her mother.

"What are you making?" Moll asked.

Her mother held up a snowy-white collar edged in lace. The fabric was bleached, so it must have been expensive. It was also a large collar, so Moll assumed it was for a man.

"Pretty," she said.

"Yes. But no one can know about them." Mama dropped her voice to a hushed whisper. "They are for the king's men. They are now called Cavaliers. I want to do my part for them."

Moll was now more confused than she had ever

been. "But…didn't the king attack our people in Ireland? And kill them? Why are you making nice clothes for his men?"

Mama sighed. "Poor Moll, life is too complicated for a child your age, isn't it?

Each time Moll thought she was becoming an adult, it seemed that she was in for a lesson about how young she was.

Her mother laid down her sewing, carefully placing it atop another scrap of cloth on the table. Moll knew that was to keep the fine linen collar clean.

Her mother kept her voice low. "You are right, it is terrible that the king attacked our relations in Ireland. But he is the best hope we have for maintaining our Catholic faith traditions, faint as that hope is. The Roundheads—and especially the Puritans—would sooner see us attached to stakes and put to the fire than to allow us our freedom of worship."

Moll shivered at the thought of what a burning would be like.

"It wouldn't do for the king to believe that any of his subjects had been disloyal to him. But if Parliamentary forces prevail, we wouldn't wish them to think we had worked against them."

"But aren't battles being fought up in Warwickshire? What worries are there, since that is so far away?"

"Not just Warwickshire," her mother said. "The king has won a battle at Braddock Down, in Cornwall. Royalists now have possession of all of Cornwall, south of us. But will they hold it?" She shrugged. "The Roundheads would also be content to extinguish us for supporting the king."

Moll pointed at the unfinished collar, which

had surely cost their family a precious number of coins. "Does that prove that we are working against them?"

Another sigh. "Yes. Which is why we must be very quiet about it. Your father and I think—hope—that the king will prevail. But who can predict anything in the middle of so much disorder and upheaval?"

"So, we have to pretend to like both sides?" How were they to do that?

"In some ways, yes. It is our goal to survive, Moll. It is others' goals to be right, or triumphant, or sit in power. We just want to *live*. Do you understand?"

Moll nodded. "Are the Martyns Royalists or Roundheads?"

"Shh." Her mother put a finger to her lips. Everyone seemed to be shushing her lately. "They are Royalists. But if the Parliamentarians take over the cloth maker's guild, I suspect they will turn and suddenly be wearing tall hats and short hair. Do you understand?" she repeated.

"Yes, Mama, I think I do."

Her mother picked up the lace collar again, but fidgeted with it more than she sewed. "There is a royal colony across the ocean called Maryland. They say Catholics can live in peace there. I've suggested to your father that now, with your Granda gone and at least one of the children about to secure a marriage, we should consider going there. Not just for religious safety but for opportunity. I once thought he was open to the notion, but now he won't hear of it. Says Devon is our home and always will be."

Maryland? It sounded much further away than Warwickshire. Would it even resemble England? Moll was glad her father had refused the idea.

CHAPTER 7

Kenn, Devon,
October 1648

AT FOURTEEN YEARS of age, Moll was getting older and taller. She was nearly as tall as her elder brother Thomas, who not only teased her mercilessly as being "gangly," but routinely informed her that, "You'll never find a husband looking like a long-necked, pointy-beaked heron."

Just as routinely, Moll told her brother that she planned to swallow him whole, like the warty toad he was.

Despite her ability to jab back quickly at Thomas, Moll was still wounded when he mocked her. "By the time you're a woman, you'll have to bend down to pass through the doorway," Thomas commonly told her before leaving home to serve out an apprenticeship with a boardwright.

She couldn't help that she towered over many women.

At the same time she was growing up, her family was getting poorer. The long stalemate between king and Parliament had ended at someplace called Marston Moor in 1644, not long after Moll and her father had visited Clapham to sell elixirs.

Not only had the Parliamentarians won, but they had created a standing army in the country, about which Dada whispered the people should be very afraid.

Yet life had still gone on. Agnes had married her William Martyn and already had two children. She only deigned to speak to her family when she ran into them at market on Fridays. The Martyns had proved quite adept at changing allegiance depending upon how the wind was blowing, thus Agnes seemed to be quite safe within their protection.

Dorothy, too, had secured a mate and then moved to a nearby town.

Everyone was astonished that Thomas had excelled in learning carpentry. Rumors drifted to the family's ears of his carousing, which would surely end his apprenticeship if he weren't careful, but that wasn't Moll's concern.

The departure of her elder siblings made Moll the eldest child at home, about which she felt pride, for she served as a mother figure to William, Elizabeth, and Christian.

William continued to be her favorite, so close were they in age and temperament. Perhaps it was also because he never held it against her that she had been responsible for his burned hand.

Despite life continuing, there were harsh realities with which the Dyers had to contend.

The Parliamentarians, with their "new model army," had been able to move more readily against the Royalist forces, despite Mama producing her little lace collars far into the nights to support them.

Dada said the Parliamentarians had secured military support from the Presbyterian Scots up north, who feared that the king had the Catholic Irish allied to his side. Apparently, the Irish troops had never equaled the numbers that the Scots had provided.

It was such a mix-up of why different people were joining opposite sides that Moll gave up trying to understand. Her parents' hushed conversations no longer even held interest for her.

King Charles had, however, surrendered to the Scots in May 1646.

"Let that be an end to it," Dada had said in disgust.

It wasn't the end, though. Moll was quickly learning that when it came to men and their wars, nothing ever ended.

One night, a loud banging scared Moll witless as she lay on her sleeping pallet.

The family scrambled to the door. Dada opened it, only to find several Roundheads there, looking very important in their steel breastplates and helmets over buff leather breeches and jerkins.

"We seek Elizabeth Dyer," one of the men announced.

Before Dada could say anything, Mama exclaimed, "What have you need with me?"

"You are accused of having aided the king's illicit campaign against Parliament," the man said.

Dada's face was flush with disappointment, surely because Mama had so readily given away who she was.

Moll's mother was hauled away in manacles and unceremoniously tossed into the back of a cart, her unbound hair everywhere and her gaze wildly unfocused. Mama looked like one of those old crones who live in the woods, muttering incantations.

It was a sight Moll would never forget as she watched from the open door.

Dada hurriedly dressed so he could follow Mama to wherever the soldiers were taking her.

"I will go with you," Moll said, already tying on her shoes in the fading light of the soldiers' torches.

"No," Dada replied. "You will stay here and watch your siblings."

Moll argued with her father. The younger three would be fine for a few hours alone, wouldn't they? But Mama might not be fine. Mama might be in great trouble. Moll's mother might need her. She might—

"I cannot concentrate on your mother's fate unless I know that everything at home is secure," Dada said. "Can I rely on you?"

He reached out a thumb and touched Moll's nose, just like Granda used to do.

Moll swallowed her disappointment and fear and nodded at her father. "Yes, you can rely on me."

Dada refused to let anyone go with him to the gaol to visit Mama. Moll didn't know how much Dada had paid or what he had promised, but two weeks later, he came home with Mama, who looked as though she had done nothing but weep the entire time.

"You'll not be making those lace collars anymore," he told her sternly. "No doubt someone at the market reported your excessive purchases. We are lucky they decided that executing a woman for making bits of clothing might not serve them well."

Mama nodded without saying a word.

After that, Moll's mother was pensive and nervous, never liking her family members to wander very far from home.

The days spent with Dada, peddling to different towns, became a relief for Moll, even if their fortunes were not changing.

Mama's one happy moment had been when she heard that Father Andrew White, who had helped to settle the Maryland colony, had been released from Newgate jail. Mama said he'd been sent back to England in chains by an illegitimate, Protestant usurper to the colony's government.

"How shameful to lock up a man of God," Mama had said. "And the condition of his release was that he never return to Maryland, even though the Calverts got control of the colony again. The poor priest, unable to return to the place where Catholics can worship in peace."

It made her start talking about that faraway settlement again.

Moll had covered her ears against it. Her father also admonished Mama, saying that there would be no emigration to a country thousands of miles across the dangerous ocean.

"Let that be an end to it," he repeated.

The king's defeat, however, had not really been a final defeat. Charles had signed some sort of agreement with the Scots to establish Presbyterianism in England. In return, they agreed fight for him, and that had started it all over again.

The Scots had invaded England back in July, but had been repulsed by Cromwell's army, their former allies, by the middle of August.

Then the unthinkable happened.

Cromwell's army demanded that the king be put on trial for treason as the cause for all the bloodshed. Charles, now under arrest, was moved around to various castles until finally brought to trial at a specially constituted court at Westminster on January 20th, 1649.

England, Scotland, and Ireland held their collective breaths as the charges of treason and other "high crimes" were brought against the king, who steadfastly refused to recognize the court because he was a king and thus not answerable to any earthly jurisdiction.

Oliver Cromwell, whom Mama said was the true source of the treason, signed the king's death warrant.

On January 27th, the death warrant was read.

On January 30th, the king was beheaded as a "tyrant, traitor, murderer, and public enemy."

Mama blanched in a way Moll had never seen before over the news that the king had been executed. "My God, what will become of us all?" she whispered. "A blade across the neck of a legitimate sovereign? What sort of country does this?"

Moll involuntarily put a hand to her throat, the horror of what must have happened frightening her.

"The sort whose citizens would do well to remain quiet in the face of such events," Dada said. "He is gone now, and we are under the rule of Cromwell. Dear God, let *that* finally be an end to it."

CHAPTER 8

October 1650

WITH KING CHARLES gone, the Parliamentarians believed they had permanently secured control of the country and had in fact declared England to be a "commonwealth" country, whatever that meant. Something to do with the country existing for the common good. Not that the Dyer family had experienced much benefit from it.

But the king's execution had only served to galvanize both the Irish and—ironically, the Scots—into fighting on behalf of the king's son, also Charles, and now the second of that name.

Apparently, the Scots had been just as mortified as Mama that a sovereign king had been executed by his Parliament.

Thus, the civil war engulfing the country entered its third phase. War had now been raging in the country for more than eight years.

Yet the Dyers considered themselves lucky, for if they lived in Scotland or Ireland, they would more likely be dead, given the devastation that had been wreaked up there.

Moll had turned sixteen, causing her mother to begin fretting over how they were to find a husband for her, given how many men had been sacrificed to war at this point.

Moll didn't care about a husband. She was quite satisfied helping her father make and sell potions. If life could just remain settled, she would be happy the rest of her days.

While Moll frequently helped Dada, Mama had gotten the idea of making ales and selling them to local taverns and alehouses. Dada was glad to see Mama occupied in a way that brought the family a little more money, although he complained about the stink of the work outside.

"Worse than goats, it is." Dada wrinkled up his nose in a way that made Moll laugh.

But she enjoyed the malty aroma produced by the ale-making process.

Mama had begun her little business by simply gathering recipes for steeping a variety of herbs in ready-made ale. Moll watched, fascinated, as Mama went through many recipes trying to find a desirable one.

The recipes ranged from tossing in handfuls of fur and orange peels to peony roots and bitter dock weeds. The work seemed to bring Mama peace.

As Moll's mother became more confident in her infusions, she began making the actual strong beer itself—the smell of which Dada objected to so greatly.

Mama combined varying amounts of malt, wheat, dried pease, oats, and hops, boiling the liquor on a "long boil" for four to five hours in a copper kettle under a small lean-to behind their cottage.

Mama said the copper was crucial to the flavor.

One day, Moll stood outside with her mother before the roiling kettle. The autumn day was crisp, so the fire roaring beneath the kettle was pleasant.

Her mother dipped a long-handled ladle into

the hot liquid and scooped out a little, bringing it toward her and blowing on it to cool it.

Once the mixture was slightly cooled, Mama took a sip from it. Her expression was disappointed. "Try it?" she asked Moll, extending the wooden utensil.

Moll took the ladle from her mother and sipped from it. It was very...tart. "I don't think it's ready," she said.

Mama nodded and pursed her lips, as if deciding what to toss in next.

Dada came outside, nose wrinkled as usual.

"Are you going to make us rich?" he asked.

Mama sighed. "Not at this rate. But the Three Sheeps did say they would try some of my honey ale. Hopefully, Cromwell doesn't decide that ale making needs be regulated to death to ensure we are all upstanding citizens."

Dada frowned at Moll's mother. "Quiet, Lizzy. Neighbors have large ears."

Mama had eventually revived from her arrest scare, but the experience had changed her. She spent her days preoccupied with the future of the family and how they would survive the war that continued to explode among Parliament, Scotland, and Ireland.

At least they lived in the southwest of England, now Royalist territory, and away from the fighting that was mostly in Scotland, but it made for terrible economic times for everyone. Food was scarce, and everything else scarcer.

It was terrible enough that Dada had returned home one evening and surprised them with a surprising admission.

"Came to tell you that I was talking to some customers in the village today," Dada said to Moll's mother. "You might like to hear what they said. You, too, Moll."

The three of them sat at the family's table, with Mama drawing back the cloth coverings on the window openings to let in more light before she joined Moll and Dada.

"Where are the others?" Dada asked.

"William took them to the village square to entertain them. Moll stayed back to help me." Her mother sat down heavily, as if already tired for the day. Fortunately for Moll, William was now old enough to be in charge of the younger ones.

Dada nodded. "A man I met—a good customer, he purchased three pots of beauty cream for his wife and two daughters—told me that the Maryland colony has passed some sort of toleration act. They've suffered some Puritan abuses as we have, and they are trying to make it tolerable for any religious sect to live there."

Moll looked at her mother, whose expression was hopeful. "Think you it's a place you'd want to go?"

Dada spread his hands. "I don't know. I don't think so. The thought is more attractive than before, but the idea of religious toleration and the actual practice of it might be two different things. Imagine sailing all that way to find out that conditions are just as bad as they are here. And would we subject all four remaining children to it? Would you go there and risk not ever seeing Thomas, Agnes, or Dorothy again?"

Mama pursed her lips tighter, and her eyes had a faraway look.

"I'll not go," Moll said flatly. "I live here in Devon, and I'll never leave. I'll—I'll—I'll find a husband and start a farm of my own."

Dada was now looking at her thoughtfully. "You

know, Agnes's marriage into the Martyn family has meant that Agnes has become so enamored of her growing status that she no longer recognizes us as family. And Dorothy's husband is, well, an addle-pate, but they live a quiet life, and no one has a harsh word for them. What if Moll made a good marriage with a Royalist to secure her own future, and then we could…"

"What?" Moll gasped. She hadn't been serious about her suggestion. "I cannot leave you and Mama." How quickly she had exposed her own bluff of finding a husband.

"Of course you eventually will. You will have your own children and your own home. You're sixteen now, child; it's almost time. And then you wouldn't be faced with a decision to leave the country."

Moll was incredulous. "Dada, are you saying you *will* go to the Maryland colony?"

Even Mama was agape at the thought.

"I'm not saying that. I'm saying that we must put more thought into how to best preserve the family. Charles's son has strong support down here, and the Royalists may win yet, but what if they don't? If the Roundheads fully take control of this country, what will happen to Catholics like us?"

Two days later, the Parliamentarians routed the Scots in a battle at Dunbar, in the southern part of Scotland along the North Sea.

Rumors began that Charles II's cause to regain his father's throne was lost.

CHAPTER 9

April 1657

FORTUNATELY FOR MOLL, discussions about getting her married had died down, despite being twenty-three now, what with so much else happening in the family.

Her beloved younger brother, William, married a woman named Agnes, making for two Agneses in the family.

Agnes then had a son that they named William, creating even more naming confusion— but great happiness—within the family.

Moll loved Agnes as though she were a sister, not only because she was William's wife, but because the woman seemed to take no notice of William's long-ago scarred hands.

It helped Moll's sense of guilt to know that her beloved brother had found a wife who did not view him as marred in any way.

Dorothy had had a son, John, last year, causing Moll's mother to spend considerable time between Dorothy's and William's homes, cooing over her grandchildren.

Mama had less inclination to insist that Moll get married off, because Mama now had less inclination to leave the country.

Mama's final word on the subject came when she delivered some news she had heard.

"Remember they sent that priest back in chains from Maryland?" she said one evening as Moll accompanied her to check on the copper kettle.

"You mean Father White," Moll said, nodding as she used the edge of her white apron to lift the hot lid on the boiling kettle.

"Yes. He has died here in England. He was never permitted to return to Maryland. Seems such a shame." Mama dipped her ladle into the mixture and took a sip. "The extra molasses helps the taste."

Mama had enjoyed some success with her brewing, despite how difficult life under Cromwell's "protectorate" had been.

The man had many rules and restrictions that had never existed before under a king. All of them came from the Puritan belief that if one worked hard, one would end up in heaven.

Conscientious toiling for a divine destination applied to all days except Sundays. On that day, absolutely nothing was to occur except attending church. One could not even take a stroll without being heavily fined, unless walking to church.

Anything remotely frivolous was frowned upon in Cromwell's England. Theatres were shut down, as were many inns, thus impacting Mama's business, although she still managed to sell some of her ale.

Swearing was punishable by a fine. The playing of sports was banned. Previous feast days to honor saints had been turned into general monthly fasting days.

If Puritan leaders smelled a goose cooking on Christmas Day, hefty fines could result. Christmas celebrations were now dour affairs, of which no one wanted to partake.

Even worse was Cromwell's standing army, something which had never been seen in England.

Cromwell had divided the country into eleven areas, each of which was governed by a trusted Cromwell associate…and whose rules were enforced by soldiers.

Women were forced to dress as modestly and as blandly as possible. Puritan leaders and soldiers would roam the streets looking for women who wore dresses that were too colorful or who had any type of cosmetics on their faces.

Fines and public humiliation would result for women who weren't dressed in black dresses with white aprons and caps.

The white aprons and caps were to symbolize women's supposed chastity, while the black dresses were no doubt intended to make them miserable.

At least the snowy hair coverings meant that Moll looked quite in keeping with everyone else while keeping her red hair hidden.

Over the past few years, as she had blossomed into a young woman, she had learned a great deal about ale-making from her mother, even as she was learning about physicks from her father.

Mama's ale—distinguished from beer by the fact that it was fermented at warmer temperatures—started with malted grains and took about a week to turn into a drinkable product.

Although work wasn't permitted to be conducted on Sundays, Mama frequently kept working and simply risked being discovered.

Barley was the usual grain for her ale, although corn, oats, wheat, and rye could be used. Malting involved spouting the grains and then drying them in a makeshift kiln Dada had built for Mama outside.

By using Sundays to soak her grain without any other activities, she wasn't likely to be caught.

On Monday, she drained the barley or whatever

grain she was experimenting with. The grains would begin sprouting almost immediately.

On Thursday, Mama collected the grains and dried them to stop the germination. Somehow, this helped the fermentation that would ensue, as well as lending sweetness to the resulting flavor.

On Friday, Moll would help her mother grind the newly created malt and make yeast.

On Saturday morning, they made wort, which was malt-infused water. By Saturday evening, they were ready to strain the grains from the wort. The leftover grains were thrown down for animals to consume, and the wort was placed into a copper kettle over a fire, along with a measure of hops, the fruit of a vine-like tree related to the mulberry bush.

Moll always liked to inhale deeply at this point, for the hops were what gave the ale its distinctive aroma.

After it performed its "long boil," Mama would extinguish the fire and let the pot cool, then Moll and her mother would add, or "pitch," the yeast into the liquid.

A sugar, such as molasses or honey, was added to help nourish the yeast.

It was at this point that the mixture simply developed itself into a tasty ale. Moll would cover a straw broom with more yeast and use it to periodically stir the ale. The additional yeast quickened the process.

By the following Monday—after Sunday's work restrictions—Mama poured the ale through funnels into cork-stoppered bottles.

They kept a few bottles for the family, but Mama peddled most of them to the remaining open taverns and inns in nearby villages.

"You should get married, Moll, but if you never do, you at least know how to make ale, so you will be able to provide for yourself."

Ironically, life unexpectedly turned for Moll, and she no longer cared about being able to provide for what appeared to be a long and contented spinsterhood.

Richard Northcutt had appeared in her life, and Moll was in love.

CHAPTER 10

August 1657

MOLL WAS READY to go by herself to the Friday market in town to purchase hops.

"Remember, only buy them from Mrs. Pagg," Mama had cautioned. "She has the best ones."

With hard-earned coins safely sewn into her somber, black dress pocket, Moll set out for the market, one of the few activities Cromwell had not forbidden as useless, immoral, or frivolous.

At least, not yet.

She was perspiring heavily by the time she got there, as her drab, wool dress was oppressively hot in the sun.

After trading her coins for a sack of hops with Mrs. Pagg, Moll decided to wander through the market, despite it not having the joyous air it used to have, except...

She cocked a covered ear. Was that music carrying across the thick, heated August air?

She followed the sound of it, curious as to who would be so daring as to play joyful music and run the risk of infuriating Cromwell's men.

Moll finally found the man, who stood tucked between a hosier selling stockings, gloves, and nightcaps, and a clutch of vendors selling men's breeches, waistcoats, and shirts. He held a long pipe up to his lips as he blew against a cup-shaped mouthpiece while moving his fingers up and down over the air holes running along the top of the instrument. His thumbs appeared to take turns at an air hole on the bottom of the instrument.

The scene reminded her of that long-ago day when she danced with abandon at a hurdy-gurdy player at the market. That had resulted in humiliation when Moll's cowl had fallen off, exposing her fiery hair to the townspeople.

She was much older now and had no intention of carrying on like a hoyden in front of a musician.

The player, whom Moll guessed to be around her age, seemed oblivious to her standing a distance away, observing him. He simply played, his eyes closed as he swayed to his own notes.

All around him, people either flashed him appreciative looks or else reprimanded him, depending upon their viewpoints.

"Terrible thing, you're blasting about as though life were all about selfish pursuits. Why d'ye not fight for the king?" some hissed.

"Thank ye, son, for bringing us a bit of joy today," said others.

"Quiet yourself, you simpleton. Will you have us all arrested and the market closed?" came from a few angry people.

The player, who wore the requisite dark clothing and a tall, black hat, seemed anything other than a Puritan.

Moll finally got the nerve to approach him. He had an old cap—from a bygone day where people were permitted to be stylish—on the ground, inside of which were a few coins.

"Excuse me," she said tentatively.

He stopped his playing and opened his eyes.

Moll took a sharp intake of breath. Those eyes

were the grayest things she'd ever seen, like mild storm clouds rolling in over the hills.

"I—I—er, I was wondering what that is you're playing," she said. Did she sound like a foolish child?

Thankfully, he smiled. It wasn't the tolerant, tooth-gritting smile of one of Cromwell's men. No, his smile stretched across his face and included his eyes.

Moll was entranced.

A million questions clanged around in her mind at once. Had he fought in the wars? On which side? Had he been injured? Was he married? Did he have sons? Had he—

"This is a cornet," he said. "Who might you be, gracefully tall and fairest of maidens?"

"Mary Dyer, from Kenn, but most call me Moll." She was certain she was blushing to match her hair.

"Well, Moll Dyer from Kenn, I'm Richard Northcutt. I'm from Teignmouth, but there's not much appreciation for music there. Not much appreciation for it anywhere these days. What do you think about music?"

The question sounded like a trap.

"I—er, when played in its proper place, music can be—ah…" Moll had no idea how to respond in a way that wouldn't get her in trouble.

Cromwell had made everyone so fearful.

Richard laughed. "You've no need to be afraid of me. In fact—" Richard removed his tall hat and showed her the inside of it. A white feather with a piece of lace wrapped around it was sewn to the inside of the hat. Moll had heard of this. It was a symbol of the Cavaliers.

"Oh," she breathed.

"I expect you are of the same persuasion?" he asked.

Moll nodded dumbly. Why was she so taken with this stranger?

She dropped her voice to a whisper. "My family is Catholic."

He nodded knowingly. "I could tell we were of one mind, Moll Dyer." He, too, dropped his voice. "Glory to the Father, and to the Son, and to the Holy Spirit. As it was in the beginning, is now, and will be forever."

Why was Moll's stomach somersaulting? It wasn't a feeling of sickness, either. It was more like she was intoxicated, like those people who drank too many of Mama's ales.

"You are brave to speak as such," she said.

He shrugged. "Life has been too difficult for too long. I find myself caring less and less for the opinions of others. I long for the day that things might return to normal."

Naturally, the only way things could return to normal was if Charles II came back and took the throne. To even utter it aloud could mean severe penalties for the person who suggested it.

There were too many people around. Best to change the subject. "Do you have employment other than serving as a minstrel in towns?" she asked. Even that was a dangerous question, given the Puritan attitudes toward music.

He shook his head. "My father wanted me to join him in his fishing business, but it held no interest for me. Then he died. So, I resigned myself to a life as a jongleur, going from town to town, playing for a little money or food. I expect one day I'll be drafted into Cromwell's army or some such thing. Until then, I play and earn what I can. Fortunately, there are people who have pity on my sad attempts to play under the Protectorate's watchful eye."

Richard winked at her and spun out a quick ditty on his instrument, interrupting the music to sing out verses.

She laughed at his rhyme about a mouse that fell in love with a cat, only to be eaten by said cat later.

Her laughter sparked him to smile even more. "May I buy you a pastry, Miss Dyer? There is a booth here that sells perfect peach tarts." He reached down and pulled the coins that had been dropped into the cap, then shoved the cap into the waist of his trousers.

She really should head home. Mama would be wondering where she was. "Yes, I would like that."

The two of them wandered through the market together. It was remarkable how different the market looked when being escorted by a handsome man. It was brighter, full of joy and hope. As if she could reveal her hair and her faith and not be ill-treated for them.

Moll took the steaming hot peach tart from an elderly woman missing a couple of her front teeth. Although dressed according to regulation, the woman wore a sprig of August-blooming blue aster on her white collar.

While Richard paid for the treat, Moll stared at the pinned flower. The woman noticed and winked at her.

Another subtle sign of rebellion.

They continued through the market, which, although small, was organized by goods. Garlic sellers, booksellers, cheese mongers, wool sellers… all offering their wares.

Missing from the fairs these days were tavern owners, play-actors, games of chance, or anything that might cause merriment.

It didn't matter, though. She could hardly believe

that she, red-haired, gangly, insignificant Moll Dyer, was walking on the arm of a man as talented and well-favored as Richard Northcutt.

Finally, though, Moll realized that her parents would soon be worried about her. It was time to leave.

"Might I escort you home?" Richard asked.

"I live two miles away," she said, frowning. What would Mama's and Dada's reactions be to her bringing home a young man?

"I do not mind."

He periodically played his cornet as they walked down the road leading back to Kenn. The further away from the market they got, the more receptive fellow travelers were to Richard's tunes.

As they neared the small scrabble of homes that included the Dyer cottage, Moll suddenly felt embarrassed by their leaky thatched roof and the illicit ale-making arrangement behind the cottage.

But Richard Northcutt did not mind at all. "Why, you're almost as poor as I am!" he exclaimed, laughing heartily.

Moll's heart warmed to the point that Richard could have tossed her brother, William, into a cistern, and she would still be falling in love with him.

To Moll's chagrin, her mother stepped outside as she and Richard stood in the dusty yard in front of the cottage. To her credit, Mama frowned briefly, then her expression turned to one of curiosity.

Moll didn't want a barrage of questions just yet. She had just met this man and wanted to nurture her feelings for him privately.

Well, there was nothing to be done about it, for Richard played like a courtier and bent over her hand. "May I have the pleasure of your company again at next Friday's market?" he asked.

Mama had surely heard that.

Moll agreed and went into the cottage, trying not to look at her mother, who was now looking at Moll curiously.

"Is he worthy of you, Moll?" was all Mama asked. Moll nodded her head and said no more. Mama seemed to innately understand Moll's need for privacy, for she asked no further questions. She must not have told Dada, for he didn't inquire about Richard, either.

Moll knew that Mama's silence was temporary, though. However, that silence also meant that her younger siblings didn't plague her with questions.

Moll considered talking to William's wife, Agnes, about her newfound happiness, but discarded the idea. Agnes would tell William, who would tell the other siblings.

No, silence was best.

CHAPTER 11

MOLL'S HEART WAS lighter than ever the following week as she practically skipped down the lane to town. More than anything, she looked forward to Richard making her laugh with delight.

It hadn't just been Mama who hadn't been joyful in a long time.

Richard was in the same place, playing his cornet for the few coins that would be thrown to him, enduring both platitudes and insults for what he was doing.

They again wandered through the market together. This time, Richard purchased her a small comb, badly carved in wood, but in the recognizable shape of a feather. It was a trifling thing, but Moll loved it. She tucked it into her dress pocket

He tapped his hat. "To always remember me and our king, who will one day return."

Richard embodied everything romantic and dangerous in the world. It seemed impossible that he could be enamored with her in return.

But she had a secret, didn't she? She must share it with him before this went too far and she got her heart broken by his rejection.

As he walked her back to the cottage again, Moll stopped when there was no one around.

"You must know something about me," she said.

Richard was ever quick to demonstrate joy. "Must

you tell me that you are the comeliest lass in all of Devon? I assure you I already know this." He reached out to take her hand in his.

Moll blushed. Such gallant words.

"I am not that, but I am glad you consider it to be true. No, there is something about me that might make you…think less of me." She was gathering her courage, but it was in short supply.

"There is nothing that could make me think less of you, Moll. My dearest," he added. Did she dare say his look was one of love?

Another lightning bolt shot through Moll.

Well, there was nothing for it but to tell him. Or show him.

"You see, I am very obviously marked as someone undesirable." She untied her cap and removed it, letting her thick, flaming hair tumble down her shoulders and back.

To her surprise, Richard's expression didn't change at all. "Ah, then the comb should set off very well against it, shouldn't it? Where is it?"

Moll pulled it from her dress pocket and wordlessly handed it to him. He tucked it into a section of her hair on the left side of her head. "There. Well done," he said.

Moll was speechless. "But my hair marks me as being of Irish descent and therefore Catholic. My parents have always had me keep my head covered, ever since one day at market when—well, they don't want me to be hurt."

She started to put the cap on again, before anyone should come down the lane and see them, but Richard stayed her hand and then entwined his fingers with hers.

"This hair of yours makes you even more unusually beautiful than before. I confess I wondered what was under that cap. Now I know all." He grinned. "Well, I know all except for one thing."

Moll was puzzled. "What do you wish to know?"

"What you taste like, my love." Richard took her face in his hands, bent his head, and pressed his lips to hers.

Moll could hardly stay upright as she gave herself over to this moment of a man kissing her, having just told her she was beautiful *because* of her red hair.

Regrettably, he broke off the kiss, but he folded his arms around Moll and pulled her to his chest.

Was that his heart or hers hammering so wildly?

Moll met Richard at the market every Friday after that, until one day, several months later, he held open his hand. In his palm was a coin, broken in half. He handed one half to Moll. "Perhaps it's time for us to marry."

CHAPTER 12

THEIR WEDDING PLANS were conducted in secret, except for telling their respective parents. Mama and Dada had voiced doubt that Richard's musical talents could support a wife and future family. But upon hearing that Richard was both Catholic and supported the claims of Charles II, they reluctantly approved.

"I only wish this marriage might have been an elevation for you, daughter," Dada had said wistfully. But Moll didn't care about that, only about being married to her sweet Richard.

Richard's father had died long ago, and his mother was remarried to another codman in the nearby Devon fishing village of Teignmouth. Richard's stepfather expressed ambivalence about whatever his stepson did but did seem interested in keeping his wife happy. Richard's mother wept every time she was in Moll's presence, always with the same emotion.

"I had given up hope that there was a good Catholic girl out there for him. These damned Puritans…" These statements were always accompanied by kisses on Moll's cheeks and fierce hugs.

The Church calendar prevented them from getting married during Lent, because of penitence for the approaching Easter. They also could not marry in late spring as the church prepared for the Ascension. May was considered an unlucky month for weddings. They finally settled on a date in June 1658.

The Puritans took no stock in the liturgical calendar of the Church, so no mention was made to friends and neighbors as to why their particular wedding date was selected.

The Puritans also insisted that banns be read in public places, not in churches, so they had them read during a Friday market in town, which somehow seemed appropriate to Moll.

Mama had a little bit saved from her ale making to purchase fabric for a new dress for Moll. Still in the required Puritan style, Mama had fashioned a beautiful coif for Moll that was embroidered with a beautiful silver-threaded floral design.

Even if Mama could have afforded more, it would have been unwise to flout an elaborately styled dress, for Cromwell's sumptuary laws prevented common people from wearing rich fabrics.

Silver, however, symbolizing purity, was the wedding color for the wealthy, making Moll feel like royalty the morning she carried a bouquet of rosemary and wildflower blooms to the altar of their private church ceremony, took her vows to Richard, and they exchanged wedding bands.

Richard had had several coins melted down and made into posey bands, with the phrase, "Two bodies, one heart," inscribed inside each of them.

The Puritans did not approve of wedding rings, considering them a leftover relic from Catholicism, so Moll and Richard did not wear them again until they were in private.

They had followed their secret marital rite with a ceremony including a few select people in front of a justice of the peace, the only allowable form of wedding in England under Cromwell's rule.

A local tavern keeper had offered them a penny-bridal, allowing them to use his business as a gathering place for the small number of friends and neighbors invited to share in the joy. Guests donated money to the tavern keeper to keep wine and food flowing.

Richard's mother, Edith, now keeping a full cup of wine at her side, turned from effusive kisses and hugs to maudlin displays of sorrow that her son, who had long ago left her breast, would now have children of his own, and thus have no care whatsoever for his bereft mother.

Richard's stepfather seemed embarrassed by it, whereas Richard didn't seem to notice his mother's behavior.

It was Moll's first flicker of discomfort regarding her new marriage.

But Edith's overwrought emotions had been unnecessary, for there was no money for Moll and Richard to move into their own lodgings; thus, Moll took up residence with Richard inside her new in-laws' cottage in Teignmouth. Their cottage was even smaller than the Dyers' home, but with fewer people living there, seemed more spacious.

The first couple of weeks were bliss. While Richard went to towns, offering his services as a minstrel for weddings and other occasions, Moll got to know her mother-in-law.

The woman's odd swings in temperament were unsettling, but she wasn't mean nor violent, so Moll accepted Edith's oddities.

Her mother-in-law was receptive to learning how to brew ale, so their initial days were consumed with it, after Moll went back to her parents' home and obtained supplies from her mother.

During the day, Moll and Edith worked over their

own secret kettle. For the first time, Moll oversaw the work.

At night, she tucked in for exhilarating nights with her new husband. They giggled and cuddled and explored, trying fruitlessly to remain quiet so as not to wake his parents.

Until late one night when, sweaty and sated, Moll had fallen asleep in Richard's arms, only to be awoken in terror by banging on the door.

"Richard Northcutt! You are hereby summoned to see the magistrate!" came a deep, booming voice from outside.

Moll hurriedly got back into her dress as Richard, too, clothed himself. They reached the door at the same time as his parents. Edith was already muttering wildly, to the point that Richard's stepfather shushed her as he opened the door.

Standing there were parliamentary soldiers.

CHAPTER 13

"WE HAVE A report that you are working against the true governing body of this country," the soldier standing at the front of the others said.

Richard said nothing.

"Just for wearing a feather?" Moll cried out without thinking.

This alerted the leader. "He wears a feather? It's quite the nest of Royalists here in Devon, isn't it?"

It felt like being boiled alive in a copper kettle, watching as her beloved was accused of ostentatiousness beyond his status.

Edith turned up the heat on the kettle. "Please, sirs, it was just a bit of frippery and didn't mean anything."

"Mother, hush," Richard whispered.

"Frippery?" the soldier asked. "What would the likes of you be doing with 'fripperies'?"

It got worse from there. Richard was grabbed roughly and taken away. It was difficult to tell in the dark in what direction the men were taking him. Edith's wailing also made it hard to focus on what was happening.

There was no sleep for Moll or her parents-in-law. Moll paced the floors the rest of the night with Richard's mother and stepfather, stopping frequently to run outside to vomit from fear and anxiety.

At daybreak, they went to the local gaol to see Richard.

"Yep," said the official, smirking as he blocked their way. "Not cooperative at all. Had to be beaten into submission." He waved to a couple of other men standing guard. "Get the Northcutt creature."

The two men disappeared into a building made of gray stones. Moll held her breath for the eternity it seemed to take them to return.

She reached out for support when they came back, carrying Richard's lifeless body between them. There was no one to help her, and Moll fell to the ground.

Near her, Edith wailed. Her keening was high-pitched and unending.

"Woman, hush," Edith's husband hissed.

"No need for dramatics," the official said without sympathy, putting a booted toe out at Moll to rouse her. "He shouldn't have resisted our kindly instructions."

Richard's stepfather helped Moll up to her feet.

She hardly knew how to react to Richard's body, now lying crumpled up on the ground. What she knew for certain was that Richard would have never "resisted" in such a way that would have resulted in his death. He was kind…and loving… and now staring sightlessly at her from a bruised and bloodied face.

"We'll do you a good deed and return him to you," the official said.

It was as if he expected thanks for it.

The three of them trudged home to wait, with Moll stopping periodically to heave in shrubbery along the path. Her empty stomach produced nothing.

The same two guards arrived later, having

unceremoniously loaded Moll's husband into in a cart. They dumped him at the front door so the family could take care of burying him.

Moll was crazed with grief, even snatching out clumps of hair in her worst moments. Knowing Richard had been her first moments of true happiness since the death of her grandfather, and happiness had been cruelly snatched away for no reason other than Richard being a man who was joyful.

The Puritans couldn't stand joy, though, could they? It was vital to them that every drop of happiness be squeezed from citizens of the realm.

Moll's grief slowly transformed itself into a slow, burning anger, marked by an inability to feel anything at all except animosity.

That anger expanded when, two days later, Edith informed Moll that she would have to return to her parents. "Not really part of the family anymore, are you? But I thank you for the ale-making lessons and supplies."

Moll was being discarded like Richard had been and would not even be permitted to have the brewing materials she had brought from her parents' home.

At least she had her ring. That and the wooden comb were all she had by which to remember Richard. Edith even snatched away the cornet, insisting that it rightfully belonged to his dear mother.

The day after Richard received a meager burial, Moll was sent packing. She walked back to Kenn, all her possessions tied up in a single piece of cloth.

Her own family greeted her with great sympathy and left her to grieve in private. The days turned to weeks as she nursed the hot fire in her soul.

The first decision she made was to return to using the name Dyer. She hadn't been married to Richard long enough for his Northcutt name to really take, and with him gone, she had no desire to be associated with his mother.

Mary Margaret Dyer she had been born, Mary Margaret Dyer she would remain.

A couple of weeks after that, she realized she had more misfortune with which to deal.

She was carrying a child.

CHAPTER 14

March 1659

HER BODY SWOLLEN with her impending birth, Moll had found a modicum of happiness, knowing that she had retained a part of Richard to which his mother would never have any claim.

Yet, she still sometimes pulled out strands of her hair when she lay on her pallet at night, away from her parents' view. The joy of a new babe did not fully compensate for Richard's loss.

Dada had moved her pallet down next to the hearth, for she was too large to make it up the ladder rungs to the loft anymore. It was much warmer here, and she wished she could be here all the time.

Dada had offered her Granda's old curtained-off space, but Moll had refused. Those memories were freshened in the wake of Richards' death, and she didn't want reminders of her beloved grandfather's suffering.

But the long, uncomfortable nights while waiting for the birth of her child made Moll miss her Granda almost as much as she missed Richard. Granda would have made her feel warm and loved right now. He would have told her she was a great Irish beauty and a sweet girl, as well.

Moll shifted many times each night, trying to find an agreeable position. It rarely worked.

Eventually, though, one early morning when she

had reached the point that she was so big she could hardly get up from her pallet anymore, she felt a great flooding between her legs.

"Mama!" she shouted without thinking.

Her mother emerged from behind her curtain. "Ah, child, it's time."

There would be no midwife for Moll, for Mama had insisted she could take of her own daughter herself.

Within a few hours, Moll prayed for either a midwife to miraculously walk through the door or for death to simply take her. The pain was so great and endless that she didn't think she could bear it.

Dada had fled the cottage, mumbling about needing to deliver some herbs to a customer. Elizabeth and Christian, now twenty-one and eighteen, also ran off on unidentified errands while Moll yowled and cried piteously.

Eventually, though, Moll was delivered of a boy. "Hmm," Mama observed as she held the freshly born child. "Not crying. I worry that he isn't strong. You'll need to make him strong, Moll."

Mama helped Moll into a seated position against the cottage wall and put the boy to her breast. He didn't seem anxious to feed.

"You will be Callum," Moll whispered, kissing his bloody head. "For you will love me as Granda did."

But little Callum did not seem to love Moll at all. Most of the time, he refused her milk, as well as refusing various mixtures Moll's father concocted from his array of herbs and powders.

He also cried endlessly.

Moll cuddled him, kissed him, and whispered words about his brave and gallant father to him. Nothing comforted him.

"Maybe your milk just isn't nourishing enough," Dada said helplessly. Mama chased him out of the cottage on that comment, telling him to come back when he had a kind word for his daughter.

It went on like this for weeks—Callum crying, Dada offering weak solutions, Mama getting furious, the younger siblings staying out of sight, and Moll receding further into herself.

All the fuss ended one day when Moll returned indoors from giving Mama's current batch of ale a stir late one afternoon while Mama was visiting a neighbor. The cottage was eerily quiet. Moll stood in the doorway, not understanding the silence.

Then she realized.

Moll ran across the floor to where Callum lay on her pallet, which had never been moved back to the loft.

Her boy was motionless, and his skin was mottled gray.

The precious link to her beloved Richard was gone. Moll released an anguished howl that she thought made her sound more like a keening wolf than a human being.

May 1659

MOLL COULDN'T BE consoled. She refused food, drink, and any manner of sympathy. Why should she care about life? Her husband was gone because of her foolish statement to the soldiers, her son was gone because of her poor milk, and their grinding poverty made everyday life unbearable.

God hated her, she was sure of it.

The only good news was that Oliver Cromwell

had died back in September. Unfortunately, his son, Richard, had risen in his place, proving the lie that the younger Cromwell wasn't interested in royal dynasties.

But Richard wasn't like Oliver, lacking the assured authority of the elder Cromwell. By May 1659, he had resigned.

The rule of Richard Cromwell, who had been nicknamed "Tumbledown Dick" for his quick fall, ended, leaving the country holding its collective breath and praying they wouldn't descend into anarchy.

The collapse of the government that she hated, combined with her overwhelming grief over the loss of both baby Callum and Richard, as well as, yes, Granda, was turning Moll into a creature she didn't recognize.

She found that hatred and grief were all-consuming on their own. Together, they threatened to devour her.

She still sometimes tore at her once long, thick hair, which was becoming lifeless and stringy. She owned no mirror but was certain she looked wretched.

Her wretchedness was reflected in her father's gaze one day when he came to her. "Moll, it's time you did something besides sit here, staring into the fire. Come with me to Exeter tomorrow. I haven't been there in about a year, so there's probably a number of people who could use my elixirs."

Moll shrugged, as close to saying "yes" as she could manage.

It was a five mile walk to Exeter the following morning, which had started with a misting rain that was quickly growing in intensity.

"Don't know that I can afford a cart ride today," Dada said.

Moll shrugged again, indifferent to the downpour. "Doesn't matter," she mumbled.

As they walked, other people with horses and carts went barreling past them in their own rush to get out of the rain. They splashed water and mud against Moll and her father. Moll's white apron was streaked with filth. The two of them were going to be unsightly by the time they finally reached Exeter.

Moll developed an idea as she watched the fourth horse and cart rush by in the opposite direction.

Letting Dada get several steps ahead of her as she heard the distinctive rhythm of hoofbeats and a creaking cart coming from around a curve, Moll put herself in the path of an oncoming conveyance.

She stretched her arms out wide, dropping her leather satchel. "Take me," she said.

The driver saw her and yelled at her to get out of the way. Unfortunately, that alerted Dada.

"Damnation, girl! Are you out of your brain?" He flew across the lane and pushed her out of the way, tumbling off the side of the road with her.

Just a few more seconds, and she would have been out of her misery.

Dada helped her up and took her chin in his palm as they continued to stand in the copse of wildflowers and vegetation on the side of the road.

"Moll, love, you can't do this. Not just because it would split your mother's heart, not to mention mine, but because this isn't your destiny. You are meant for more than just giving up. It's hard for you to hear, but you're young yet, and you could still have another husband and another child."

Moll shook her head. There would never be anyone like Richard Northcutt. She wouldn't allow anyone else to touch her.

Dada sighed. "You'll see. I promise."

CHAPTER 15

September 1669

"I DON'T UNDERSTAND," MOLL repeated, her mind not registering her brother's words.

"I've told you many times. I've accepted a contract for indentured servitude to a sugar plantation in the West Indies. The proprietor is paying passage for Agnes, me, and young William, provided my son also accepts a contract when he turns fourteen. When my servitude is over, I should have enough money to get to the new world."

Moll had to admit that her brother was nothing if not patient. He probably *had* told her many times. She just couldn't believe he was leaving and had refused to listen to him.

"Where will you go from there?" she asked.

"Maryland, I hope. There are settlements in the new Carolina colony, but Mama always said that the best hope for Catholics was Maryland."

Moll felt a familiar pang. Mama and Dada had died within days of each other when the grippe had swept through their town two years ago. It had blown over her parents like a tempestuous storm, ravaging them overnight into mere shadows of what they had been. Chills were followed by fever, then dreadful headaches, muscle aches, and a cough.

None of Dada's elixirs were helpful, and her parents had quickly died within a fortnight of becoming ill.

Ten years had passed since she'd lost Richard and baby Callum. Her father had been wrong when he'd told Moll that she would find another husband.

He was wrong because she had refused to look for anyone new.

Now, she was a thirty-six-year-old woman, so old and dried up she might be referred to as a crone. At least she no longer had to wear the drab Puritan clothing, although she still kept her hair hidden away.

William told her she was being dramatic to refer to herself that way, but she knew it was true.

Mama. Dada. Granda. Richard. Baby Callum. So many of her people gone. Moll had been barely scratching out an existence over the past four years by taking over her mother's ale-making business and carrying her father's case of elixirs to the Friday markets in town and selling them to passersby.

Yet, the people of Devon had to count themselves as lucky. Despite the relative peace and calm that had arrived with Charles II's ascension to the throne, London had experienced great tragedy, from a plague in 1665 that had torn through the city and killed many of the poor inside its walls, to a hellish fire in 1666 that had consumed much of London.

They said that the king himself had assisted in fighting the fire, for all the good it did. Displaced lower-class peoples had flooded into the countryside, seeking refuge.

No, life in England had not improved much for the poor since the return of Charles II.

During the war, many people had fled the disease and poverty of England for plantations in the West Indies in hopes of starting anew once they'd served out their indentures. Even with the war over, plague and fire were causing many to still board ships and head west.

It had never occurred to Moll to do so. Life had been tolerable because her favorite brother and his family were nearby. She loved him so much that it didn't even cause her to feel envy that he had a relatively happy life with his wife and children.

Now he planned to leave her like all the others.

"When will you leave?" Moll swiped a finger across a tear that spilled down her face.

"We leave from Bristol in early December."

December. That was months away. There was still time to change his mind.

She worked on this with a vengeance, constantly reminding her favorite brother that his entire family was in England, that he would never see any of them again if he sailed away, that the ship's crossing was dangerous and he would likely drown in a storm, that he had no idea what wild animals there might be on the island, and—

William sat down with her in the tiny cottage where she now lived alone. He guided her to the table, which had become worn and scratched through so much use over the years. They sat down, and he took her hand in one of his, covering it with his other scarred palm.

Moll always felt discomfort at seeing his hands, that reminder of what she had done to her beloved brother.

"Moll, dearest sister, look at you, your expression always sour and gloomy now. And don't think I can't see that when hair escapes your coif, that it has faded and become dull. Come now, you must be happy for me and happy in your lot. Mama and Dada would want to know that you've taken care of the cottage and carried on their businesses. See how you've done both Mama's and Dada's work single-handedly. I'm proud of you." William patted her hand and smiled at her.

"I promise to send letters. There must be people in St. Kitts who can write one out for me."

Was her brother a simpleton? "I don't care about letters. I care about *you*," she bit out. "I will never see you again! How can you abandon me? Must everyone abandon me?"

Moll heard the growing desperation in her voice but was unable to stop it.

"I will be completely alone without you here," she said, removing her hand from between his. He held both hands up in supplication.

"Sister, you know that our siblings are still—"

"*I don't care.* What, is Thomas going to accompany me to fairs? Is haughty Agnes going to invite me to feast with the Martyns?" She followed this with a snort at her brother. Combined with her tears, it sounded like she was choking.

William dropped his hands to his side, opened his mouth to say something, then stopped. He stared at Moll for several moments before speaking again. "Moll, you mustn't become so...unraveled... by my plans. There are seven of us Dyers alive. You will be surrounded by the remaining five and their children. You have a means to care for yourself. You should find another husband, a widower with his own children that you can care for. Dear sister, you are still comely to a man. Despite what I regrettably said about your hair and eyes, you are still shapely with clear skin, and you have all your teeth. You are still sweet in spirit."

William reached a hand to her shoulder. "Promise me you will be well when I'm gone."

But Moll's mind was working furiously. A new

husband was of no interest to her. Unless he could be a means to an end. Could a marriage help her? Of course, attaching herself to a husband would bind her over in a way she didn't want.

She wanted to be bound to her beloved brother, not a widower who wanted a handmaid to care for his squalling children.

Moll retreated into herself for days, alternating between weeping piteously and nursing anger at a God forcing her into such an unfair life.

She needed a better life. Caring for children. Being loved by others. Escaping her wretched life.

Slowly, she stopped nursing anger and began nursing an idea.

That idea grew like wild periwinkles in her mind until finally her mental vision was full of happy blooms.

Yes, Moll knew what she would do. She would follow her brother to the West Indies.

❦

Moll marched to Kenn without reserve and had soon accepted an indenture contract with a Thomas Lugg in St. Kitts, after confirming that Lugg's plantation was near that of William Salter, to whom her brother had signed his own indenture contract.

Mr. Salter sought no more servants, so she was unable to join her brother directly at the Salter plantation.

The agent in Kenn agreed to give her a contract after she explained that she had ale-making skills as well as a good hand in elixirs, pain powders, and poultices.

"Yer not much to look at and yer not likely to survive the climate, but Mr. Lugg might make good use of your height, reaching up for things and such," the agent said, having Moll sign an "X" on the signature line.

At seven years, her contract was longer than William's by two years. Ironically, her ship was to leave much earlier, on October 25th.

Back in the village, William expressed disbelief, then outrage, then pleasure, at knowing Moll would be in the West Indies with him, even if not on the same plantation.

Moll merely announced to her other siblings that she was abandoning the meagerly furnished cottage, taking nothing but her spare dress, Dada's potions case, and some of her hops and barley for brewing ale.

She had no idea what might happen to the cottage, and she didn't care.

Moll walked for two days over hilly terrain to reach Bristol, where, starving, she boarded a small ship that took her along the River Avon to the mouth of the Severn River. From there, Moll boarded a much larger ship for the journey west into the Bristol Channel and finally into the Atlantic Ocean.

At least there had been a bit of food provided on the journey.

The sailing was every bit as torturous as she had cautioned William it would be. Storms pitched the ship to and fro one day, complete calm preventing the ship from making distance the next. Women cried belowdecks, men vomited above deck.

Moll herself was sick on multiple occasions. Her shapeless dress became even more sack-like. None of it mattered to her, as this journey put her steps closer to a future near her beloved brother.

The Madness of Womanhood

Nevis Plantation, St. Kitts

CHAPTER 16

December 1669

THE SHIP FINALLY made it to the island of St. Kitts at the end of December. As they sailed near the island, Moll thought she had never seen anything so beautiful in all her life. Green-covered mountains, so much larger than the hills back home, dominated the small island, which was blanketed by warmth and sunshine, even in December. Puffs of white clouds dotted an impossibly blue sky.

It was as if she'd entered paradise.

She would never miss the bitter rain and cold of England.

She was let off the ship with the instruction, "Anyone knows where Nevis Plantation is." The ship then departed for other islands in the West Indies to continue dropping off passengers and cargo.

With her father's case in one hand and the rest of her belongings wrapped in a blanket in the other, Moll spent a moment finding her balance now that she was on firm ground.

She was struck by how busy it all was. People bustling about, some shouting at one another, some singing tunes, while men loaded and unloaded crates from ships with ropes and pulleys.

Unlike the docks in Bristol, the air wasn't heavy with the smell of rotting offal. The warm breezes must have carried away putrid odors. Instead, the air was perfumed with just pure briny sea, a sea whose color reminded Moll of the French limes she had seen for sale at Friday markets.

She couldn't wait for William to experience this perfect place. His ship was underway by now. She prayed he would have a smoother sailing than she had had.

Some of the men working were the darkest she'd ever seen. They were of a nearly ebony color, so dark that the whites of their eyes featured prominently in their faces. They were being instructed by an Englishman dressed in their same modest breeches and tunics, but distinct from them by the wide-brimmed, straw hat on his head.

Moll realized that she was standing there with her mouth agape at the scene before her. However, it didn't appear that anyone had even noticed her presence.

It made her wonder if she could remove her cap and let her hair flow freely for the first time in years.

She untied her cap and removed it, shaking her head to let her hair tumble out.

Praise the Mother, that felt marvelous. The sun beamed its approval upon her.

Her attention was caught by a pair of beautiful birds with black underbellies, mottled black and white feathers, and a funny white streak from their heads to the feathers, started calling out along the shoreline, their voices shrill and insistent.

Moll laughed in delight. They reminded her of black-robed judges, with their long, fancy wigs, and ominous demands.

"You find our little, black-bellied plovers funny, miss?"

Someone had noticed her. She turned to find the

man who had been shouting orders at the dark-skinned workers had approached her.

"I—I'm only just arrived, and I've never seen birds like that before," she said, feeling embarrassed although she wasn't sure why.

"Lots of birds here you never saw in England," he replied. "I'd cover up if I was you."

Moll instinctively reached a hand to her head. The warmth still felt so pleasant on her head. "Oh, sorry, sir, is this a Protestant—"

He shook his head. "With that hair and fair skin of yours, you are going to burn like roasted meat. It feels pleasant now, but it won't feel that way come March. Have a care for yourself."

It seemed impossible that this place could be anything but idyllic, but Moll merely nodded. "Yes, sir. Do you know where I can find Mr. Lugg's place?"

The man pointed off in the distance at a home set along the rise of a hill. It was gleaming white in the bright sunshine. To Moll's eye, it was a palace. Was she to live there?

The man returned to what he was doing, and Moll made her way to her new home.

***

Six months after her arrival, Moll understood what the man at the docks had meant regarding the climate. There might be breezes, but the sun felt as though it were close enough to boil one alive.

Her pale skin fared poorly under the blistering sun. She had burned so badly that Mr. Thorpe, her overseer, had allowed her to recuperate in her hut for a couple of days, much to the disgruntlement of the other servants.

"The tall white witch has the master's favor and gets days to laze about," she overheard them grumbling.

Healing from the burn resulted in her skin peeling in scaly layers. During those periods, everyone avoided her as though she carried leprosy.

She would hardly be healed before she would get burned again.

The more she burned, the more the other servants grumbled. Soon, there was open hatred from them.

It wasn't just the sun and the other servants making Moll's life miserable. It was the work itself which made her yearn for the days of ale-making and elixir peddling. As far as she could tell, neither of these skills seemed to have any value here on the island.

Growing and harvesting sugar cane required many hands to plant, weed, and cut the cane plants. Mr. Lugg had planted cane in different parts of his plantation every month, so that weeding and harvesting went on continuously.

It required about six months for an individual field to go from planting to harvest.

Many of Mr. Lugg's fields were planted in unusual rows along the hills behind the big house. "Terracing," the sugar master, Mr. Roland, had called it.

She had never seen such a thing back in Devon.

Before a field could be planted, it had to be cleared and burned. The remaining ash would then be used as fertilizer.

Moll's job was to collect the ash in buckets, first sweeping it up into trays and dumping the trays into the buckets. Not only did her back feel like an anvil had been sitting on it by the time the day was over, but she had no relief from the sun.

Irrigation networks had been built all over the plantation, so the plants—which flourished in the sunshine—received far more water than any of the indentured workers did.

During intense periods, when there was a profusion of sugar to be harvested, the work didn't even stop at dusk. Torches were lit, and the servants were expected to work into the night.

Moll spent her days longing for her brother—whom she had not yet seen here on the island—and her nights quietly crying herself to sleep so that the other women in her hut couldn't hear.

She was unpopular enough without appearing to be weak.

In her precious little spare time, Moll traversed the plantation, staying out of everyone's way while she examined its workings.

The sugar cane plants were thick stalks topped with thin leaves, which dried out when the plants were ready for harvesting. The stalks themselves were where the sugar cane was located. On the day that Moll walked along a row of these plants, she realized how impossibly tall they were. Why, they were taller than most buildings she had ever seen.

Once the sugar cane stalks were cut down at their bases, the leaves stripped away, and the tall stalks cut into manageable pieces, they were hauled in an oxen-led cart to the plantation's mill. Some of the stalks would be reserved for planting again.

In the mill, servants used hand presses to crush the cane. The juice from the crushed cane was then boiled in huge cauldrons. Those cauldrons were voracious eaters of timber for the fires that roared beneath them. That timber was cut and hauled from the nearby hillside, known as Mount Misery.

The liquid resulting from boiling the cane was

poured into large, cone-shaped molds and left to set. The result was twenty-pound sugar "loaves."

The loaves were then thoroughly dried to ensure they were as white and pure as merchants demanded. Apparently, it was difficult to achieve in the tropical climate of places like St. Kitts.

The quality sugar loaves were then packed and loaded onto ships for foreign destinations.

Resulting sugar of a brownish color was considered inferior. Not to Moll, though, since Mr. Lugg saw that the brown sugar was distributed to the servants and also used to make preserves for the Lugg family.

Moll had never tasted such luxury as this leftover, off-color sugar. She could only imagine what the finer quality was like. Nibbling sugar was the only bright spot of being on this miserable plantation.

Mr. Lugg's plantation had more than a hundred people working just the mill. There were at least a hundred more like Moll, working at various other jobs around the plantation. That didn't count those who worked as house servants, only sometimes visible as they carried messages to certain plantation managers.

The Luggs must be rich indeed to afford to pay passage for so many servants. Not that she had met any of the family members. Moll's only contact was with the sugar master.

Mr. Roland had, thankfully, been patient with Moll, seeming to understand that her inability to acclimate wasn't her fault. "They shouldn't have brought over an Irish," was all he said.

Of course, it was his kindness that drove most of the other servants to despise her.

CHAPTER 17

O NE NIGHT, MOLL sat in her normal, balled-up position in the tiny cabin she shared with two other women. There had been four of them in the one-room structure, but one had finished out her indenture soon after Moll's arrival and left on a ship bound for the New York colony.

The cabin was one of dozens dotting the sugar plantation where she now lived. It was even draftier than her cottage back in Devon. That meant that air and light more easily permeated the building. It also meant that rain did, too.

Tears again ran silently down Moll's face, as she awaited sleep, knowing she would be woken before dawn by the banging of a wooden spoon against a metal pot. Then the torturous work would begin again, day after day, until she was released to be on her own each Sunday afternoon.

Moll regularly ignored the other two women, Joan and Bridget, who had spent time in London's Clerkenwell workhouse and elected for servitude to escape their circumstances there. Both were much younger than Moll and didn't seem to be suffering nearly as much in the Caribbean sun. While Moll withdrew, the two of them sat and gossiped in the dark, as the plantation's servants were rarely given candles for light.

"Did you see Arthur lifting the sugar cone packages onto the wagon? A fine form, that one." Joan smacked her lips, a revolting sound.

Bridget responded, "No, but I've got my eye on Isaac. His cut is a handsome one. And I think he admires me, too."

Moll put her hands over her ears. Listening to silly young girls run on about silly young men held no interest for her. Why weren't the two of them as miserable as Moll?

The door suddenly opened, and a woman was thrust inside by one of the overseers, Mr. Thorpe, who held a glowing lantern up as he peered inside.

"This here's Hannah. She's to start off picking insects." The overseer's gaze caught Moll. "You show her tomorrow."

In the light, Moll saw that this woman was dark like the men who cut trees on the mountain and who worked at the docks. She clutched the same bundle of cloth that Moll had been given upon her own arrival; thus, Moll knew that Hannah held two shapeless dresses that weren't long enough to reach the ground, a cap, and a petticoat, in addition to a length of fabric with which the new servant could do whatever she wanted. Moll still had hers folded up tight and planned to save it for the day this trial of servitude was over, to make a dress in which she could proudly depart this dreadful place.

The woman stank terribly. Her voyage must have made her very sick.

The overseer shut the door again, casting the cabin back into darkness. The other two paid no attention to the new servant—after all, servants came and went regularly—but Moll had glimpsed the terror in Hannah's eyes and felt pity for her.

She rose and put an arm around the woman's painfully thin shoulder. Hannah flinched at Moll's touch, so Moll released her. "Your pallet is here," she said, pointing down next to her own, not that the woman could see her.

Hannah didn't respond, so Moll gently tugged on her hand, which caused the other woman to recoil from her.

What was wrong with her?

"All you can do tonight is sleep. I will show you what to do in the morning." She knelt and patted the mattress covering stuffed with dried sugar cane plant leaves.

Moll's motions must have made Hannah understand, for she knelt next to the pallet and placed the clothing bundle at one end of it, then collapsed upon her new bed. Soon, Moll could hear Hannah softly sobbing.

How could she comfort the new servant when she spent most of her own nights in the same state?

Early the next morning, just as the sun was rising, the usual beating of the pot awoke Moll.

The new woman bolted upright, her face stricken with terror.

Moll signaled for Hannah to follow her, leading the other servant out to use the communal pit, which consisted of long benches with multiple holes in them for seating and deep trenches beneath them for catching waste.

Hannah seemed unclear about using one of the sticks with discarded sugar cane plant leaves attached to it, located on the bench, so Moll demonstrated using one of them to wipe herself.

Hannah frowned but imitated what Moll did.

Next, Moll led her to the food shed, where they received salted cod fish that had been spiced and mixed with onions and tomatoes, then cooked inside banana leaves that they used as plates.

Two female servants, whose English skin was darkened with time in the Caribbean sun, walked past Moll and Hannah. "Old white witch," one hissed as she spat at Moll.

Hannah recoiled from the action. Although tempted to sling her food at the woman, Moll restrained herself and returned to eating. Starting a fight would only result in punishment, no matter who instigated it. She needed to survive the next seven years of servitude, however she could.

She just left the globule of spit on the hem of her dress. It wasn't as though it was noticeable in all the other smears and marks on it.

Hannah offered a sympathetic glance and started to bite into her banana leaf, but Moll pushed it away from the woman's mouth. "No," she said, shaking her head. The banana leaves were inedible.

To this point, Hannah had said nothing but had instead just obediently followed Moll. As they sat down near the food shed and opened their banana leaves to pluck food out with their hands, Moll studied Hannah for the first time.

The woman's skin was a glossy ebony that hung on her slight frame, as though she had lost considerable weight in a short period of time. It made her look at least Moll's age of thirty-six, but Moll suspected she was much younger. Hannah's eyes were a brown so light that they almost seemed golden.

Moll was fascinated.

Not just fascinated. For the first time since she had arrived on the island and felt that brief moment of hope before learning the realities of plantation life, Moll was once again feeling something akin to...

contentment. Perhaps it was having someone more frightened than her to care for.

"Time to go, Hannah." Moll signaled for the other woman to rise. Servants were only allotted around fifteen minutes to sit and eat, as there was no wasting time while the sun shone.

"No Hannah. Yaddy," the woman said, shaking her head.

Moll tilted her head, confused. "Your name isn't Hannah?"

"No Hannah. Yaddy." This time she pointed at herself as she said, "Yaddy."

Hannah. Yaddy. They sounded similar. Her contract agent must have misunderstood when she signed on.

Moll motioned for Han—Yaddy—to follow her to a field of flourishing sugar cane. At the edge of the field, Moll picked up a sack for collecting insects. Spider mites, mealybugs, and grasshoppers all loved the plants, and it required constant attention to keep the plants clear.

She led Yaddy down a row, demonstrating how to reach into the plants and pull them forward to examine them for the offending creatures.

Once Yaddy appeared to understand, Moll handed her the sack so she could leave to attend to her own back-breaking work.

Yaddy grabbed her arm, her expression terrified.

Moll had no idea how to tell her that they would see each other again at the end of the day. Moll's pity for the new servant made her own misery seem less important.

She did her best, pointing to the sun and the direction of their sleeping hut, as well as pantomiming eating supper.

Yaddy's expression went from terrified to doubtful,

but she eventually nodded, and Moll fled, worried that the overseer would be displeased with her day's efforts if she didn't get working soon.

In a small blessing, clouds rolled in as the day progressed, giving Moll relief from the daily searing heat from the sun. By the time the supper bell rang at twilight, she felt that she had scooped up as much ash as she did on any other day.

Moll immediately sought out Yaddy. She led the other servant back to the pits and then to receive their supper allotments. Tonight, they had raw conch mixed with vegetables and spices.

Life in St. Kitts was difficult, but she certainly ate better than she had at home. The amount of food that men simply waded into the waters and caught was unlike anything she had ever known.

After eating, they returned to their hut. The other two servants weren't there. Moll suspected they were out enticing Arthur and Isaac. She shook her head. It would be a serious offense if they were caught with the men, and it would most likely result in beatings.

Moll was very careful to never give enough offense to earn punishment.

As she sat down on her pallet, Moll realized that for the first time, she didn't have the urge to turn to the wall and cry.

Yaddy was scared enough without Moll crying.

Her new friend would never get by, though, without knowing their language. "I'm going to teach you English," she said.

"Eeen-gloos," Yaddy repeated.

From that point, Moll did her best to help Yaddy learn some English words so that she could get by. She also taught Yaddy how to show respect to the overseers and the sugar master whenever encountering them.

Yaddy was a quick learner and was soon able to communicate with Moll using a combination of words and gestures.

As more weeks went by, Yaddy relied less on gestures.

One morning, as the wake-up banging startled Moll out of sleep and she quickly sat up, she noticed that the other two women were not there.

Yaddy also appeared to notice. "Gone already?" she said.

The door banged open, startling Moll once again, and the two missing hut mates were shoved in by the overseer. "Yer expected to be in the fields with all the rest," he growled before departing.

Even in the perpetual darkness of the cabin, it was obvious that the two of them had been severely beaten. Joan's right eye was swollen shut, and blood trickled from Bridget's mouth.

"Save yourself and don't pursue any men on this plantation, witch," Bridget said before Moll could ask a question. "Mr. Thorpe don't like it."

Moll was very glad she had no interest in any romantic pursuits. How did the two of them even have the energy for it?

But Joan and Bridget managed to hobble out of the hut behind Moll and Yaddy, although the two stayed apart during their quick repast and quickly disappeared into the fields. Yaddy seemed thoughtful while they ate their morning meal, only finally saying, "Masters here bad like ship masters."

"What do you mean?" Moll asked, licking her banana leaf clean of its bits of food and tossing it into the scrap heap, where it would be used for animal feed.

Yaddy shook her head, finishing her own meal and also tossing the leaf onto the scrap heap.

That night, they received an allotment of inferior sugar and chunks of pineapple on which to sprinkle it. Yaddy's expression of surprise at the sweetness delighted Moll.

The treat's pleasure was tempered by the fact that Joan and Bridget had been made to work late in the fields, part of their punishment for having behaved "indecently."

With the other two women gone, Moll and Yaddy stayed awake deep into the night, discussing their pasts.

Moll learned that Yaddy's father had stolen something from a wealthy tribal leader, intending to trade it for food and clothing for his family.

He was discovered in the act, resulting in the entire family being sold into slavery. Yaddy, her parents, and her brother were all boarded onto different ships to further humiliate them.

"Slaves?" Moll said. "You mean, you won't be freed at the end of your indenture?"

Yaddy shook her head. "I have no *en-dint-chure*. They say I never be free. Master Lugg owns me. Forever."

Moll frowned. Forever? She knew vaguely about slavery but had never met someone who was actually in bondage.

"All Africans here slaves," Yaddy said. "I come over on a big ship. Stinks. All food rotten. They give us almost no water. Sleep in chains. Many die and are thrown to the sea." There was a catch in her voice.

Moll reflected on her own sea voyage, which had been difficult, but certainly no one had been dumped into the ocean.

Yet here they were together, living in the same circumstances. She didn't understand it.

Moll told Yaddy of her family, of her losses, and of the curse of her red hair.

"When I came here, I thought my ale-making skills and my experience with elixirs might give me a better opportunity. But here I am in the fields."

"*Ee-lick-shures*," Yaddy repeated slowly.

"Yes. Medicines and potions. For healing."

Yaddy nodded vigorously. "Yes, my father a healer."

"He was?" Moll clambered up and sought her own father's case. To her surprise, the very early rays of the sun were coming up and beaming through the slats of the building. Had they really been talking all night?

Moll sat back down and opened her case to show Yaddy the contents. Sometimes Yaddy expressed surprise, sometimes she nodded her head. At other times, she asked whether Moll used certain ingredients, such as boa constrictor fat or baboon bones.

All of it was incomprehensible to Moll. Dada's remedies were based on plants and much more…common…ingredients. Although he did occasionally scoop the turds of a goose or hen to use in his curative pastes.

But their friendship was deepening. Moll had never had a friend such as this before.

Joan and Bridget had not returned to their hut by morning, but Moll knew better than to inquire about it. It was just good to have only two people in their tiny quarters.

Soon, the morning banging began. With no sleep, it was going to be a long day.

It wasn't just a long day; it was a brutally hot one.

Once again, Moll's skin burned such that it was painful to have her thin frame rub against the rough fabric of her dress.

Days like this almost always left her weeping, but now she needed to put on a brave face for Yaddy.

As she scooped the last shovelful of ashes into her bucket, a young boy, towheaded and deeply tanned, came running across the field toward her. "You know medicine?" he asked, panting from his exertion.

Moll nodded.

"Mistress at the house needs help. Heard you have treatments."

"What does she—?" But the boy was already gone.

CHAPTER 18

DESPITE THE SUN'S burn on her skin, Moll hurried back to her hut and grabbed her case before heading to the big house.

It was intimidating to do so, as if she were standing before a palace in rags. The house wasn't all that much, being constructed of wood like everything else, but it was large and had real windows in it, and the paint over its boards was fresh.

She stood at the front of the house but realized she should enter through the back. At the rear of the house, the same boy was waiting for her. "Come," he said.

He led her up a back staircase to the next floor. Despite the rush up toward the unstained, raw wood stairs, Moll was still overwhelmed by the luxury in the house. Not just because of the windows, but the painted plaster walls, the draperies, and the framed paintings.

It really was like what she imagined a palace to be.

The staircase led them to a doorway. The boy pushed it open. They were at the end of a hallway. He walked down the long corridor, whose herringbone-laid floors were topped with a long run of patterned carpet. Candles shone brightly in their sconces along the wall.

He reached a doorway near the other end of the

hallway and scratched at it. "Madam?" he said quietly.

"Benjamin?" came a plaintive voice from behind the door. "Benji, do you have her?"

The boy opened the door and ushered Moll in. She was aghast by what she saw.

A young woman, at least fifteen years younger than Moll, lay panting in a large bed that was a jumbled mess of bed coverings. Panting until she began violently coughing, that is.

This must be Mr. Lugg's wife, Alice. Moll had seen Thomas Lugg walking about the plantation a few times but had never laid eyes on Mrs. Lugg. All servants were, however, aware of the owner's wife.

But was he aware of his wife's sorry condition?

Mrs. Lugg's skin was papery, and her body beneath her thick, pale blue nightdress was even thinner than Moll's. Her disheveled hair, which appeared to have once been a beautiful shade of gold, was wrapped in green ribbons that were coming loose.

The room itself was startlingly beautiful. Framed pictures adorned painted walls, and the dark poster bed with its floral canopy and stuffed pillows and mattress was simply glorious. Moll couldn't imagine sleeping under such rich finery.

Mrs. Lugg's bed chamber smelled foul. Not of bodily excretions nor from the hazy smoke from the fireplace. No, it reeked more of misery and despair, conditions with which she was well familiar.

"Help me," Mrs. Lugg rasped as her gaze locked onto Moll.

Moll cleared her mind of the luxurious room to concentrate on her master's wife. Approaching the bed, she said, "Mistress, what ails you?"

Up close, Alice Lugg wasn't just disheveled, but red like a rooster's comb. Moll was no physician, but to her eye it appeared to be from strain rather than fever, even though there was a fire blazing in the hearth across the room.

"I can't stop coughing. Throat hurts so very much." The woman placed a hand over her neck. "Help me," she repeated. "No doctors on this awful island."

"I will try my best." Moll put her case on the floor next to the bed and knelt before it, searching through it and removing several jars.

Fortunately, the boy Mrs. Lugg called Benji was still in the room, cowering next to the door. "Can you bring me a cup of very hot water, a spoon, and a small jar of honey?" she asked him.

"If you please, Mistress?" she added, turning toward the plantation owner's wife.

Mrs. Lugg nodded. "Go. Talk to Mrs. Barnes. Get whatever she wants."

Benji scampered out of the room.

Mrs. Lugg went into a coughing fit. It took her at least a minute to recover.

Not sure that it was her place to offer comment without being spoken to first, Moll silently opened the jars she had pulled and sniffed at them to ensure they weren't spoiled.

She also removed a fuming pot from her case. From the jars, she sprinkled cinnamon, rosemary, and clove into the top bowl of the pot. Taking the pot, which was about as large as her hand, to the hearth, she swept some embers into the bottom chamber with the small fireplace shovel resting against the stone wall of the hearth.

Moll imagined that the Africans who cut down trees along Mount Misery had also dug out the rocks that were artfully placed here on the wall.

"I've put a blend of spices in here, Mistress," Moll

said, rising and holding the piece of pottery by its handle. "They will fill the room with a sweet perfume that will help you feel better."

Mrs. Lugg expressed no interest as Moll placed the pot on a table near the bed.

Benji returned with Moll's requested items on a tray and set the tray next to the fuming pot before moving to stand at the ready at the bedchamber's door.

Moll went to work, remembering Dada's instructions for curing a cough, hoping this was a genuine cure and not akin to his love potions.

Into the jar of honey went a bit of the hot water from the cup and a couple of pinches of dried roses. She stirred it all together into a thin mixture and left it to sit, not only to let it cool, but to let the roses "bloom" within the liquid.

She then dropped some dried petals of coltsfoot, which resembled dandelions, into the cup of hot water and stirred, also putting it aside to steep.

Mrs. Lugg struggled herself into a seated position. Moll arranged pillows behind the woman, then offered the cup of coltsfoot-infused tea.

Mrs. Lugg sipped at it then handed the cup back to Moll.

"No, maum, please drink it all." Moll stepped back to signal her refusal to take the cup.

The woman narrowed her gaze, no doubt unused to being told "no." Nevertheless, she drank the rest of it.

Moll now offered the honey-rose petal infusion. "All of this, too, please. It will help your throat."

This time, Mrs. Lugg took it without comment. Her expression at handing back the empty jar to Moll suggested that this infusion had tasted much better than the tea.

The plantation's mistress coughed again, but it wasn't with the same intensity.

She closed her eyes and lay back against her pillow, a hint of a contented smile upon her lips.

"Much better."

Moll was relieved. "May I recommend that you have these two elixirs made for you every day for a week, Mistress? I can leave you with some—"

Those eyes flew open again. "What? No, you shall make them for me."

That was impossible. "I—I—work in the fields. If I stop my tasks to come here to attend to you, maum, I will be beaten for sloth. I mean, you are of course the most important person on the plantation, and your needs are the greatest, but already I have been gone for far too long and I—"

Mrs. Lugg airily waved a hand. "I shall tell my husband that I require you to serve me temporarily, and he will tell your overseer. Who is he?"

Moll's stomach churned. If she received additional special treatment, how much more would the other field workers hate her?

"I—er—Mr. Thorpe might not—"

"That's settled, then. Benji, find Gabriel Thorpe and have him come to me as soon as possible."

It seemed to be a unique talent of Benji's to scamper in and out of rooms. Out he ran.

Mrs. Lugg coughed again. It was even more subdued than before.

She pointed to a chair. "Sit," she commanded.

Moll sat.

"You are certainly a curious shade of red," Mrs. Lugg said, tilting her head.

"Yes, maum. I—I don't do well in the sun here. I wish I'd known before signing my indenture contract."

"Hah!" Her laugh was a sharp bark. "I wish I'd known about this place before signing my marriage contract, too."

Moll didn't respond. But Mrs. Lugg seemed to want to talk and didn't expect it to be a conversation.

"I hate this place. 'It will be just like home,' Thomas promised. That liar. Had I known the pestilence of this place, I would have never agreed to come here and marry him. My God, the heat. And because all the fields need to be near the water for irrigation and such, the house must be too far inland for the best breezes."

This woman was spoiled. The Lugg home was glorious compared to her shared hut. Warm breezes did not make up for her own harsh living conditions.

Mrs. Lugg changed topics. "Where are you from?"

"Devon, maum. Well, my family is originally from County Donegal in Ireland."

"And why did you take an indenture contract?"

"My brother took one to get himself and his family to the new world. I decided to follow. But I haven't even seen him yet." What had been a clever thought last year now seemed like the most foolish decision she had ever made.

Mrs. Lugg's expression was thoughtful. "Is he here on the island?"

"I think so. Or maybe on Nevis? He should have arrived in January, but I don't know if he did."

Nevis was a neighboring island, yet the plantation on which she worked was also called Nevis, making it confusing. Regardless, she'd heard nothing of her brother.

Could he have perished on his journey? Moll might never know.

"Help me to a chair," Mrs. Lugg commanded. She apparently felt much better.

Moll did so, assisting the woman into a wooden chair with an upholstered seat and arms. The pale-yellow fabric had a sheen to it such as Moll had never seen before.

"Yes, much better." Another cough, but it was barely to the level of throat clearing.

There was scratching at the door again. Benji entered with Mr. Thorpe, who scowled at seeing Moll standing there.

Mrs. Lugg informed the overseer that Moll would be temporarily serving as her maid.

"Making ale for you, madam? Her contract said she has some ability with it." He was obviously bewildered by a lowly field worker like Moll standing in the plantation mistress's bed chamber.

"Ale? You are an alewife?" Mrs. Lugg turned her attention back to Moll.

"Yes, maum, I have some brewing skills. My mother taught me." *Perhaps I have two routes for getting out of field work.*

"Aren't you an interesting creature, then?" her new mistress said. "Very well."

With that, the overseer was dismissed, and Mrs. Lugg said, "You will come back to tend to me with your teas and such until I'm well. Then we might have use for you in the kitchens. Benji, show Moll to the staircase closet."

The staircase closet was aptly named. It was a tiny space that had been built under the staircase on this floor, not far from Mrs. Lugg's chamber.

"I'll need to bring my pallet from my hut," Moll said to the boy.

He shook his blond head. "Mistress won't like that. I'll bring you another one."

The room was airless and stuffy, and Moll couldn't have been happier. Here she was in a space that was probably five feet square, but it had actual wood flooring in it instead of being dirt. And she was to have a new sleeping pallet.

Here she was, a thirty-five-year-old woman, and for the first time had a room—with a door!—all to herself.

Yes, Moll's fortunes were miraculously improving. She only hoped she could maintain this good fortune for the duration of her servitude.

Without, of course, enraging the other servants.

CHAPTER 19

I N ADDITION TO a new pallet, Moll was given two more pieces of clothing—castoff nightdresses from the mistress—and was required to bathe once per month to live in the house.

She hadn't done so in such a long time that it was almost an uncomfortable experience to have one of the other female house servants take her down to a protected cove surrounded by trees and to be handed a rag-topped stick for scrubbing herself, as well as a jar of scented powder for her hair.

How odd it was to be naked here, with a view across translucent green waters that went on seemingly forever.

Moll was reminded of her impression of the island when she had first arrived. Before life had become so unbearably hot and difficult.

She rubbed the rags across her arms and involuntarily yelped. Her skin was still sensitive from frequent burnings.

The servant who had accompanied her, named Ruth, laughed at Moll's discomfort.

"Is it amusing to you that I'm in pain?" Moll asked as she applied the stick with less force against her skin.

"You deserve it," Ruth said. Like most of the women on the plantation who weren't Moll, her skin had grown accustomed to the sun and was deeply tanned, even if her face looked like she had once been ravaged by some sort of pox.

Moll shrugged. Some field hand must have told Ruth that Moll was a witch.

"How did you come to the house?" the other servant asked.

"The mistress heard that I have knowledge of healing herbs, and she wanted my help for her cough." Moll didn't like this conversation. She quickly finished scrubbing and rinsing in the warm Caribbean waters, then stepped out and slid the loose-fitting dress over her head.

She then removed her caul, letting her hair tumble down, and used the scented powder, which smelled of rosemary and lavender, on her hair, scrubbing it in so that it would absorb all the accumulated oils and dirt. It was the most heavenly experience she'd had in a long time.

However, Ruth's gaze narrowed at her. "So, what they say is true. You're a red witch, towering over all the other women."

"I'm no witch, I'm just a plain woman and a servant, just like you." Moll was glad she was clothed once more. It made her feel…safer.

"They say you cast a spell so that the mistress would call you up to the house and give you special treatment." Ruth now stood with her arms crossed. Whether in anger or to ward Moll off wasn't clear.

"Only a fool would say such a thing," Moll said, scrubbing furiously at her hair roots.

"They also say you cast a spell on Mr. Thorpe so that he would falsely accuse Joan and Bridget of being trollops and beat them."

Moll stopped what she was doing. "What? Why would I do such a thing?"

Now it was Ruth's turn to shrug. "Jealousy.

They're prettier than you. Or you're haughty and think you shouldn't have to share quarters. Look at you now with your own room near the mistress. I've been here three years, and I sleep in the attic with the other house servants."

Moll knew the field servants didn't like her, but she'd hardly been in the house a few hours, and her undeserved reputation had already followed close on her heels.

The wisest course of action would be to ignore Ruth, just as Moll ignored most of the field hands. Yet she couldn't resist an insult as she gathered her hair back up inside her caul.

"If I were a witch, do you think I would be stupid enough to end up on this island with the likes of you?" She strode off, barefoot, without waiting for a response.

Her happiness over her new situation had been chewed through an instant, like she was merely bait for one of the sharks that prowled the waters off the shores of St. Kitts.

CHAPTER 20

THE EVENING WAS even more unsettling. Moll retreated to her compartment, leaving the door open a crack, both to allow candlelight from the corridor's wall sconces in and to be sure she could respond instantly if Mrs. Lugg called upon her.

Unfortunately, it made her privy to an argument she did not want to hear.

Heavy steps trod the flooring in the corridor at some point in the evening, waking Moll from the light doze she was in.

"Alice!" a voice boomed. It sounded like Mr. Lugg. That was followed by Mrs. Lugg's bed chamber door creaking open.

Everything in this humid place seemed to creak.

"Thomas, must you be so loud?" came Mrs. Lugg's voice. "I've just found someone to cure my cough, and here you bang in, enough to wake the dead."

"That's what I want to talk to you about. What is this about you pulling one of the field servants into the house to serve you? I need every available hand outside." There was rustling in the room. Perhaps it was Mrs. Lugg rising from her bed.

"Oh, Thomas, one weak woman in the field isn't going to be the reason for the success or failure of this plantation. Besides, I like Moll. She's rather... motherly."

A pang hit Moll so hard she stepped away from her open door and put a hand to her midsection. Did Mrs. Lugg really think that of her? It had been a long time since she'd thought of herself as a mother.

Mr. Lugg wasn't done. "Do you seriously believe that the servants on this plantation won't notice that you've specially selected one of the worst workers to tend to you as though she's a lady's maid? We are always just one incident away from an insurrection, and now you do this?"

Mr. Lugg made some kind of choking noise, which was drowned out by Mrs. Lugg having a mild coughing fit.

The master's tone changed. "You do seem… improved. What did she do for you?"

"Moll made me a restorative. It started working immediately, although I believe I need more attention to be entirely well. I don't think I am asking for much, husband. After all, most successful planters live in town or even manage their plantations from back home in England. They don't live on their pestilent plantations as we do here."

"It is not the mark of a successful man to try to manage his holdings from far away. I must be present to supervise the overall workings of this endeavor, and to ensure that I'm not being cheated by everyone, from servants to paid employees to sugar buyers. As my wife, you should support me, since you will benefit richly by our success."

The next words were garbled, and Moll couldn't understand them. Then Mr. Lugg raised his voice again.

"You know it's my intent to slowly replace all the indentures with slaves. They're cheaper and hardier. They don't burn red every morning when the sun comes up, as your favorite does. Although they do require more…supervision. I'm having watch towers built around the property so that when I begin importing Africans in earnest, we can ensure that they remain…contained."

"'Tis a bit foolish what you say, Thomas. The indentures don't run away, and so they don't require watch towers and people to man those watch towers. And naturally, the slaves run away. Wouldn't you in their situation?" Mrs. Lugg coughed briefly.

Her husband ignored her. "Once we have a fully complement of slaves, we can start releasing the indentures and send them wherever they want to go. But if you want to keep Moll by your side, we won't let her out of her contract early."

"Thank you, Thomas, that does make me happy."

The pang turned into resentment. Were others going to be released early, while Moll would have to stay because she had done something beneficial for the master's wife?

But then, where would she go without her brother?

"You'll need to be careful with her, Alice. I hear rumors that the other servants are suspicious of her. The sugar master has already been too permissive with her because her skin burns easily. Now she's been given a privileged place in the house. I can't have discord among the workers." His tone had gone from demanding to wheedling.

"Thomas, there's something you should know." Mrs. Lugg's voice dropped to a whisper, so Moll couldn't hear anything until Thomas Lugg exclaimed, "Why, that's wonderful! Why didn't you say so, my dear? Of course, you shall have the servant of your choice at your side. Don't worry about anything, I'll have the slave, Hannah, who shared Moll's hut, pick up Moll's duties in the fields while she comforts you until you are safely delivered."

Moll heard a loud, wet kiss, then Mr. Lugg's heavy footsteps retreated away from the room.

Moll let the door to her compartment slowly shut so that it made little creaking noise in the quiet corridor.

More than six years left in her contract. Between Mrs. Lugg's affection and the other servants' hatred, Moll wasn't sure which was going to kill her first.

CHAPTER 21

MOLL KEPT HER head down as she picked her way across the plantation to find Yaddy. She had been at the plantation house for several weeks already, but had never been out of Mrs. Lugg's sight long enough to return for a visit.

This evening, though, the Luggs were entertaining a neighboring plantation owner, so Mrs. Lugg had freed her until tomorrow morning.

Moll lived in a strange realm. On the one hand, she had the privilege of being in the plantation house. Very few servants lived inside—just Benji, the errand boy; Mrs. Barnes, the cook; and Ruth, who lit fires, swept rooms, and generally kept the house in order.

And now Moll, who had undefined duties except for keeping the mistress happy and healthy.

Not only did she have her tiny room, but her food rations improved in quantity and quality, as she now received scraps from the Luggs' table in addition to additional servings of secondhand sugar.

On the other hand, Mrs. Barnes, Ruth, and seemingly all the field hands despised her for her quick elevation. Except for Yaddy, Moll had not made a single friend in her time on St. Kitts.

Serving Mrs. Lugg was not difficult. Moll continued to help the woman with her cough, and the mistress's improvement was marked.

The mistress's pregnancy elevated her mood, too. With the baby to focus on, Mrs. Lugg was less worried about the climate or her boredom. In fact, her pregnancy was all-consuming, and Moll sat in her mistress's bed chamber for hours, listening to all of Mrs. Lugg's hopes and dreams for her child.

In her own way, Moll looked forward to the arrival of the Lugg baby. Mrs. Lugg had already implied that Moll would be employed to tend to the child. The new baby couldn't replace Callum, but what joy it would be to hold a gurgling infant again.

It would be worth all of Mrs. Lugg's pattering.

Hearing a loud rasping, Moll paused in her walk and looked around to find the source of the noise.

In the distance, she saw a square, wooden building under construction. It was taller than the main house, was topped with a flat platform, and was surrounded by a fence comprised of wood poles whose tops were sharpened to fine points. The noise was caused by several workers sharpening poles that lay across workbenches on the ground.

She frowned. It was very forbidding. Was this one of the watch towers Mr. Lugg had mentioned?

She had no time to consider it, for it would be dark soon. She wanted to have some time with Yaddy and still return to the big house before nightfall.

At the hut, Yaddy expressed surprise to see her, gripping Moll in a fierce hug. "You live?" she asked. "Mr. Thorpe gives your pallet to new girl. I think you must have died."

Moll told her what had happened.

"You don't come back?" Yaddy responded. "You live up there now? I do not like new girl, I think she is…not good. She leaves during the night many nights. But I try to teach her English. She is slave, too."

It seemed that Mr. Lugg was being true to his word to begin replacing indentured servants with slaves.

Moll shook her head. "Once the baby is born, I will help Mrs. Lugg with him. Or her."

Yaddy looked doubtful. "You will miss your own child too much when you do this. It will not be good for your spirit."

Poor Yaddy, to be so sweet and concerned for Moll. But nothing could be worse than remaining a field hand. "I'm sorry you have to remain here. I wish I knew a way to bring you to the house with me."

Yaddy shook her head. "Don't want. I...I have another friend here."

"Who is that?" Moll said. There were many servants on the plantation, but Moll had had little success with them. She envied Yaddy's ability to find friends.

"He is Sumbar. He is big and strong. Works as a sugar boiler. Very important job. Not many can do."

It was indeed an important job. It was critical to the entire sugar-making process to know when the sugar was ready to set. She had witnessed many a worker place two fingers into the hot, sticky syrup, rub them together, and declare it ready when it was not yet the proper consistency.

Those workers were quickly sent back to the fields.

"But isn't that dangerous, Yaddy? Remember what happened to Joan and Bridget. They're gone, and we don't know where."

Yaddy was dismissive. "It's not like it was with those two. They were chasing men who not care about them. Sumbar, he loves me. He wants a better life for us. Says one day we will be free. For now, we have piece of land together for our own crops. Mr. Thorpe say slaves can work their own fields on Sundays. We plant sweet potatoes, maize, and beans."

Even in the low light of the hut, Yaddy's face glowed. Moll was torn by gladness that Yaddy had found some happiness, and a stabbing fear that Yaddy would be foolish in that happiness.

She knew how easily one's hopes for the future could be callously drowned before one's eyes.

"I must leave before it's too dark for me to find my way back." Moll grabbed her bundle of fabric and hugged her friend fiercely before leaving. "Please be careful," she whispered in Yaddy's ear.

"I always careful," Yaddy whispered back.

But Moll feared that this new-found love would make Yaddy rash.

CHAPTER 22

ALTHOUGH MOLL CONTINUED to worry about Yaddy's romantic entanglement, she had more pressing matters to occupy most of her thoughts.

The other house servants were venomous, even more so than the field hands had been. Not content with merely spitting in her direction and hissing that she was a "red witch," Mrs. Barnes intentionally made Moll's meals intolerable. Some days, there was so much salt in Moll's serving of a soup that it was like drinking the Caribbean Sea. Other times, the cook would reserve an especially bad cut of meat that would normally be given to the pigs and serve it to Moll. Whether too brackish, too tough, or partially rancid, Moll ate all food presented to her without complaint, wishing for the food she had had as an outdoor servant. She knew that if she said anything to Mrs. Lugg, the slights and tortures would just get worse.

She just needed to survive her indenture so she could start a new life.

Moll had a fright, though, when she went to her compartment one time, exhausted and planning to fall into a quick sleep right away. As she found her pallet in the dark, her hand touched something that moved. Emitting a yelp that she hoped had gone unheard, she quickly jumped up and opened the door so that the corridor's light would bathe her room.

There was a snake on her pallet. With a gray back and an orange underside, it resembled a very large worm. With one hand on her chest to quell her heartbeat while the other held the door open, she examined the little beast, which indeed writhed like a worm.

Perhaps that's all it was. She knelt for a better look, which was when the snake stuck out its tongue, causing her to yip again.

She rose and decided she would have to dispose of the snake the way she did food.

Silently and without comment.

Using the rough sack which she had used to carry her meager belongings across the Atlantic, Moll emptied it and threw it over the reptile, capturing it. She trod down the stairs as quietly as she could, went out through the servants' rear entrance, and made her way a distance from the house, where she dumped the snake out among some berry plants.

Ruth revealed herself the following morning with smirks and sidelong glances. Moll ignored her, not giving Ruth the satisfaction of knowing how badly the other woman had frightened her.

Mrs. Lugg's cough was gone, only to be replaced by vague complaints. "The baby makes my temples throb," or "I feel unsettled this afternoon."

Moll dutifully worked up cures as she could, even daring to ask if she might have a bit of ground near the family's food plot to grow some herbs and flowers for drying. Mrs. Lugg quickly granted the request.

Mrs. Barnes's gaze glittered at that, but Moll stayed focused on keeping her employer happy.

Mrs. Lugg's requests for medicine seemed to be

secondary to her need to have Moll sit in her bed chamber with her and listen.

One day, when Moll was summoned, Mrs. Lugg was particularly excited. Two male servants were in her room, nearly done hanging a painting.

"See what Thomas bought for me?" she said to Moll as the workers climbed down from their ladders and departed with courteous nods to their mistress.

"It is beautiful, maum," Moll said.

"Step closer. It's by Frans Wouters. Flemish artists are all the fashion now, you know."

Moll wouldn't have any idea of that.

"Wouters was painter to our King Charles when he was Prince of Wales. Wouter is dead now, so his paintings are so much more valuable. Thomas wrote to a dealer in London, who found this Madonna and child painting by him. Thomas said it is to remind me of how important I am to the future of the Lugg family. He also said it is a reward for my upcoming labor pains."

At Mrs. Lugg's urging, Moll approached the large painting. She had never been in the presence of important art before. It was remarkable how the painter had brought a Biblical scene to life. The folds of the Virgin Mother's tunic were so lifelike that Moll wondered if she would be able to feel fabric if she touched the canvas. The artist had portrayed light shining down on the Child so accurately that Moll herself was warmed by it.

"It is very pretty, maum," she said, unsure how to describe the feelings it had instilled in her.

Mrs. Lugg nodded. "It is. Wouters was also the court painter for the Holy Roman Emperor, Ferdinand II, back in the thirties. So, he must have been a Roman Catholic. What of you, Moll? What are your religious inclinations?"

Moll was rooted to her spot. It had been a long time since she and her family had been swept up in religious controversies. She remembered how her father had satisfied the vendor in Clapham without admitting to anything.

"I worship in the true way," she said.

But Mrs. Lugg was not a simple pie seller. "What is that supposed to mean?" she asked. "Are you a Reformer or a Papist?"

The word "Papist" likely meant that her employer did not think highly of the Roman Catholic Church.

"I—I—" Moll floundered on what to say.

"I presume you are a Papist, then. There is a chapel for you on the island. I'll have Benji show you where it is so that you may attend on Sunday afternoons."

Moll expelled an audible sigh of relief, immediately wishing she had been more circumspect.

Fortunately, Mrs. Lugg laughed at that. "You needn't be afraid, Moll. Truthfully, with all the heathen religions coming from Africa, it is well enough that you worship our Lord Jesus Christ. Oh, how I warn Thomas that bringing slaves in will result in ruination, to us and them, but he does not listen to me."

Moll had not heard the word "heathen" before. "Maum, what are heathen religions?"

Mrs. Lugg sat down in her favorite chair, the painting now seemingly forgotten. "Those who do not worship the Lord. Some are Obeahists; they believe in magic and spellcasting. Some are Myalists, a heathen faith that uses magic, dancing, and spiritual possession. I'm sure there are others I don't know about, but in general, these traditions go against what we know to be true. Stay away from such practices, Moll."

Magic. That sounded frightening. And powerful. Did Yaddy follow either of these religions? She had said her father was a healer.

She wondered what Dada would have said about it all. Some of his elixirs were medically doubtful yet worked, he said, because the recipient believed they would cure an illness.

Maybe that was what the Africans' magical practices were like.

It was all confusing. She couldn't imagine a world without God and the Church, and yet…the Africans had been forced to emigrate to this island and abandon their lives; now, they should be forced to abandon all their knowledge and rituals?

"Yes, maum," she said, keeping all her thoughts to herself.

CHAPTER 23

THE NEXT MORNING, Mrs. Lugg was cheerful. "Thank you, Moll, for caring for me and my babe. In fact, as a reward…"

Mrs. Lugg went to a trunk at the foot of her bed and knelt before it. The trunk looked as if it had endured a very difficult sea journey. The dark stain was worn off in spots and the wood was chipped in some places.

She opened the trunk, which contained many dresses.

"These are some of my things that I no longer wear. Pick a dress for yourself. Look, this deep blue would complement you."

Mrs. Lugg held up a dress the shade of the Atlantic Ocean. It had an ivory underskirt that was stained, as well as sleeves with lace trim that were stained and tattered in places.

Moll had never worn anything so elegant in her entire life.

"It is beautiful," she said, while not moving to touch it. Her thoughts were thoroughly jumbled. It would be a gift like no other that she had ever had before. It suggested that Mrs. Lugg was truly pleased with her. It also suggested that if Mrs. Lugg expected her to wear it, Moll's days of hard work might be truly over. Perhaps she could assume the rest of her indenture would be pleasant. She would feel like a queen to wear such a gown.

But…when the other house servants saw Moll in the dress, what then? If they were already making her food inedible and putting serpents in her bed, it was unimaginable what they might do if she were to be deemed uppish for wearing it.

Mrs. Lugg was frowning. "What's the matter? Do you not want it?"

She did want it, but more than the dress, she wanted peace in her life.

"Yes, thank you, maum." Moll reached for it. She would decide what to do with it later. It was so full it was likely going to occupy every square inch of her compartment. Perhaps she could get Benji to help her put a nail in the wall to hang it.

Begging her mistress's leave, she took the dress to her room and laid it against the wall. It was of such quality that it stood on its own instead of collapsing to the ground. She quickly returned to Mrs. Lugg's bedchamber.

Mrs. Lugg seemed pleased with herself for having given Moll the dress and spent the next hour chattering idly about her plans for the baby. Moll's mistress was growing heavy with the child and frequently required Moll's help in sitting, standing, and dressing.

As Moll stood by, listening to her mistress, a small bird flew into the open window, landing on Moll's head. The bird offered a shrill *tweet-tweet-tweet-TWEET*, then took off and flew back out the window before Moll could even register that a bird had dug its feet into her scalp.

Mrs. Lugg laughed in delight and indicated that Moll should help her from her chair. Moll did so, and together they went to the window to see where the bird had gone.

It was easy to spot the bird, whose golden yellow body topped with smoky gray wings were brightly visible on a branch.

"It must have thought your caul made for a good nest." Mrs. Lugg was still highly amused.

"Yes, maum." In the distance, Moll noticed another tower being erected. She squinted. Were those Africans working on its construction?

"Mrs. Lugg," she said, hoping she sounded innocent. "What is that over there?" She pointed toward the structure.

"Oh, that's to guard us against outside threats." Mrs. Lugg's tone was strained and high-pitched. As well it would be, given that her answer was vague and not at all what Mr. Lugg had said.

"Do you mean pirates, maum?" Pirates were rumored to sail stealthily around the Caribbean, seeking to capture ships that carried valuables aboard.

"Of course. And the Spanish, the Dutch, and the French. They all want control of the islands to dominate the sugar trade. As though tropical diseases, pests, and dead soil weren't enough to make my husband's work difficult. Although he certainly doesn't listen to me when it comes to—" Mrs. Lugg stopped and took a deep breath.

"I think I'll work on my embroidery now." She held out her hand. The conversation was over.

Moll retrieved a piece of fabric that her mistress had been stitching.

Even Moll's untrained eye knew that it was very amateurish work, but the sewing kept her mistress occupied for part of each day. Moll had never learned embroidery, as Mama had never had time for idle stitchery, unless one counted the lace collars for the Cavaliers as idle sewing.

Moll shivered at the memory. She also trembled at the thought that the watch towers might be to repel pirates, and they might be to prevent foreign invasion, but it was obvious that their main purpose was prevent escapes.

As Mr. Lugg had said.

Moll gazed back out across the expanse of the property while her mistress stitched. Today's sea breeze was the perfect temperature and strength. One could almost forget how difficult—

She frowned and squinted again. Who was that man, escorted by Benji, up the long drive to the house?

Moll trembled again. "Mrs. Lugg—maum—I do believe that—oh my heavens—"

Mrs. Lugg lumbered up and tossed her embroidery hoop to one side to join Moll again at the window.

Mrs. Lugg broke into a smile. "This is a surprise I arranged for you."

Moll's brother, William, deeply tanned and thinner but otherwise looking just as he had when Moll had last seen him nearly a year ago, was stepping onto the white-painted wood porch of the house.

At the same moment, Mrs. Lugg cried out. "Oh, I believe the baby is coming!"

CHAPTER 24

1673

REUNITING WITH WILLIAM had been Moll's most joyous moment since bearing little Callum. Mrs. Lugg furthered the joy by giving Moll every Sunday afternoon to meet William and Agnes at a small church on the island, having written to William's master and obtained permission for William to also have every Sunday afternoon free to take a barge across to St. Kitts.

With her beloved brother back at her side, Moll found some peace, which made the time pass tolerably.

And after a difficult labor full of screaming and tears, Mrs. Lugg had delivered a sweet boy courtesy of Mrs. Barnes.

Moll had been stupefied that a woman who was so foul and disagreeable could not only have midwifery skills but could also be so tender and loving over the care of her mistress and the newborn.

Several coins were dropped into Mrs. Barnes's hand once the infant has been cleaned and settled to his mother's breast.

The boy was named Thomas after Mr. Lugg. Although the child was now the heir to Mr. Lugg's plantation, Mrs. Lugg called the boy "Massie" instead of Thomas.

Moll wondered if there was intent in that, but it was none of her business.

Mr. Lugg didn't seem to mind, for he soon presented his wife with a pair of drop sapphire earrings as an additional reward for producing a son.

Moll's days were spent entertaining both Alice Lugg and Massie. Neither was difficult. Massie was an agreeable baby and turned into an even more agreeable toddler. Cuddling him gave her immense satisfaction.

Her dress collection had grown by two more, as well.

Additionally, Moll was more than halfway through her indenture and had not suffered a calamitous illness. She now saw William, Agnes, and their children every Sunday at a tiny chapel in Basseterre. There were few Catholics on the island, so the Dyer family made up the majority of attendees.

Moll would have happily climbed over one of Mr. Lugg's sharp watchtower posts to not miss those sacred Sundays with her family. Fortunately, Mrs. Lugg never interfered with Moll's Sunday afternoons.

It was the only time she wore one of the fancy dresses Mrs. Lugg had given her. The other servants seemed to think it acceptable that she was dressed in finery to stand in church, so miraculously, they didn't plague her over it.

Religion also came to the forefront when Mrs. Lugg casually mentioned one day that a missionary was scheduled to arrive from Bristol any day.

"Thomas has hired Mr. Sparrow to give Christianity lessons to the slaves," she said as she plucked a sweetmeat from a tray that Mrs. Barnes had prepared. "He says it will give them benefit by offering them the opportunity for eternal salvation.

And that will make them more valuable." Mrs. Lugg frowned as she bent down in her chair to offer Massie one of the treats. He popped it into his mouth and swallowed it after two bites.

Mrs. Lugg smiled at her son but turned serious again. "But I don't know how enslaved people will react to a message of salvation from their enslavers. Although they certainly need to abandon their spells and incantations. I shall do my best to make the missionary welcome." She sighed. "This place is terrible. How I wish I were back home. Would you like to be back in England, Moll? You could serve me there."

"Yes, maum, it sounds wonderful," Moll said dutifully. She would never leave her brother to make a grueling journey back to poverty.

Three more years and she would have her independence.

THE MISSIONARY ARRIVED on a day of torrential rains. Work rarely stopped on the plantation, so servants simply continued making their way through the muck as they plucked bugs, harvested cane, and processed sugar.

The drudgery was visible from Mrs. Lugg's window. Moll was both relieved and guilt-ridden that she was no longer part of the field work. Yaddy often crossed her mind, and Moll prayed to God every night in her compartment that her friend would remain safe.

Moll crept to the top of the main staircase to listen as Mrs. Lugg swept down with her husband to greet the missionary. The rain drummed heavily on the roof and against the windowpanes, making it difficult to hear.

"Mr. Sparrow, you do us honor by bringing the Gospel to our shores. We are especially grateful considering our weather. Be assured, it is not always like this." Mr. Lugg sounded over-enthusiastic.

A voice Moll didn't recognize laughed heartily. "Fear not, sir. If I were to permit a bit of rain to hamper me, I should not be long for missionary work."

There was polite laughter from the Luggs. "May we offer you a repast?" Mrs. Lugg asked. "A servant will take your trunk to your bedchamber."

As the group moved into the dining room, Moll went back upstairs and made her way to the rear servants' staircase. She moved quietly down the stairs and made her way into the rear entrance of the dish pantry to observe more and to avoid servants carrying the newcomer's trunk up the main staircase.

She also prayed she wouldn't be discovered by Mrs. Barnes or Ruth, who would surely tattle on her immediately.

The Luggs and their guest sat down at the table. Moll had never been near the family dining space and was amazed at the fine furniture and the number of beeswax candles hanging from a chandelier, bathing the room in light. Silverware clacked against decorated china plates and crystal glasses.

How very rich the Luggs must be.

"I noticed cannons being unloaded on the docks upon my arrival," the missionary said. "Is this tiny island planning on a war with its neighbors?"

"Indeed not," Mr. Lugg said. "The Dutch island of Tortola has been put under the protection of Sir William Stapleton, the Governor General of all the Leeward Islands. He did not have sufficient men to occupy Tortola but burned its forts and sent its cannons here for storage."

Mr. Sparrow speared a piece of meat with his knife and carefully placed it in his mouth. "So, the Dutch have been run off? Who occupies Tortola now?"

"Right now, it's sparsely populated with English settlers, but they are starting up more sugar plantations there, so I expect it will be bustling like St. Kitts in no time. I suppose I should be wary of more plantations, but the English craving for sugar means that there is no end to the demand for it." Mr. Lugg laughed as he drank deeply from his glass.

Mrs. Lugg dandled Massie on her lap while Mr. Lugg asked Mr. Sparrow about his background.

"Ah, my tale is not a happy one, I'm afraid. Lived most of my life in Bristol and have been a member of Nicholas's Church there for nearly as long. I lost my wife, Mary, a couple of years ago. A good woman, but not constitutionally strong." Mr. Sparrow also drank deeply from his glass.

"My son was already pastoring his own congregation, and I knew I had to develop a new meaning to my life, lest I become a bedlamite. The vicar at Nicholas's Church, Samuel Crossman, said I might find that meaning in missionary work."

Moll studied the missionary. He was probably ten to fifteen years older than she was, lean of frame, with snowy white hair that was still full.

If she was not mistaken in the shadowy candlelight, Mr. Sparrow's eyes were…deep green, just like hers.

"We are fortunate that the vicar recommended you to such work and that you answered our advertisement," Mr. Lugg said. "More wine?"

Mr. Lugg tipped a bottle into Mr. Sparrow's glass.

"Yes, thank you. Not everyone follows Reverend Crossman's suggestions, I must say. He had Puritan leanings and ran into some trouble during the war when he joined a group attempting to update the Book of Common Prayer so that Puritans and Anglicans alike could use it. The effort failed, and after our present King Charles took the throne, the reverend and about two thousand other Puritan leaners were expelled from the Church of England."

Mr. Lugg again took a long draught from his own glass. "Yet, he is now Vicar of St. Nicholas Church?"

Mr. Sparrow laughed. It was a low, pleasant sound, coming from deep within his chest. "Mr. Crossman is a wise man. He quickly renounced his Puritan affiliations, was ordained in 1665, and became a royal chaplain. Two years later, he became Vicar of St. Nicholas Church. Four years later, he convinced me that I should dedicate my life to missionary work, and today I am in your hospitable home drinking your delectable wine."

His laughter rumbled through the room again.

The men talked idly of Sparrow's ocean voyage, of the state of the plantation, and then, finally, about the missionary's suggestions for proselytizing to the slaves.

Mr. Sparrow spoke passionately about the saving of souls. Mr. Lugg spoke equally passionately about keeping the slave population under control, particularly as he was planning to import many more of them.

Mr. Sparrow quieted and seemed to focus on his food. For a time, the only noise in the room was Massie chattering happily on Mrs. Lugg's lap.

Mr. Lugg eventually spoke up again and asked the missionary what assistance he might need. "You seem to have traveled entirely by yourself with no assistant."

"That is true. Not everyone has the stomach

for this type of work. Since you mention it, I would indeed appreciate a helper, if you can spare someone, to assist me with distribution of tracts and the recording of baptisms. Reverend Crossman is also a hymn writer, and I have a book of his works that I want to use in conversion efforts, so having someone who can sing them while I play my instrument would be very helpful."

Mrs. Lugg spoke up for the first time. "You brought a musical instrument across the ocean with you?"

"Yes. I have a violin in my trunk and would be happy to entertain you with it. I flatter myself that I have some marginal talent with it."

So, Mr. Sparrow played an instrument. Just like Richard had. But whereas Richard was all lighthearted and carefree, this man seemed much more…intense.

Richard's memory was fading now. Thinking of him made her wistful and a little sad. However, his memory didn't offer quite the same blow to the stomach that her son's did.

Massie's laughter and antics soothed her soul, but Moll knew that she was leaving in a few years, and when she did, she would never see him again. Moll had to protect herself from loving the child too much, lest her heart get broken again when her indenture was finished.

"We would welcome some music, sir," Mrs. Lugg said. "It isn't often that we have entertainment."

She rang a bell, and Ruth entered the room from the direction of the entry hall. "Retrieve Mr. Sparrow's violin from the trunk in his room." Ruth dashed out and returned quickly with a shaped case that had multiple leather-strapped buckles along it.

Ruth started to move in the direction of the

pantry where Moll stood, but seemed to change her mind and went back out the way she came.

Moll heaved a mental sigh of relief.

As Mr. Sparrow opened his case, Mrs. Lugg said, "I know just who to lend to you as your assistant. My healer and companion, Moll Dyer, is very obedient and helpful. She's also a mature woman, so she won't be foolish and silly like some servants can be. I can spare her for a few hours each day."

Just like that, Moll was no longer calm. She put a hand over her heart. *What?* She was supposed to assist a religious man who was not Catholic? Did she have to hide her religious views from him? How would the field hands react when they saw that she was back to "instruct" them on abandoning their ways?

No, no, no. She couldn't do this. Except…she had no ability to tell her mistress no.

Full of dread, Moll left the pantry and found her way back upstairs without being caught. She sat in her compartment with the door ajar to continue allowing light in while she fretted over what was to be expected of her.

Downstairs, Mr. Sparrow's alternately sorrowful and happy tunes went on into the night, long after the rain had stopped beating the island into submission. Moll finally got tired, shut the door to her compartment, and went to sleep.

CHAPTER 25

ON THE FIRST Sunday, Moll met Mr. Sparrow early in the morning at the rear entrance of the house at his request. He was carrying a handled box that seemed to be heavy.

"Where do you think most of the workers will be right now?" he asked after they made introductions.

In the morning light, Mr. Sparrow was even more impressive, carrying himself with an ease and assurance far beyond Richard's.

Moll glanced up. The sun was starting to make its way into the sky. "I think they will have eaten and will be in their own fields, working their crops."

"Then that's where we shall go."

Moll led Mr. Sparrow to where there were about a dozen male slaves and couple of females, performing the work of hoeing, seeding, and plucking vegetables in various stages of growth.

"Do they speak English?" Mr. Sparrow asked.

"I don't know, sir." Moll had taught Yaddy English, but had Yaddy taught others? Moll did not see Yaddy among the group in the field today.

The missionary considered this for a moment as he dropped his case to the ground. "Well, God will help us."

God's help appeared in the form of Mr. Thorpe, who was suddenly there and told the slaves—in broken English—that they were to stop what they were doing to attend to Mr. Sparrow.

Their irritation was obvious to Moll, even as they dropped their tools and gathered around her and the missionary where they stood on the path next to the field.

Mr. Sparrow started out brightly. "Welcome to today's lesson on Christianity. I am here to share with you the Good News that will save your mortal souls and make them immortal."

From there, the missionary launched into a long treatise on the life of Christ and the life of the church. He spoke eloquently, but what he was describing was complicated.

Even Moll, devoted to the Church, was confused.

A slave glanced up at the sky. The sun would be fully overhead and hot soon.

Moll interrupted the missionary. "Sir, I don't mean to tell you your business, but I believe they are anxious to get back to work. They might be more interested if you continued another day."

Mr. Sparrow started, as if he had just noticed their attitudes. "What? Oh, yes, yes, of course you are right. Thank you, Mrs. Dyer, for your wise counsel. I am quite new at this and can use all of the assistance I can muster."

Moll blushed. Had anyone ever called her wise before? Mr. Sparrow was treating her as an equal, too, and the feeling was both peculiar...and warming.

He might not understand the people on St. Kitts yet, but neither had Moll when she first arrived. She flattered herself into thinking that Mr. Sparrow would prove to be quite successful on the island... with Moll's help. Her thoughts of the impracticality of converting the African arrivals fled as she contemplated a different life for herself. Not a mere servant, but an instrument of God.

The vision was intoxicating.

Mr. Sparrow knelt before this box and unlatched the lid. Moll peered over his shoulder. It was as if he had carried with him everything from his chamber except his clothes.

He rifled through papers and quills and seals until his hand touched something that made him say, "Ah." He withdrew a sack and handed it to Moll, who pulled open the drawstring.

Inside were a plethora of bracelets, each made of a leather thong with three beads knotted onto it.

Moll looked at the missionary quizzically as she held one in her hand.

"Give them out. These will help them remember what I have told them today. The beads represent the Trinity. See? One for the Father, one for the Son, and one for the Holy Ghost."

Ah. But...

"Sir, I don't mean to contradict you, or to suggest you are not..." Moll stopped. Perhaps she had flattered herself too much, and her words would not be well received.

"Yes? What is it?" Mr. Sparrow rose from his box. He was very tall and broad-shouldered, and carried himself with ease. He looked nothing like the wizened old ministers she had known in her life.

"I—well, sir, I think perhaps you are expecting too much at once. The workers have not been here long, and have so many cares and concerns, that it seems as though tending to their needs first would open their ears a little wider." Moll stared directly at him. If he reported her brash behavior to Mrs. Lugg, there could be trouble, but Moll saw this as an opportunity to help improve life on the plantation.

"What cares and concerns are those? Come, let us walk and talk."

To her relief, Mr. Sparrow's gaze was intense but genuinely interested.

He took the bracelet and bag from her, dropped them back into his box on and held up his hands to the group. "We are done today. God bless you all."

Leaving the box on the ground, he nodded his head at Moll to follow him. The slaves seemed to be confused at first, but quickly realized they no longer had to listen and returned to what they were doing.

She walked alongside the missionary, anxiously waiting for him to open the conversation. Would he listen to her?

"What are the concerns you believe must be cared for first?" he asked.

"Well, Mr. Sparrow, I know that they have endured much worse voyages than you or I have, and their misery is compounded by having been sold by their countrymen into a place where they don't know the language and receive little in the way of clothing or comfort."

"How do you know about their journeys?" he asked.

"I am an indentured servant and started my time here in the fields, so I lived in one of the huts that—"

Mr. Sparrow stopped. "You are? I thought you were simply…paid help. I did not realize…" He became thoughtful.

"This is why Alice Lugg said you would be a perfect helper for me, as you are an ideal bridge between them and me. Yes, Mrs. Lugg is quite clever. And I am most fortunate in you, for you have maturity and wisdom." He nodded in satisfaction. "You must call me Alexander from this point. I believe we shall be very good friends. May I call you Moll?"

Moll felt herself blushing yet again. She nodded, and they resumed walking.

"How much time remains in your indenture?" he asked.

"Three years, sir. I mean, Alexander." Because she was nearly as tall as he was, she was able to match the missionary's steps.

"I presume you lived under hardship at home?"

"Yes." She explained briefly why she chose to come to St. Kitts, following her losses and desire to follow her brother.

He listened intently. "Your sorrow nearly matches my own. I lost my wife tragically, although, praise God, my son is alive and well."

"Yes, I know," she said, without thinking.

"How do you know that?" He stopped walking again.

Moll wished she could bite her words back. "Er, I just meant that I know it is tragic to lose your spouse."

He seemed satisfied and they walked on.

She talked about her time on the plantation, what she knew about the slaves' lives and how she came to live at the house because of her healing skills. "I also know a fair bit about ale making, but the mistress hasn't asked for me to make any."

He nodded. "It will serve you well for earning an income when you finish your indenture. Perhaps you will find a new husband at that time, too."

"Perhaps." Would she not ever stop blushing?

"Tell me what you know about the slaves' needs." Alexander's interest seemed genuine and it warmed Moll.

She told him of what she knew about their harrowing journeys to the Caribbean and how they received a cloth allowance upon their arrival, as she had, but not much else.

"Did you make that dress from your allowance?"

Moll looked down at her dress, which was finer than the sacks the female slave swore or even the modest clothing of the other house servants. "Mrs. Lugg gave this to me."

His glance was appreciative. "Another wise decision on her part."

Moll was ready to faint from the pleasure of his flattery, mostly because he seemed so genuine.

"I presume you also understand the sugar-making process," he said.

Moll told the missionary of how the sugar cane was planted, harvested, and processed.

"Fascinating. Your perspective is unique, Moll. Do you personally know many of the slaves?"

"No, but I have a friend among them. Her name is Yaddy and we—"

"Well, then, this Yaddy shall be our first convert, and she will help us with the others. Shall we meet again tomorrow afternoon to make plans?"

Moll spent the remainder of Sunday at church with William and Agnes, afterward telling them little about Alexander Sparrow's arrival except that the plantation now had a missionary visiting and that she was helping him.

William brushed over her news with his own news that Agnes had started earning her own money by offering her seamstress services to people in Charlestown, the capital of Nevis.

"I am proud of you, Agnes," Moll said, glad that William's wife had proven to be such a prized pearl.

Moll now wished to be a prized pearl, too.

CHAPTER 26

THE NEXT DAY, Moll tended to Massie and Mrs. Lugg for a few hours, mixing up a draught for her mistress's vague complaint of a sore throat and answering her questions about the previous day's work with the slaves.

Once Mrs. Lugg had lain Massie down for a nap and decided to lie down awhile herself, she released Moll, who sought out Alexander Sparrow downstairs. He was near the servants' entrance, looking over his violin. His smile was wide when he espied Moll.

"Might you like to practice some musical entertainment that we can present along with our Gospel presentation on Sunday?"

He led her outside behind the house. "We will sing a hymn called '*Sweet Place*.' It was written by the vicar of my church, Reverend Crossman. Listen."

First Alexander spoke the words, then came back around to sing them.

Sweet place; sweet place alone!
The court of God ostensibly high,
The heaven of heavens, the throne
Of spotless majesty!

O happy place!
When shall I be, my God, with Thee,
To see Thy face?

The song went on for several more verses.

Alexander's voice was surprisingly strong and pleasant. Much like his laughter, Moll supposed.

"Do you think you can sing the song back to me?" he asked.

Moll stumbled, but after several tries was able to sing the song without error.

"Now I shall accompany you on the violin," he said.

They went through it again. It was much easier to sing with music in the background.

"Good, good," Alexander said, removing the violin from under his chin. "We shall rehearse a few more times this and then will be ready to lead the unfortunate souls in singing."

The slaves seemed very confused by the initial proceedings the next Sunday, as Alexander opened up with his violin playing and Moll's singing accompaniment. He followed this up with a repeat of his Gospel discussion from the previous week.

This time, though, Alexander told the slaves that he understood their predicament and knew that they were living in the wilderness, much as the Israelites had so long ago. God would rescue them and give them succor, as He had the Israelites.

Moll had to give the man credit; the story was a compelling one, but it seemed to fall on deaf, bewildered ears. Moll knew that, ultimately, the missionary's offering of spiritual "bread" was no replacement for tending to their crops, which resulted in actual food.

Today, Alexander insisted that the Father-Son-Holy Ghost bracelets be handed out. The slaves took them with bewildered expressions on their faces.

At the conclusion of Sunday's lessons, Alexander spoke to Moll as an equal, as he had before. "What did you think of today's lesson? Are we making progress?"

Moll shrugged. She was hesitant to tell him what was truly in her thoughts, but if she couldn't be honest to a man of Alexander's goodness, then when could she be?

"Truthfully, you are taking away time from their only day to themselves. I know I spend my Sundays in church, but that's because I am already Cath— Christian, and I see my brother and his family there. If I were, as you say, a heathen, and had to spend most of my free time listening to something I didn't understand, I don't believe I would be inclined to accept it."

Alexander tilted his head and seemed to be considering her words thoughtfully. "So, what do you propose that I do?"

This had to be the first time in Moll's life that someone was taking her opinion seriously. Her heart beat rapidly in gratitude to Alexander Sparrow. "I don't know that you will see great success unless you can convince Mr. Lugg to give the slaves additional time off for hearing your lessons. But Mr. Lugg doesn't like anything interfering with the plantation's workings. I don't think he would agree."

Alexander slowly nodded. "It is a conundrum, for certain."

"A what?" Moll frowned in confusion. Alexander Sparrow was very learned.

He made that low rumbling noise in his chest. "It is a puzzle, Moll. One I shall work through. Once again, I thank you for your wise guidance."

Moll's face flamed once more in both embarrassment and pride. She was glad that her skin had improved dramatically now that she spent most of her time indoors.

That evening, she overheard a heated argument between Alexander and Mr. Lugg downstairs. It seemed to start as a pleasant conversation, with Alexander suggesting that Mr. Lugg give the slaves more time away from their labors so that they might hear his message, as well as recommending that they be given more clothing and better food.

Mr. Lugg was clearly offended and replied that Alexander should stick to proselytizing and leave plantation management to him.

After several minutes of raised voices, the men must have come to some sort of resolution, because Moll then heard the clinking of glasses.

THE PATTERN MOLL and the missionary established was strange. Every evening, Moll would retreat to her compartment while Alexander would dine with his patrons. She was fully equal to him during the day, but at night she transformed into a lowly servant once more.

A week later, Alexander inquired as to whether Moll had had a chance to talk to Yaddy. "For if you can open her ears to the Gospel, she might influence others. I believe this to be your special, God-inspired duty."

Moll agreed to talk to Yaddy.

Yaddy did not greet her with her customary warmth, which was odd. But then Moll saw that her friend was eyeing Moll's dress, which, although worn and stained in places, was vastly different from Yaddy's sack dress.

It was a mistake to have worn this to see the woman with whom she once shared mean lodgings.

Moll broached the topic of God, but Yaddy was far more enthusiastic over the topic of Sumbar, and she freely interrupted Moll's efforts. "Sumbar has the strength of three men. All Africans here follow him. He is wise leader. Our garden grows big."

Moll did not have Alexander's Gospel spreading talents, and her attempts to engage Yaddy in it fell on deaf ears. Finally, she tried a different approach.

"Mr. Sparrow had bracelets for people at his last lesson. They are—"

"Yes." Yaddy bobbed her head. "They break apart bracelets and use beads as money with one another." She knelt, reached under her pallet, and pulled out a handful of beads to show Moll.

Alexander would be heartbroken to hear this, but Moll had warned him that he was moving too fast.

"If you would only be baptized—" she said, trying once more with her friend.

Yaddy frowned. "Sumbar likes what man says about more freedoms, but does not care about *Jeez-oos*. I follow Sumbar."

This would break Alexander's heart even more.

To her surprise, he listened to Moll's report without emotion and, when she was done, he smiled. "What you say is that he has heard me. He does not yet believe, but we can be patient. Now, what say we practice more singing?"

They were outside, on a trail leading from the house to the smoker, where hams and other meats hung for preservation. Although the sea provided much of the food for the plantation, Mrs. Lugg insisted that animals be kept to provide the family with the meats with which she was familiar.

Alexander had his violin with him and retrieved it from his case to play. At first, he started playing hymns and Moll sang along, as he had taught her.

The stranger homeward bends,
And sigheth for his rest:
Heaven is my home, my friends
Lodge there in Abraham's breast.

Earth's but a sorry tent,
Pitched but a few frail days,
A short-leased tenement;
Heaven's still my song, my praise.

Alexander removed the violin from his neck and put it on the ground, whereupon he clapped. "Brava, dear lady. You have learned these songs so well. Perhaps we might impose upon the Lord to forgive us if we now spend a few moments on a tune a bit more lighthearted."

Alexander picked up his violin once more, but this time the sound was brighter and faster. It reminded Moll of that time long ago at the Friday market, where she had twirled like a ribbon in the wind until her red hair had been discovered and she had been set upon.

Some of the workers still whispered *witch* at her, although accompanying Alexander, who in turn was there at the master's request, had silenced many of the tongues.

The music made light of her heart, and her feet began to move of their own accord. At first, she simply swayed to the music, but its tempo did not permit that for long. Soon, she was stepping and spinning and laughing like that young girl from long ago.

She was so caught up in the moment that she untied her caul and let her hair go free.

The music stopped abruptly, and so did Moll, opening her eyes with the thought that she had done something wrong.

But Alexander Sparrow was looking at her with something akin to admiration in his gaze.

"By the love of the Savior," he whispered. "Look at that hair. It's like a bottle of sherry tumbling down your back."

"It doesn't...bother you?" Moll asked. She knew her hair had faded some with age, but it was still an unusual shade of copper.

Alexander was breathing heavily. "Quite the contrary. You are...a vision. I had not thought— not since my wife died—that I might ever again—" He sighed and picked up his violin again, assuming his tune where he had left off.

At first hesitant, Moll again picked up with her dancing, eyes closed, feeling completely free and unburdened as she did so. It was as if she were immediately transported back to a time before the loss of Granda, and her parents, and Richard, and Callum, and the weight of her current circumstances. She moved without care, and each step and jump made her feel more like a young girl again.

Alexander's encouraging laughter receded into the back of her brain as she simply let herself meld with the buoyant music.

Round and round and round—

With a thud, she landed against something. Opening her eyes, she realized that she had twirled herself right against Alexander Sparrow.

His gaze caught hers, and he tossed his carefully

kept violin to the side as though it were an inconsequential rag poppet.

Moll tried to step away from him, but with both his arms free, he caught her up to him.

Her heart continued to race, but no longer from dancing.

"I—I'm sorry, I didn't mean to—" Was she babbling like the girl she pretended to be?

"Moll…" Alexander's voice was husky. He cupped her face in his hands and brushed a thumb over her lips.

His face was so close to hers that she could feel his raspy breath. He smelled of the sea and of rain-laden clouds and of sugar loaves.

What was this feeling overcoming her? It was as if her blood was on fire.

Alexander briefly pressed his lips to hers, which made that hot blood race through her veins.

He drew back and gazed at her with his sparkling green eyes as if she were a glass of that sherry, to be drunk deeply.

"The Lord works in mysterious ways," he murmured, and kissed her again.

Suddenly, Moll felt like she was Job, and all her previous deprivations over the years were just God's requirement for her to finally gain blessings.

CHAPTER 27

IT WASN'T LONG before Moll was leaving her compartment during the night to creep along to Alexander's chamber, returning to her own pallet before the dawn's light. She knew that if the Luggs discovered that their house servant and missionary guest were illegitimately behaving as husband and wife, that they would likely have him marched onto the next ship leaving the island, and Moll would be subject to not only a beating but be returned to the fields.

Yet, she couldn't help herself. Alexander was older and wiser and still very handsome for his age. He looked at her not as if she were a woman for whom life had been harrowing and painful, but as if she were still a girl in her first blush of womanhood.

Moll quickly learned how to keep their relationship hidden. During the day, she was Mrs. Lugg's faithful servant and Alexander's dutiful assistant. At night, she was his wanton lover.

As the weeks and months went by, Moll became less concerned about the state of souls and more worried about continuing to maintain the secrecy of her relationship with Alexander. The further she fell in love with him, the more difficult it was to disguise her feelings around others.

For his part, Alexander also seemed to be

struggling to behave decorously. He brushed up against her and winked at her multiple times a day.

It was so very difficult to concentrate on their vital work.

While their nighttime activities were sweet and rewarding, efforts with the slaves' lessons were of little value. Not many of the slaves acted genuinely interested in Alexander's Gospel messages. Those who made professions of faith seemed to either be confused or were simply expressing thanks for the gift of a beaded bracelet, which, according to Yaddy, would be quickly turned into currency.

Others were outright hostile to Alexander and Moll in their glares, although of course they didn't dare do anything untoward to a guest of the master.

Late one night, as she lay with Alexander atop the bed coverings in his chamber, Alexander did the unthinkable and began talking of the future.

"The life of a missionary is a difficult one," he said in a low tone as they lay on their sides facing each other. He brushed a thumb over her lips, as had become his custom. "That of a missionary's wife is more so. She has all the work of her husband but none of the credit for conversions. What do you think of that?"

Was it possible that once her indenture was over, she would become a wife once more? To live a life that, while not one of wealth, would at least not be in poverty? She controlled her trembling as best she could.

"I think a wife follows her husband wherever he goes, as God dictates."

His laughter resonated softly in the room. "Ah, Moll, you are too clever for me by far."

She kissed him and started to break away from

him. Soon, it would be time to return to her compartment.

But Alexander pulled her close again. "You have completely bewitched me," he whispered.

This alarmed Moll and she scrambled up to a sitting position. "I am no witch!"

There was that rumbling laugh again. "Do not mistake me, dearest, I only mean that you are enchanting. Beautiful. I can hardly believe that you are nearly forty years old. You look like a girl in the fresh flower of her youth to me. It has made me behave like a lovesick boy and not like a widower who has dedicated his life to God. But I think I can be both in love and dedicated to service."

Moll let his words wash over her like a long, cool drink of fresh water. No one had ever spoken to her as such, not even Richard. Alexander's words made her feel…queenly.

She lay back down in the crook of his arm. His chamber was small as compared to Mrs. Lugg's room, with only the barest of furnishings, but to Moll, it was the most stately room in the world.

She briefly fell asleep, dreaming of a possible future with Alexander. Moll at her husband's side, being his helpmeet as he converted heathens all over the Caribbean—nay, all over the world. Retreating each night to a cozy bed chamber, murmuring their love for one another, as they lay with their limbs intertwined, not caring about the oppressive, damp heat.

As she reluctantly returned to her compartment, Moll contemplated for the first time whether she might be able to get out of her indenture early. Surely Mr. and Mrs. Lugg would see that Moll was indispensable to Alexander and would be agreeable to allowing her to leave so she could help him spread Christianity throughout the Caribbean.

Moll's desire to leave her indenture early became more acute when she learned one Sunday that William was leaving Nevis to go to Dorchester in the Maryland colony.

"I bought out my contract early," he said as they were walking down the path away from the chapel. Agnes and the children were several steps behind them, as William's wife wrangled the young ones into obedience.

"I don't understand. How did you do that?" Moll asked.

"It was my dear wife. She has been sewing and baking her heart out and selling her goods wherever she can. She kept every penny and presented the money to me last week. My master was so impressed with her that he told me I was the most fortunate of men, and he agreed to take the money in exchange for releasing me early. I think he's planning on replacing all his indentures with Africans, anyway."

Moll was thrilled for her brother, but…this meant she might not see him again for years. Unless she, too, could get released.

Suddenly, her dream of marrying Alexander to gain her freedom didn't seem so far-fetched. Surely, they could spend time in Maryland for rest periods in between missionary journeys.

"Congratulations, brother. Agnes is indeed a clever wife. I—" Moll hesitated.

"Yes, what is it?"

She shook her head. It wasn't the right time to tell him. Not until Alexander knew.

Moll had a secret she was hugging to herself. A

miraculous secret, dropped down by a merciful God upon a woman too old for such a blessing.

For Moll was quite sure she was with child.

CHAPTER 28

ALEXANDER HAD SAID little more of marriage, as his focus on his lessons became more intense.

One of the slaves named Osay, had sought him out to ask a question about "this God who rules the master and the master's people."

Alexander enthused over the slave's interest and became wholly devoted to spending as much time as could be mustered with Osay. Thomas Lugg had agreed to more time off from laboring in the fields for slaves who were interested in Gospel lessons, and Moll worried that Osay's interest was purely for the free time, but it wasn't for her to judge.

Alexander's joy was infectious, though, and Moll was happy, despite being unable to be open about their relationship.

But Osay, a quiet, slightly built young man, ultimately refused to convert, communicating in halting English that he would be cast off from the others if he said he no longer trusted in the power of spells and incantations.

He thanked the missionary, however, for "make me understand truth of things."

Alexander was bitterly disappointed. "I thought we were so close with him, Moll."

We.

She was sorry that Osay refused, yet she floated

the rest of the day on that one word. She also decided that tonight would be the night she told her beloved of her pregnancy. That would dispel his sadness over the lost soul, and they could begin planning their life together.

Alexander must have been sadder than she realized, for at the conclusion of the day, he said to her quietly, "I believe I'd like to be alone tonight, sweetest."

Moll reeled. He had never suggested they spend a night apart since they had first taken up with one another.

"Of course," she replied evenly. Her momentous news would keep until the morrow.

After an evening of letting Massie chase her around on his new hobby horse, a stick with a carved horse's head on its top, Moll collapsed onto her pallet, exhausted from the exertion.

The next morning, she found it more difficult than usual to rise. Massie's lusty shrieks and rough, tumbling play the previous night had been harder on her than she realized. Was she too old for such activity?

She swept the thought away. It would be different when she and Alexander set up housekeeping together. Their son or daughter would be perfectly behaved, would be—

"Miss Moll?" came Benji's voice from outside her compartment.

She opened the door, and he handed her a folded note. Moll opened it and recognized Alexander's handwriting, but she couldn't read the words on the page. Humiliated by what she had to do, she carried the note to Mrs. Lugg and asked her to read it.

Dearest Moll,

It has given me more joy than I can possibly say to have known you during my stay at Nevis Plantation. I learned great things about human nature from you, and our hours together were passed in what I trust was mutual joy and sweet companionship.

However, my repeated requests for better conditions for his unfortunate slaves—more substantial clothing, better food, and more free time so they might receive Gospel lessons—have been met with pure obstinacy by Thomas Lugg. He has not agreed to a single suggestion of mine. This has translated into the slaves refusing to hear the message, as you have witnessed.

I do not see how widespread conversions can occur on St. Kitts, and, as the Lord Jesus once said in the book of Matthew, I must shake the dirt from my feet when I leave the house or city where my words are not heard.

I am sure my days on earth are shortened due to my advanced age of fifty years, and I wish to see success in my endeavors before I die. It will not happen on St. Kitts, thus I am boarding a ship for the Leeward Islands, a place where I believe I can be of more use.

I have been in correspondence with their governor, Sir William Stapleton, and he assures me that there are nearly nine thousand Africans there with a great need for the Gospel message, as well as around ten thousand English settlers who have largely forgotten our Lord.

As you still have several years remaining in your indenture, I knew you could not come with me. I thought it best to leave without a scene of tears and sorrow between us.

I hope you will say prayers for me each night, Moll, for my success. I, too, will hold you in my own prayers every night for the rest of my life.

Mrs. Lugg looked up. "He signs it, 'Yours, Alex.' Highly improper to talk to a servant that way. How very rude of him to sail off to another situation without properly taking his leave of us. Dreadful. And his ingratitude toward his host, my husband. Well." She dropped the note to the ground between them.

"He must have been quite useless as a missionary if he was willing to give up that easily. We are better off without him. As are you, Moll, dear. Now, now, you look as if you are about to cry. No sense in that."

Moll was trembling, but not because she desired to weep. No, this was something else entirely. It was pure, white-hot wrath. The wrath started down in her toes and slithered up her body in dark, painful tendrils that wrapped themselves around her stomach, her heart, and her lungs. She could hardly breathe for the intense turmoil created within her.

"I am not crying, maum, I am—I am—" What was the point of telling Mrs. Lugg of her feelings?

"Ahhh!" Moll cried out. A sharp, stabbing pain pierced through her innards.

"Whatever is the matter? If you are that sad about Mr. Sparrow's departure, I have just the thing to cheer you. Would you like to pick out another dress from my trunk?"

Claiming to feel unwell and begging leave to go and make herself a posset, Moll quickly fled back to her compartment.

Unable to sob as noisily as she would have liked, Moll sat on her pallet with her back to the wall in the dark room and allowed tears to flow freely down her face. The pain of Alexander's betrayal was so wrenching—and unexpected—that she found herself staring blankly at the wall, frozen in grief and unable to contemplate what was next for her.

At some point, Ruth knocked roughly at the door. "Mrs. Lugg says you're to have some soup."

A tray and some dishes clattered outside the compartment.

Moll ignored her fellow servant, who muttered against Moll as she left.

More time passed, she had no idea how long. It was at least long enough that she thought perhaps she should take a spoonful of soup to be nourished enough to attend to Mrs. Lugg in the morning without raising any suspicions.

As Moll rose from her pallet, she was attacked by stabbing pains in her stomach. She yelped, then clapped a hand over her mouth. It wouldn't do for anyone to hear her.

But now she really was sick. Was she going to vomit?

She pulled her tin chamber pot near her to prepare for the expulsion.

But no, she wasn't nauseous.

It dawned on Moll that her womb was opening, far, far, too early. The realization of what was happening was worse than the associated pain.

She crouched over the chamber pot while her innards cramped repeatedly, willing herself not to cry out.

Eventually, there was a sickening splash into the pot, and Moll's tears resumed coursing down her cheeks.

When all the spasms had receded, Moll cleaned herself as best she could, then crept downstairs with the chamber pot, slipping outside and making her way to the place where she had danced while Alexander had played his violin.

The moon was large and full, and the stars overhead provided countless points of light as she found a place off the path and, gently putting down the chamber pot, dug with her hands until she had made a hole that was large enough for her poor, stillborn babe. So very tiny, yet she could make out a head and arms from the tiny little corpse that lay in the pot.

Once she had buried the body, she remained on her knees at the makeshift grave, motionless.

A second child gone, and there was no doubt now that there would never be another. She was far too old, and she no longer had marital prospects, anyway. She was stranded on this terrible island with more than two years left to her indenture, surrounded by fellow servants who mostly despised her. Even Yaddy no longer regarded her well.

Even worse, her beloved brother and his family were leaving for Maryland.

What would William think about the wretched mess she had created of her life?

She should have known that God would snatch joy away from her as soon as it was within her grasp. What she wondered now was how much more He planned to take.

CHAPTER 29

MOLL TRUDGED THROUGH her servitude, her only point of light being Massie. At least Mrs. Lugg was a reasonably kind mistress and hadn't returned Moll to the fields.

Another missionary had shown up with his wife and two daughters. He had the personality of a turtle, and the slaves completely ignored him. He was gone within six months. Moll had hardly bothered to learn his name.

Trouble started when the next missionary came. He stayed in lodgings in town rather than at the house and was also far more heavy-handed than Alexander or the second missionary had been, even encouraging Mr. Lugg to punish those who would not convert.

It was terrible, especially since one of the new overseers seemed to take joy in punishments and was overly fond of his whip.

Between punishments and guard towers, deprivations and forced conversions, the plantation had truly turned into a very large, outdoor prison.

It was painful to watch from Mrs. Lugg's window, not only because she knew how hard they were working in addition to now being sorely abused, but it was a reminder of how gently—if slowly—the conversion attempts were with Alexander.

Moll refused to even acknowledge the hateful

missionary. He, too, eventually left, and Mr. Lugg had not yet replaced him.

Massie was growing up, to the point that Thomas Lugg decided he was too much attached to his mother's strings and began taking him out to survey the sugar works. "He needs to learn as soon as possible," Massie's father said on almost a daily basis.

Mrs. Lugg protested that he was still too young for such doings, but her husband was adamant.

Thus, Massie was slowly taken away from Moll's care as well as his mother's. They shared a common grief over it and spent their days together, with Alice Lugg weeping and moaning about her lot in life, and Moll stoically pretending to be content with her situation.

At least she had a reprieve in her little herb plot adjoining the kitchen garden behind the house, where she could spend time nourishing and harvesting plants in peace. She also found serenity in hanging sprigs from a string between two posts, watching them dry sufficiently so she could bottle them up for future elixirs.

Early one evening, she had just hung some sage, lavender, and marjoram, a new combination she had come up with to infuse in tea for Mrs. Lugg's various pain complaints, when she heard multiple men shouting from somewhere on the plantation. It didn't sound like overseers chastising workers. It was something else, something more urgent.

She made her way back to the rear of the house. Inside was turmoil, with servants she didn't know darting back and forth, wringing their hands.

What had happened?

Moll made her way up the servants' staircase and to her mistress's bed chamber, lit only by candles because the draperies had been pulled shut.

"There you are, Moll. Where have you been?" Mrs. Lugg's voice was plaintive.

Mr. Lugg was attempting to calm his wife by rubbing her shoulders. He looked up at his wife's words. "Very good, you can take care of my wife while I take care of this silly little uprising. Stay here and keep the bolt fastened." He kissed his wife's forehead and stomped out, angrily muttering about the punishments that would be wreaked after today.

Massie was in a corner playing with a set of carved dragons and knights, seemingly unaware of the tension in the room.

"Maum, what has happened?" Moll asked.

Alice Lugg, her face haggard in a way Moll had never seen before, merely pointed nervously toward the window.

Moll drew open the draperies. The chaotic scene outside shot terror through her. A sea of angry African faces, many carrying hoes, spades, and rocks. Some carried torches.

"Heaven, help us," Mrs. Lugg moaned, collapsing heavily onto her bed and briefly distracting Moll from what was occurring outdoors. The ropes holding the mattress inside the frame creaked in protest. "We shall all be murdered tonight. I *told* Thomas to stay with indentured servants and not bother with bringing over these enslaved souls. I knew no good could come of it. Why didn't he listen to me?" Moll's mistress started rocking back and forth on the bed.

Moll sighed. Alice Lugg was going to be of no use in this situation. Whether it was because of her mistress's delirium or her own harrowing experiences, Moll felt utterly calm.

Moll unlatched and pulled open the window to

hear what was happening. She was sure the men outside could see her, as well.

They had surged several feet closer as Mr. Lugg exited the front door with the sugar master and the overseers. Moll recognized them all by the backs of their heads. "What is the meaning of this gathering? Why are you not working?" Mr. Lugg demanded.

There was a loud *CRACK!* in response. Moll saw that one of the slaves toward the back of the crowd carried a whip and was snapping it around randomly and viciously. Others gave him a wide berth to avoid the sting of it.

Mr. Lugg bobbed his head, looking for the source of the noise. "Who is that? Show yourself."

The crowd was silent. The only sound came from the hissing and sputtering of torches.

"Again, what is your purpose here?"

Mr. Roland and the overseers drew in closer to Mr. Lugg.

Moll thought it a sign of fear.

Emerging from the crowd of angry men was a tall, broad man with an angry welt across his chest. His expression as he crossed his arms in front of Mr. Lugg held no fear whatsoever. In fact, it was almost as if he welcomed the confrontation.

"I tell you the meaning," the African said.

Before he could continue, the sugar master called out to him, "Sumbar, I give you an esteemed job as boiler, and you become a traitor?"

So, this was the man with whom Yaddy was so enthralled. The word "traitor" clearly confused him, but he hesitated for only a moment.

"Other missionary men tell us to be happy as slaves. Missionary man, Mr. Sparrow, tells us in *Jeez-oos* we are free. Since you want us to follow this *Jeez-oos*, we demand to be free."

Moll's heart plummeted at the mention of Alexander. She had almost stopped spending every single day thinking of him and his treachery.

Mr. Lugg and his men visibly relaxed. In fact, Mr. Lugg laughed. "You are not following the teachings properly. You are free to have salvation. For eternity. Not to determine your destiny in the temporal realm. On Earth, that is."

Sumbar did not budge. "We want to be free and to have voyage back to our homeland. You pay."

The man was built like an ox cart. Mr. Lugg would be wise to be very careful before—

"You will be lucky if you are not whipped within an inch of your life," Mr. Lugg replied.

CRACK.

The sound caused Sumbar to smile slowly as his gaze remained focused on Mr. Lugg.

Mr. Thorpe leaned over and whispered to the plantation owner.

"And just how did they get possession of your whip?" Lugg hissed. If Moll could hear it, surely the slaves could, too.

"No more whip," Sumbar said. "More food, more clothes. No rags. And you send us home."

Lugg whispered to the sugar master on his other side. Mr. Roland stepped backward out of Moll's view. She heard the front door open and bang shut.

Lugg became conciliatory and spread out his hands. "You are right. I am an agreeable man and apologize for not caring for you in a proper manner."

Sumbar frowned. He must be confused over the master's quick concession.

Stepping out from behind Sumbar was a woman.

Yaddy. Her belly was swollen with child, while her gaze was wild and unfocused. "No trust the master," she said, pulling at Sumbar's arm.

Lugg continued. "Surely, we can come to an agreement together. I am a man of God, and I see that I am not following His teachings." He held out his hand.

Now Sumbar nodded. He stepped forward and took Lugg's hand in his own.

Yaddy went on a tirade in her native language. Moll couldn't understand her, but the other slaves started stepping back upon seeing that Sumbar and Thomas Lugg had reached an accord.

Moll turned to tell her mistress that the crowd appeared to be dispersing. Now in the room were all the house servants. How had they entered without her noticing? One of them must have been in possession of a key to the room.

They were all cowering at the door. Moll couldn't help but feel a sliver of satisfaction at seeing Ruth trembling uncontrollably.

"Your husband has calmed the situation, maum," she said.

Mrs. Lugg had a miraculous recovery, sitting up on her bed and issuing instructions to the other servants. "Mrs. Barnes, Ruth, whatever are you doing there, shaking like week-old puppies? We must prepare a good supper for Mr. Lugg after his trying day. Benji, take Massie downstairs so Mrs. Barnes can give him a treat. He's such a good boy."

The other servants stared at one another in expressions of disbelief.

Before any of them could unbolt the door, the front door banged open again. Moll returned to the window, but this time Mrs. Lugg rose from her bed and followed Moll.

What passed before her eyes occurred both in an instant, like sugar poured into a mold, and inexorably slowly, like molasses from a jar.

Mr. Thorpe passed an object to the other overseer. At the same time, Mr. Lugg stepped back from Sumbar, who was staring curiously at whatever had been handed from one man to the other.

There was a loud pop and a flash of smoke near the other overseer. One of the slaves near Sumbar crumpled in a heap on the ground, and scarlet fluid spread rapidly around him.

Yaddy's shriek was ear-piercing.

"Now perhaps you will understand your rightful place," Mr. Lugg said, his tone that of someone in complete command of his surroundings.

The house servants remained frozen at the door, having never even gotten as far as unbolting it.

Sumbar shouted at Yaddy, who stopped her screaming. He then called out to the other slaves in a sing-song voice.

It was apparently a call to attack, for they all rushed forward. Moll involuntarily took a step backward herself.

Sumbar was upon Mr. Lugg at dizzying speed. A flash of a blade, a shout, and a crimson line at the master's throat occurred in less than a second.

Sumbar laughed heartily as the plantation owner crumpled to the ground

Where had he even hidden the knife, used for cutting sugar can stalks, in his meager clothing of breeches and a ragged vest?

Mrs. Lugg screeched and ran back to the bed, jumping in and pulling the coverlet over her head. She moaned like an unsettled spirit.

Massie's eyes filled with boyish tears.

He rose and ran to his mother, crawling into the bed with her.

Moll was just as fearful as everyone else in the room, but it was of no use to cower and tremble.

They were all in danger, particularly as some of the slaves were glancing up at her and raising their torches in her direction.

First, though, they had other murderous intent. Fighting broke out among the sugar master, the overseers, and the slaves. The other pistol popped in a haze of smoke but seemed to miss whatever its target was.

However, the second pistol firing had the effect of infuriating the slaves. In a mass, like ants coming out of a hill, they set upon Mr. Roland and the overseers, wielding the implements that had been given to them by the same men. The three went down quickly, their screams for mercy unheeded among the shouts and laughter of the slaves.

With anyone of any consequence now no longer in the way, many of them were looking up at the window again, raising torches and laughing in an unearthly manner. Yaddy, too, had murderous intent in her eyes.

Moll knew they intended to set fire to the house. And perhaps worse.

Without taking time to think it through carefully, Moll stuck her head through the window, willing herself not to shake.

"Yaddy!" she shouted. "What do you mean to do? Are you going to burn your fellow servants alive? Is that justice for your situation?"

Sumbar stopped the unruly crowd, waiting for Yaddy to respond.

Moll's heart was thumping so hard it hurt. After everything she had survived, she might now die a tortuous death. Could she face it bravely?

"You talk fancy now," Yaddy replied. "You wear fancy dress. You live with master. You not one of us anymore. You don't care about slaves."

Moll glanced down at her dress, stained and worn but still much better than her previous rags, rags like what Yaddy wore. Yet, that could not be Yaddy's sole consideration of their friendship. Wouldn't Yaddy have moved into the house if given the opportunity?

Moll cupped her hands around her mouth to ensure she was heard as far back as possible. "It is you who does not care about me. You would burn your friend alive? There is a young boy in here. Would you roast an innocent child to death?"

Behind her, Mrs. Lugg moaned, but Moll couldn't pay attention to that, for Yaddy's gaze was darting back and forth between Sumbar and the other slaves.

Yaddy was wavering.

Moll thought quickly on how to press her advantage. An idea formed fully in her brain. Mrs. Lugg might wreak punishment on her later, but for now, Moll was determined to save everyone in the bed chamber.

"Mrs. Lugg agrees to free you all," she shouted down.

There was restless murmuring among the slaves.

Surprisingly, Mrs. Lugg made no response to this at all; she just continued her unearthly moaning.

Yaddy and Sumbar conferred together, then Yaddy called back up, "All of us? No punishment?"

Who was even left to punish them? They had killed the plantation's leaders.

Moll shook her head. "No punishment. But you must let Mrs. Lugg, her child, and whoever else she wants, have safe passage off the plantation."

Moll intended to be part of that group.

Yaddy and Sumbar talked together in low tones. This time, he put a hand to her growing belly.

"My husband…" Mrs. Lugg interrupted her own groans long enough to say.

"Also," Moll added. "You must allow Mrs. Lugg to collect her husband's body. You will not desecrate it."

More conferring between the two. This time, it was Sumbar who responded. "We need ship home."

How in heaven's name could that be provided?

If this was all that stood between Moll and death, she had to find an answer. Oh!

She nodded. "Yes. You board the next of Mr. Lugg's sugar transport ships bound for England. It will stop in—" Where would it dock?

She turned back into the room. "Maum, where do the sugar ships stop for resupply?"

"Bermuda." The word drawled out, as though it required all the woman's effort to say it.

"It will stop in Bermuda, and from there you can all take another ship to Africa." Moll had no idea if what she was saying was even true, but she was desperate.

Sumbar nodded. "Slaves be free. You may leave. But we make sure you leave."

Whatever did that mean?

CHAPTER 30

SUMBAR ENSURED THAT they all did, in fact, leave.

Overnight, he and the other slaves burned the fields and the sugar mill. Yaddy came to the house, brazenly entering without knocking, to tell Moll that the house would be set aflame at noon the next day.

"Yaddy, there is no need to destroy this house. Mrs. Lugg will leave. It is a fine home to live in. *You* could live in it. With Sumbar and your child."

Yaddy shook her head resolutely. "There is bad magic here. House built to keep slaves. Must be burned so we can be free."

"But—" Moll started to argue further but realized it was of no use.

"You go at first light," Yaddy continued. "Spell being cast on house at dawn, before burn, that will make you sick if you stay."

Moll didn't sleep at all that night. She took charge of bundling up the household, since Mrs. Lugg was hardly able to lift her head. In fact, she instructed her mistress that she needed to take Mrs. Barnes, Ruth, Benji, and herself on the same ship that Mrs. Lugg would take to England with Massie.

Moll also instructed everyone to pack their belongings for the sea trip, then packed for Mrs. Lugg and son.

Before dawn's light, she told Benji to fetch a cart and load their belongings on it. She then changed into her old sack dress and stowed her favorite hand-me-down dresses into a bag, which now sat next to her medicine case, waiting for Benji to load it.

Moll also told Mrs. Barnes and Ruth to wrap Thomas Lugg's body in sheets and place it on the cart. To her surprise, they obeyed without question.

Mrs. Lugg had sufficiently recovered by the morning to thank Moll. "You have saved my darling Massie and me, and I won't forget it. In fact, I want to give you a reward. I have some money—" Mrs. Lugg reached into the folds of her dress and pulled out a pouch. "I know that your brother has gone on to the Maryland colony, and I'm sure you'd rather be there than back in England. Take some coins and purchase your own passage there."

Moll's jaw slackened as Alice Lugg emptied a pile of silver into her cupped hands. She'd never seen this much money before in her entire life.

"I will sell the plantation once I get to England. With the slaves gone, someone else can start the entire thing over. And someone will want to, because sugar is so profitable. But I have no doubt that the next owner will make the same mistake of transporting Africans once again."

Moll nodded solemnly in agreement. Inside, though, she was dizzy with happiness. Mrs. Lugg was giving her money to start a new life.

"Maum, I—I'm—" She had no words for thanking Mrs. Lugg, who, overall, had been a good mistress.

Alice Lugg folded Moll's hands around the money. "Be well, Moll. I've no doubt you shall rise and become a lady's maid to someone important in Maryland. But be careful of men of God who take you to their bed, claim to love you, and then abandon you. You have too many years of life behind you to fall for that again."

Mrs. Lugg nodded knowingly at her.

Moll didn't have the wits about her to respond. So, her mistress had known about her and Alexander. Well, no one knew about the loss of her baby. And now she had to leave the tiny, unmarked grave behind.

Aware of the impropriety of it, Moll threw her arms around the other woman, clasping her hard to herself. Mrs. Lugg responded in kind.

She saw the others off to a ship bound for Southampton at the port in Basseterre, kneeling first to hug Massie for the last time before he boarded. "Miss Moll, this is for you," he said, handing her an object.

It was one of the dragons from his play set.

Moll's eyes misted. "I shall treasure it always."

She turned away without watching him board the gangplank. Massie had been the closest she'd ever come to raising a child. It was painful to watch him leave.

It was a relief to watch the others go.

She found passage aboard a merchant ship called *Friendship*, ultimately bound for Boston with a load of molasses and sugar, but intending to stop in colonies along the way, including Maryland.

It had been nearly seven years since she had arrived here, full of hope and excitement. Now, as she stood on the departing ship's deck, she saw a dark, swirling cloud of black smoke rising from the hills where the plantation house was located.

Moll turned back to face the bow of the ship and removed her cap to let her long red hair, fading from time, flow freely. She would never again hide it from view, come what may. The winds were favorable, and they were soon out in the open seas. It was time for Moll to forget about St. Kitts and look to her future in Maryland and what it might hold.

The Madness of Old Age

The Maryland Colony
St. Mary's City &
Newtowne Hundred

CHAPTER 31

1677

THE VOYAGE HAD been remarkably smooth thus far. The ship had stopped in a place called St. Augustine for resupply. The ship's captain warned them that the Spanish fort here was small and not friendly to Englishmen, so no disembarking by any of the passengers would be permitted.

Moll did stand on the deck and noticed the loud foreign chattering. More interestingly, in addition to swarthy Spaniards, there were other men working on the docks who, although also dark, had a reddish cast to their skin. They also had glossy, ebony hair. They bore no resemblance to the English, the Africans, nor the Spaniards. Who were they?

The ship also stopped in the city of Charleston, in the Carolina colony, with the captain announcing that they would pick up indigo and rice here while disgorging some passengers and picking up more.

Because Charleston was an English colony, Moll was permitted time to leave the ship. She did so in one of her better dresses. The town was fresh and pretty, with many buildings constructed of some type of pink stone with slate roofs.

"Bermuda stone," said a fishwife she met along the pier. "Most of us came here from Bermuda seven years ago, and we are already a great port."

Seven years ago, while Moll was sailing to St. Kitts, settlers were coming to this town in hopes of making it prosper. It appeared as though the Bermudians had accomplished it.

Finally, leaving the vastness of the Atlantic Ocean, *Friendship* moved into the Chesapeake Bay and quickly into the James River, continuing to the shores of Virginia. By this point, Moll felt like the world explorer she thought she would have become in a marriage to Alexander.

But she was doing this by herself, without any assistance. Her heart swelled with pride in herself. She would be able to face anything the future had in store for her.

In Virginia, *Friendship* docked again, this time in the capital city of Jamestown, to drop off some rice, as well as to pick up both passengers and dried bales of tobacco.

Moll was fascinated to watch the tobacco, with its enormous brown leaves tightly packed together, being loaded onto the ship. "More valuable than gold, tobacco is," said a passenger standing near her.

The most valuable thing to Moll, though, was the notion that she was now very close to rejoining her brother.

As they left the James a few hours later, the captain announced that they would be re-entering the Chesapeake Bay shortly on their way to St. Mary's City, Maryland's capital.

Moll approached the captain. "Excuse me, sir, how far is St. Mary's City from Dorchester?"

"Not terribly far by ship," he said.

"Might you be able to take me there?"

"Sorry, no. As soon as we make our stop there, we are heading back south through the Chesapeake Bay and back up the coast to Boston. If you've money, you should be able to find a ship to take you."

Moll had to be satisfied with that. She had plenty of money left over from Mrs. Lugg's generosity to take care of another voyage.

Soon, William, soon.

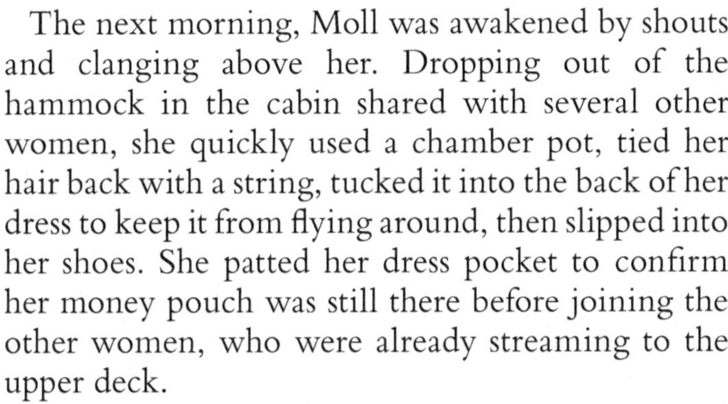

The next morning, Moll was awakened by shouts and clanging above her. Dropping out of the hammock in the cabin shared with several other women, she quickly used a chamber pot, tied her hair back with a string, tucked it into the back of her dress to keep it from flying around, then slipped into her shoes. She patted her dress pocket to confirm her money pouch was still there before joining the other women, who were already streaming to the upper deck.

The stairs to the deck were narrow and steep and required her to hold on to anything she could to prevent stumbling inside the folds of her dress.

Going up was easier than going down, however.

On deck, the women were joining their husbands, who all slept in a different cabin but had also emerged from the quarters. All was a state of confusion as the ship's mates were scurrying around without explanation, as though preparing for—what?

The captain was one level up on the foredeck, a spyglass to his eye as he surveyed the bay.

Moll glanced out over the water and realized the trouble. There was a ship gliding smoothly toward them. Its movement suggested it intended to intercept *Friendship.*

Beneath her feet was a great rumbling. Other ship's hands must be rolling the few cannon the ship had into place on the orlop, two decks below.

What was this other ship's intent?

She knew soon enough, for *Fearless Sybil* pulled smoothly alongside *Friendship* and immediately began lashing ropes to her, as well as heaving wide planks over the side of their ship that were landing with loud thuds on *Friendship's* deck.

They were now too close for *Friendship* to fire her cannon without destroying herself.

The name *Lionheart* was faded but still visible beneath *Fearless Sybil*, which was considerably larger than *Friendship*. Her men rode on a deck that was higher than where Moll and the others stood.

This must be a ship that had been captured and renamed. Which meant that these were seafaring pirates.

Moll already knew that pirates prowled the waters of the Caribbean, looking for ships full of valuable merchandise—or weapons—to take. *Friendship* had not encountered any in the Caribbean nor the Atlantic, yet suddenly, here was a pirate ship in the Chesapeake Bay?

It was as if no matter what route Moll chose in life, misfortune was close on her heels to bark and nip at her.

It was infuriating.

However, Moll was strangely calm, as she had been in the face of the plantation rebellion. So much had befallen her that to be on a ship boarded by pirates seemed to be of no consequence.

Many of the other women began to wail and, at the urging of the men, made their way back down the impossible stairs to their quarters.

"No!" Moll shouted. "Don't trap yourselves down there. Stay here, and we shall band together."

Not a single woman paid her any attention and,

like geese about to be slaughtered, ran to and fro in fright, but eventually all tumbled belowdecks.

Moll stood alone among the men as several sailors from the other ship descended over the planks, while the rest of *Sybil's* crew stood and watched. All of them were armed with pistols and cutlasses, and it was easy to see that *Sybil* had a lower deck full of cannon.

Among them was a tall man with a closely cropped beard and a wide smile, acting as though he were having a day out at a fair. He was dressed like any man, except for a long, brown, wool cloak over his clothing.

The ships rocked back and forth next to each other in a dizzying, opposite, up-and-down motion. Yet Moll had developed sea legs and was as well-planted on her feet as any of the men.

"Come down, now," the cloaked man called up to *Friendship's* captain, pulling open that cloak to reveal several pistols tied to his waist.

The captain did as he was bidden, but slowly, climbing down from the foredeck as if to transmit that he had no care in the world.

"I am Roger Makeele," the pirate announced. "I'll not trouble you nor your womenfolk for long, provided you are cooperative. What do you be carrying?" He sounded far too practiced at this.

The captain seemed practiced, too. "Nothing, just some passengers headed to Boston."

Sybil's captain made a motion to his crew members on *Friendship's* deck that Moll could not understand. However, his men seemed to take pre-arranged positions. Among them was a squat, tanned man, resembling one of the mammy apples that grew wild in the hills of St. Kitts.

The man sidled up to Moll, staring at her as though

she were a strange curiosity. His heavy breath stank of ale and tobacco.

It was hard to concentrate on the two captains with this malodorous dolt standing next to her. She tried to ignore him.

"Now, sirrah, you must take me for a complete fool," Makeele said. "I'll ask you again. What cargo do you have?"

Friendship's captain relented. "Only some indigo, rice, and tobacco."

Makeele nodded. "Have you come from the islands? Have any sugar or molasses aboard?"

Friendship's captain nodded, his expression one of defeat.

"We'll be taking your ship, then. I must say, Captain, *Friendship* is a better prize than I had thought her to be."

The pirate captain turned his attention to Moll and the mate standing next to her. "Hungry, leave that poor woman alone. My apologies, madam, Hungry forgets his manners when he be in the company of a handsome woman such as yourself."

Moll refrained from rolling her eyes at the excessive flattery.

"Muh name's really Simon, miss," the man Makeele called Hungry said to her. "Do you have a husband on this ship? Do you need one?"

He reached out and caressed her sleeved arm, smiling as he did so and revealing teeth thoroughly twisted inside their gums.

Without thinking about what she was doing, so repulsed was she by his touch, Moll reached out a hand and slapped Hungry—Simon—across his gaping mouth.

Friendship's captain stared at her in what could only

be described as horrified dread, and Moll believed that she had committed a grievous, no, a deadly, error.

The utter silence, except for the creaking of the ships as they sloshed in the water, was unnerving.

Then, Makeele threw back his head and laughed. His open mouth revealed missing and blackened teeth, far more than most people back in Devon.

Pirating on the Chesapeake must be unhealthy work.

Everyone else laughed nervously, too.

"Well, aren't you just full of sass and spirit?" Makeele said, his grin even broader than before. "Just what I've been seeking in a wife. Imagine the children I could have with a woman as tall and slender as a willow tree, such as you are."

Was he truly proposing marriage to a woman long past her flower and likely barren by now?

"I'll be no man's wife. Not yours nor Hungry's." This was nearly as bad as talking Yaddy and Sumbar out of their ungodly plans.

Makeele cocked his head to one side, contemplating her. "Methinks you are in no position to refuse me, Miss—?"

"Mary Margaret Dyer. My friends call me Moll."

"Well, then, Moll—"

"You are not my friend, captain." Moll was nervous, but she was not about to let this fool of a man have the better of her.

Makeele seemed to be even more bemused by her. "Look at that fiery hair to match the fiery temper. Let me see it all."

Moll was about to refuse him, but *Friendship's* captain was giving her a pleading look. *Satisfy him so he will go on his way.*

Knowing her hair was no longer flaming red, she

slowly pulled the long bundle out of the back of her dress.

Makeele made an appreciative smack with his lips. "Like a sorceress you are. What an addition you would make to my reputation."

"I am no sorceress," she said. Why did men perpetually accuse her of special powers? It was best to tamp this down right away, for she knew that sailors could become unnerved at the thought of a witch being present on a ship. Such a thought could result in her being hanged or thrown overboard to dispel their fears of being "cursed" by her supernatural presence.

Makeele followed it up with an exaggerated sigh. "Very well, you may keep to yourself, Mary Margaret Dyer. I suspect you might be more trouble than you are worth. But I imagine you might have something else of value—"

In a move that was faster than lightning streaking across the night sky, Makeele was upon her, running his hands all over her dress. Before she could even catch her breath to protest, he had pulled her money pouch from her dress pocket.

"Aha!" The coins clinked as he dangled the pouch in front of her face. "Perhaps this is more significant than you are, dear lady."

"It is far more significant than the likes of you," Moll said, purposefully gathering her hair back up and tucking it into the back of her dress again. She refused to let him see that he had just cast her back into poverty, perhaps this time permanently.

More silence ensued, then Makeele again roared with laughter.

"Are you sure you wouldn't like the freedom of sailing the Chesapeake with me and becoming rich in your own right?" Makeele asked.

Moll could think of nothing worse than being on a ship for eternity. She raised her chin and turned her head away from him without a word.

More laughter.

Leaving several men aboard to steer *Friendship* while he returned to *Sybil*, Makeele announced from his own deck that he would be dropping passengers off at St. Mary's City before taking *Friendship* to Watts Island to use her as part of Makeele's growing fleet. "I don't rightly care for kidnapping subjects of His Majesty's realm; I only desire growing my purse."

Once more, he dangled Moll's pouch in front of him. Moll's meager fortune had just disappeared onto *Fearless Sybil*.

"However, I do believe I'll rename your ship to *Magnificent Moll*." Grinning at his own cleverness, Makeele disappeared from view, and the ships were once more separated, with *Sybil* presumably continuing to wherever Watts Island was, and *Friendship* now being steered toward St. Mary's City.

Moll stumbled wearily down to her hammock, wondering what she faced in Maryland and how she was going to survive there without a single penny to call her own.

She also wondered if Watts Island was near Dorchester. Would it have been worth whatever she would have had to endure to reach the place where her brother now lived?

Perhaps I have made a ruinous decision. The thought caused her to pick and tear relentlessly at the thin coverlet on her hammock for the remainder of the trip.

"She's tetched," whispered some of the women, no doubt believing Moll couldn't hear them.

"Maybe she really is a witch," muttered others.

But Moll was beyond caring about the opinions of others.

CHAPTER 32

MOLL WAS DYING; she was sure of it. All her time in the heat and sun of St. Kitts hadn't prepared her for the climate and unhealthy air in Maryland.

How could this be? She was forty-three years old, and, despite the continual sunburns that had left her skin mottled and patchy, she was of a hardy constitution. After all, she had engaged in a battle of wills against a rotten, poxy pirate without blinking an eye.

Yet here she lay in a room at the Dove's Rest tavern in St. Mary's City, alternately weeping when feverish and praying for death when attacked by what the tavern owner's wife said was "grypes of the gut." It was more like endless demonic attacks on her bowels, which every day caused her to be weaker.

Mrs. Stoke had stood over Moll one day. "Yer a bit old to be a settler. 'Tis why the seasoning is hitting you so hard. If you survive, you'll live a long time. I'll need proof that you can pay for your stay here. No free nights."

Which was a reminder to Moll that even if she lived, she didn't have anywhere else to go.

She was also reminded that Yaddy had told her there was magic being worked upon the plantation house the morning of her departure. That if she didn't leave quickly enough, she would become ill. Was this the effects of that?

Impossible. Moll Dyer was a Christian woman, not subject to spells and incantations.

As her bowels slowly improved, Moll was attacked in her lungs and nasal passages. Everything filled with so much thick, slimy fluid that she thought she might drown in her sleep.

It was still more tolerable than her gut grypes.

Finally, she became passably well enough to go downstairs and ask the tavern's mistress as to where she might inquire for work.

"You seem improved," Mrs. Stoke said before Moll could ask. "I imagine you'll survive. There you are. Most people don't live past fifty here, and looking at you, I imagine you're most of the way there. I'll need fourteen shillings for your stay before you go."

Moll asked her question, hoping the woman would extend her a little more grace if she realized Moll was looking for work.

The woman nodded toward a board, covered in papers, on a wall of the tavern area where the dining tables were. There were only a couple of men in the tavern now, and both seemed to be so far in their cups that they were sleeping with their eyes glazed open, so Moll walked past them to look at the board.

Naturally, she could read very little, but it was obvious that some were notices about slaves—either adverts for the capture of runaways or for new stock coming into town—evidenced by the sketches of dark men in minimal clothing. Other notices seemed to be for items for sale. These had numbers on them to indicate prices.

She plucked several notices that, in her mind, might be for employment situations, and took them back to Mrs. Stoke, who was busy folding bed linens in a back room. "Can you tell me which of these is for employment?"

"Are you looking to take a contract?" the woman asked, smoothing out a freshly folded coverlet.

Moll sighed. She didn't really want one. It might mean never seeing her brother again if she had to take one for yet another seven years, but did she have much of a choice?

"I'm willing to do so."

"Very well." Mrs. Stoke led her out to the dining room and sat down, inviting Moll to sit down with her. Reading through the advertisements, the tavern's mistress pulled out three of them. "This one's for only four years, but it's to apprentice to a wool fuller. You don't want that."

Moll wasn't sure what that meant. Was it shearing a sheep? Combing wool fibers? Caring for the animals themselves? It didn't sound terrible. "Why is that?"

Mrs. Stoke looked at Moll as though she were a simpleton. "Yer marching on the spot in a vat all day to clean the wool. Boring and tiring, but you also have to wee in the vat, for that's what gets the grease and dirt out, and whitens the wool. No, that's a job better suited for children. Here's another one."

Hopefully, it was better than working for a wool fuller. Which sounded much like the stink of a tannery back in England.

The tavern keeper's wife was quiet as she read the advertisement thoroughly. "Hmm. Lord Baltimore is looking for a 'clean, respectable woman' to help his wife care for their passel of children. His Lordship is administrator of the colony. A very important man. A Catholic, you know."

Moll froze at this, unsure how to react.

"He demanded that the assembly take an oath of fidelity to him a couple of years ago. Everyone got heated up, thinking he was going to impose Catholicism in the colony. But he just seemed to want loyalty. Anyway, he wants seven years from you, and he's offering passage anywhere within the colonies at the end, with 'as much food and drink as the hireling wishes' during the servitude."

Lord Baltimore was Catholic. That would be a relief. Maybe there was even a chapel on his property. However, she would have no money at the end, although she could end up in Dorchester. But in seven years, she would be fifty years old. According to Mrs. Stoke, Moll might well be dead by then.

"This one might suit you well," Mrs. Stoke said. "Mr. Hugh Woodall has a tobacco plantation and needs someone to—"

"No," Moll said flatly.

"You haven't heard what it is."

Moll shook her head. "I'll not work on a plantation again." The movement hurt and reminded her of how full of phlegm she still was.

The tavern owner's wife broke into deep laughter. "My dear, what else do you think there is in this colony? Tobacco, wheat, and animals. And you're a woman who doesn't have the back for most of the work."

Moll was resolute. "I cannot. It's—I must find something else. What about here? Might I serve as your maid?" The idea had just come to Moll.

But Mrs. Stoke put her boot heel to the idea. "No, my husband and I are barely getting by. In fact, I need *you* to pay *me*, remember?"

Moll sighed again, which resulted in a sneeze.

Faced with three terrible choices, she chose the one she thought was best.

"Will you help me write to Lord Baltimore?"

It took nearly a week for someone to deliver the message to Lord Baltimore and to then receive a reply. Moll's heart sank when Mrs. Stoke read it to her.

Lord Baltimore had already hired a servant for the position.

Moll was now a week deeper in debt to the tavern with no other prospects, although the mucous and misery seemed to be finally leaving her body.

Despite every inch of her skin crawling with the notion, she said, "Maum, could you help me write to this Mr. Woodall? I should like to see if he would settle my bill with you in exchange for some of my labor."

The woman opened her mouth, and Moll knew that "no" was about to come out since no doubt what Moll was suggesting was highly improper, but then, in an apparent mind change, the tavern owner's wife pursed her lips. "You've had a hard time of it here, getting used to our pollens and wee mites and bugs. I'll extend you some mercy."

Mrs. Stoke wrote another letter for Moll. Within a day, an acceptance arrived along with coins to settle Moll's bill in full.

Moll signed her "X" at the bottom, and a passing farmer agreed to take it back to the Woodall place.

It was only as Moll began walking a path to the plantation that the tavern owner's wife had described for her that Moll realized she had no idea what her employment was to be.

CHAPTER 33

1681

MOLL QUICKLY LEARNED that any homestead in the Maryland colony did not have enough people to work on it, no matter how many resided there.

Moll's position was therefore a varied one. One day she might help Mrs. Woodall scrub walls free of candle and fireplace soot, the next she might work in the garden—a task to which she was well-suited, and then the next she might help whitewash the house.

Every day was completely different. Much of her time with Mrs. Woodall, though, was spent in food preservation.

Back home in Devon, the family scrounged for whatever food they could manage, usually relying on the chickens and goats they kept.

In St. Kitts, everyone had access to fresh fish and other sea creatures. And, of course, sugar seconds.

Now, she was learning how to dry that fish, as well as other wild game and vegetables. Mrs. Woodall also gave her instructions on pickling foods by turning beer and wine into vinegar and soaking foods in stoneware pots full of the tart substance. Moll loved the added flavor pickling gave.

In addition, the mistress salted meats, especially when preparing to carry her family over the winter. She demonstrated to Moll how to separate salt from the river's water and to use the salt to "cure" pork and beef.

In return, Moll demonstrated the fermentation process in ale making to her mistress. Although Mrs. Woodall expressed interest in it, Moll soon realized that her mistress didn't have the time to do it. Moll was left completely on her own to make as much ale as she thought necessary.

In fact, Moll was permitted to sell her ale to local taverns in her free time, which, admittedly, wasn't many hours each week.

Also helping domestically was Mrs. Woodall's mother-in-law, Constance, who had lost her husband in a hurricane more than a decade ago.

The family still spoke of that storm in hushed tones. It had completely devastated swaths of Maryland and Virginia, they said, killing around fifteen hundred people and forcing nearly every settler to start over.

Moll imagined Constance to be around seventy years old, a great age, but even so, time seemed to have worn poorly on her, no doubt because of hardships like the great hurricane. Constance's hair was pure white, and her skin was leathery. She shuffled along with a hunched back. Yet, the elder Mrs. Woodall clearly adored her son, Hugh, and doted on him every moment he was in the house.

Constance Woodall performed tasks with Moll and Lucy but was unable to move at the same pace and frequently forgot what she was doing.

Moll understood why Lucy had sought a servant.

As in St. Kitts, she was free on Sundays, except the Woodalls invited her to attend church with them, which she almost always did. There was a flourishing Jesuit mission in nearby Newtowne Hundred, and the number of priests flitting about on various work projects was astonishing. That must have been where Father White, whom Mama had talked about, had worked before being sent back to England.

Moll spent the latter part of Sundays pulling a cart to sell her ale to Dove's Rest and other taverns along the docks. It was gratifying to see Mrs. Stoke frown in confusion at her but then purchase multiple small casks, commenting on the quality of Moll's brew. "When Mr. Stoke's father ran this place, he never had ale this good."

It was as if Moll had stepped into her mother's place here in this new land.

There were six Woodall children, ranging from the eldest, Lawrence, to the youngest, Isabel. At just three years old, Isabel was the only girl among her siblings and needed perpetual tending.

This time, though, Moll wasn't about to become attached to any young ones. Her only reminder of the past was the little carved dragon that Massie had given her, which she kept tucked next to the straw-stuffed mattress of her bed. Her room was a makeshift one, built in the rafters of the house so that it was sultry hot in the summer, like St. Kitts, except without the same sun intensity. It was also bitterly cold in the winter, but it was private, and, best of all, she had floor space. Even if she couldn't stand up straight in her long room with its downward slanted ceiling.

The stairs leading to her garret room were almost as steep as the ceiling, which meant that no one wanted to climb them, and she never had to worry about noses poking in at her.

Mr. and Mrs. Woodall slept together in a chamber on the second floor. The six children all slept in a single chamber together on the first floor, in a combination of beds and trundles. The elder Mrs. Woodall also had her own bedchamber, on the second floor at the opposite end from the master and mistress.

The Woodall's plantation house was much smaller than that of the Luggs's, but seemed much...happier.

The only distasteful part of her servitude this time was watching the slaves toil in the tobacco fields, which did remind her of the Lugg plantation. However, Mr. Woodall did not have overseers, nor any sort of "master" of the tobacco.

Instead, he was in the fields himself all day, working side by side with the slaves.

One day, she witnessed Mr. Woodall baptizing several slaves in the river. There had been no visiting missionary—praise God for that!—but she was curious about it, nonetheless, asking about it one breezy day as she helped her mistress hang laundry to dry on a rope hung between two trees.

"Hugh shares the Gospel stories with them," Mrs. Woodall said. "And some agree to be baptized."

No one had ever been baptized on the Lugg plantation during her time there.

"Once they are baptized, are they free?" she asked.

Mrs. Woodall tossed a pair of her husband's breeches over the line. "No. The Maryland assembly passed a law many years ago that baptism does not free a slave, else none of the owners would ever allow them to be Christianized."

Moll frowned as she chased one of Mr. Woodall's shirts that had blown off the line. Given a choice between becoming a Christian and being free, she rather thought she'd choose freedom and then worry about her soul.

But she could see that the only way the plantation owners would be willing to assist the Church in

Gospel work would be if they didn't run the risk of losing their investments.

It was a sorry business.

Unlike Mrs. Lugg, Lucy Woodall did not seem to expect Moll to work while she lay about complaining of headaches. She worked as hard as Moll did. Her dresses were nearly as worn as Moll's, too.

Very little of the political world landed on Moll's ears, except for what she heard in taverns on days she sold ale.

She knew that there had been skirmishes between the colonists and the remaining native tribes for most of her time here, but that violence had waned.

Mr. Woodall frequently talked about the Virginia colony. He said they were a colony of Reformers with no love for Catholics. "You never want to live in Virginia, Moll."

The idea was absurd. How could she possibly get to a place as far away as Virginia?

There had been a rebellion against the Maryland government earlier in the year, instigated by two men, John Coode and Josias Fendall, a former governor. Fendall had been banished from Maryland, while John Coode had escaped punishment.

"Coode will be back, for certain, to foment more trouble," Mr. Woodall had said, shaking his head.

But as long as no one came banging at the door late at night, Moll had no interest in the affairs of men.

There were stories of pirates occasionally stopping at St. Mary's City and raiding homes and businesses along the docks, but they never went further into the city, so Moll felt relatively safe, despite her own encounter with sea thieves.

Moll's equanimity was only disrupted during these first few years in Maryland by the death of

Constance Woodall, Hugh's mother, whom Lucy found motionless in her bed one morning.

The house had a somber air for many weeks after that. "The old generation has passed," Lucy Woodall said without further comment.

That was like a slap, given that Moll was a bit closer to that "old" generation than Lucy was. However, life was overall better than it had ever been.

But would she ever see William again?

CHAPTER 34

1682

MOLL WAS A full four years into her second indenture, this one for five years, and it had certainly proved better than the first. The master and mistress treated her as part of the family, even helping her find William.

Mrs. Woodall had assisted with a series of letters back and forth to various people in Dorchester. William was making his living oystering and fishing along the shores there.

Moll begged him to visit her, but William was hesitant. *It's not safe. Too many pirates in the Chesapeake Bay to come across,* he'd said in one of his letters.

She couldn't argue with that.

Moll determined that once her indenture was done, she would travel to William. The overland journey could take weeks and was also full of danger, according to Mrs. Woodall, but what did that matter?

Mama had been right in her instincts about Maryland. The hot, oppressive moisture that hung in the air like a sticky blanket every summer notwithstanding, the colony showed promise of someone like Moll.

The soil was fertile, and so were people's ambitions. Already, she had made some meager coins selling ale. By the end of her indenture, she might be able to secure land rights somewhere.

She could hardly imagine being able to start her own farm. Moll was filled with a different sort of hope than ever before. Not just a hope for love, but a hope for success. For respect. For security.

The general tolerance of Catholics was an unexpected relief, too. "If only you could have seen this, Mama," she whispered like the little girl she once was.

The most important difference in the colony, though, was that the settlers seemed to freely help one another and teach whatever skills they had.

It seemed to be a response to how few people had yet settled in St. Mary's. They all relied on one another for survival, and everyone benefited from valuable members of their community.

Thus, Lucy Woodall was happy to teach Moll her letters and, ultimately, how to read. She also taught Moll more complicated money transactions, as well as how to write bills of sale and other financial documents.

Mrs. Woodall even attempted to teach the plantation slaves what she had taught Moll, but few of them spoke English natively, making the effort difficult.

Moll knew she was becoming powerful with so much knowledge.

Meanwhile, she spent her days serving the Woodalls and never seeing anyone outside the family until one afternoon, when a traveler arrived at the Woodall plantation, dusty from the road and seeking overnight shelter. He had seen the smoke rising from the chimney of the pleasant-looking home and decided to inquire about a short stay.

He said he was pursuing available land rights in

St. Mary's to start his own farm, having heard that the colony—and St. Mary's City in particular—was friendly to Catholics.

Hugh Woodall heartily welcomed the traveler, Peter Quince, agreeing to help the man in securing information on available properties and inviting him to stay for a few nights.

Mr. Woodall locked himself away privately with the man, where they stayed up until all hours, with Moll and Lucy Woodall taking turns serving them pitchers of Moll's ale along with smoked oysters.

On one of Moll's visits to the room to replace candles and re-light them, she overheard an interesting part of the men's conversation.

"What is sorely lacking in your colony is lodgings," Quince complained. "I had to travel south from Charles County to St. Mary's with no opportunity to stop somewhere civilized and refresh. I spent last night in the woods. Although it was well worth it, I must say, to have a sampling of your fine ale."

Moll secretly glowed with pride.

"There are a couple of lodging places in the city," Mr. Woodall said.

The other man laughed. "On the docks."

Mr. Woodall nodded. "I see your point. Of course, most people travel by river."

"But I did not. And as the colony grows, there will be more land travel. It is a shame that one must be forced to sleep in the cold and rain with no victuals to reach St. Mary's City by land."

"T'will no doubt be solved in time as the colony settles more," Mr. Woodall said. "More ale? Moll, a refill, if you please."

Moll poured full cups of her brew and finished lighting the candles before leaving the men to their continued discussion for the remainder of the evening.

She couldn't sleep that night for the thoughts that crashed against one another in her mind.

In the morning, Mr. Quince was already gone. On his bedside table, he'd left a couple of coins, which Moll promptly took to Mrs. Woodall.

Her swirling thoughts were congealing into a firm idea.

What if Moll were to start her own inn, somewhere along the road from Charles County to St. Mary's City?

CHAPTER 35

August 1682

FINALLY. FIVE YEARS had passed, and Moll's second indenture was complete. Hugh Woodall lived up to the terms of the contract and more. She received the monies she was due, which, combined with the money she had saved from selling ales, was a tiny sum to put toward the purchase of a place. Mr. Woodall then surprised her with a cart and an old nag.

"She's not got much life in her, but she's yours for as long as she lasts," he said.

He also told her she could have a couple of piglets when she was settled. "Send for me when they're ready, and I'll slaughter them for you."

He offered to sell her a couple of slaves, but Moll refused him. He shrugged. "You'll find it difficult to farm without them."

Moll told him of her idea to open her own establishment. "I'm going to call it 'Mrs. Dyer's Inn and Alehouse.'"

Mr. Woodall looked at her in astonishment. "I didn't realize you had a business mind. Although with all the dealings you've had with your ales at the wharf, I shouldn't be surprised. I still think you will have a rough go of it alone."

Lucy Woodall cried upon Moll's departure. Not

self-pitying, Alice Lugg tears, but tears of genuine sadness to see her go.

It was so touching Moll almost didn't want to leave.

Almost.

Moll was furiously busy for the next several months. She found an abandoned property with a middling-sized, ramshackle house as well as an old barn and a couple of other decrepit outbuildings on it.

It was in Newtowne Hundred, near Breton Bay and along the road to St. Mary's City.

Not only was the location ideal, but Moll could envision the house as an inn, with her own quarters on the top floor. The barn would be a stable for travelers. The outbuildings would be transformed into a kitchen and a laundry.

After securing rights to it, Moll cleared away brush and brambles herself from the buildings to better assess the repairs they needed.

She also planted a garden near the kitchen and set up an irrigation system, as she had learned in St. Kitts. Creating small mounds offset at the ends of each planted row, she put an open barrel on each mound to collect rainwater. She then dug trenches from the barrels that ran alongside the mounded plants. A rough door made in the side of each barrel near the bottom ensured that Moll could water her plants whenever necessary by opening the door and letting the water run down the row and seep into the ground.

She managed to order furniture, linens, and cookery from England on credit. She had no idea how she would ever pay the money back, but at least she could open her doors.

On a trip into Newtowne Hundred to find all

manner of supplies, such as candles, a locking box, garden tools, and whitewash, as well as to find someone who could print a list of fares for the inn, Moll was distracted by two boys loitering near a public cesspit.

The boys were clearly brothers, with similar wide-eyed expressions and dark hair. She guessed them to be within a couple of years of each other, perhaps around twelve and fourteen years. The younger one pointed at her. "Look at that! Have you seen such hair in your life, Daniel?"

Moll sighed. She wore a cap today, but had let her hair flow down beneath it. Few people in the county made comment upon her looks so she had rarely given thought to completely covering her head since her journey to Maryland.

Best to take these two urchins on directly.

She approached them both. "Have you a problem with my hair? You know the Devil himself lit it aflame one day so that I could take care of the likes of *you*." She reached out as if to snatch the one who had called out at her.

He yelled in terror and grabbed the other boy, who also looked frightened.

Moll laughed at having startled them. "What are you two doing here, anyway? The smell is like rotting corpses. Haven't you anything else to do?"

The first boy eyed her warily. "No. Our mama died last year, and Papa stopped coming home, so we were told to leave our lodgings. Not sure where to go."

Moll thought furiously about these two boys, who were effectively orphans. She had an idea. "What are your names?"

"I'm Daniel," the second, older boy said. "This is Jack."

She nodded. "Do you want some work? I'm opening an inn just outside of town and can use some help."

Daniel still eyed her with suspicion.

"I can pay you and let you sleep in my barn."

That broke through his reserve. "Yes, miss, we will work for you."

Moll had them help her as she collected supplies from various shops and stalls, then loaded it all in her cart. They sat on top of the goods as she steered the nag back to her inn.

Moll was satisfied with the day's effort. The only purchase she was unable to make was for her fare list. "You need to see William Nuthead in St. Mary's City," she was told. "He's the only one with a printing press." That would keep for another day.

She set the boys up in the loft of what was to be the stable. She then set them to work on a variety of tasks, including more brush clearing, painting, and tilling the new kitchen garden.

With Daniel and Jack busy for the foreseeable future, Moll went to work at brewing. She found good recipes for both cider and honey-based mead, which she would offer in addition to ale at her establishment. Moll could provide cider and mead more cheaply, but they contained far more alcohol in them. That would make plenty of men happy.

By the time all was done, and a shingle was hung both on the house and at the side of the road to attract weary travelers, Moll had used up half of her coins.

━━━∾∾∾━━━

To Moll's gratification, once she was ready for customers, she didn't have to wait long for tired travelers to stop by for refreshment and a bed for the night.

Unfortunately, she also didn't have to wait long for arguments and fisticuffs to break out.

But Moll was getting much older, and with that maturity came a lack of patience for such mischief.

She tossed out two miscreants one evening with an angry, "You'll not bring shame upon my establishment." As Daniel and Jack brought the men's horses around from the stable, she was aware that a new customer had come up the drive.

Torches lit along the pathway showed that it was the county's sheriff, Joshua Doyne. "Trouble here, Mrs. Dyer?" he asked mildly.

"No, sir. I was just helping these two find their way out." All Moll needed was trouble with the law to ruin her business before it had even taken hold. "May I tempt you with some mead? I make it myself, you know."

The sheriff accepted her offer with a smack of his lips. Disaster was avoided for the moment.

CHAPTER 36

October 1684

MOLL ENCOURAGED DANIEL and Jack to accompany her to church one Sunday, but they refused, so she left them in charge of the inn while she attended Mass.

It would only be a few hours in the middle of the day. They couldn't possibly get into too much trouble.

She was never quite sure if she regretted bringing them into her establishment. They were enthusiastic, but clumsy and stupid. Well, Jack was the more inane of the two, but Daniel tended to follow his brother's lead.

Which was ironic, given that Daniel was the elder of the two. But whereas Daniel was still slight, Jack was already growing into a man.

Moll hadn't asked them to take indenture contracts, but instead paid them as they went. She'd had enough of indentures to last a lifetime, even if she would be on the other side of the signing table.

Moll steered her nag and cart to the fence outside the church. Nearby, a large oak with a spreading canopy was burnished red from the encroaching autumn season. It was like God's reminder that there is always beauty to be found, even with impending bad weather.

Climbing down the steps from her cart, she tied the horse to the fence and went inside and sat down in a pew in the middle of the church.

During the Mass, she noticed a husband and wife sitting together near the front. The woman was regularly holding a hand to her head while her husband murmured to her.

Singing hymns seemed to particularly bother the woman.

At the conclusion of the service, Moll waited outside for the couple. The wife was bent over, no doubt from the pain of what Moll knew was a migram. Given how small the woman was, her bent-over stature made her look ancient. The woman was also most unfortunate looking, with thinning hair and a scarred face.

The years had not been kind to the poor soul.

Her husband was taller and wore a beard far longer than was fashionable. He had one eye that wandered separately from the other, and part of his face sagged.

He, too, must have endured a difficult life.

Moll stepped into their path. "Pardon me, I couldn't help but notice that you seem to have a migram."

They stopped and the woman looked at her in wonder. "Yes. How do you know?"

Moll introduced herself, then said, "I have seen them before. And I believe I can help you if you will permit me."

After introducing themselves as Morris and Rebecca Fowler, Mrs. Fowler said, "I've been assured of a cure before, and nothing has worked. But I am willing to try."

Moll nodded and returned to her cart to poke through her medicine case. She had learned to always keep it with her, as she never knew what sort of accident or animal bite or other injury she might encounter in her travels.

Finding the vial she wanted, which contained vinegar of roses, she returned to the couple. "Take this with you. Mix just a touch into your tea. T'will help the pain, I promise."

Rebecca's expression was doubtful as she took the vial. "Thank you."

"If the physician we saw in St. Mary's City couldn't help you, why do you think that this time you've found the right elixir, eh, Rebecca?" Morris Fowler's voice boomed. "You don't know that she isn't giving you ground cat bones." He laughed at his own clever comment.

Rebecca's husband was too bluff and hearty for Moll's taste, but maybe that came from attending to his wife's affliction for a long time.

"It will work," Moll said firmly.

She returned to her inn. To her great surprise, all was well. Daniel gave her a report of what had happened in her absence, mostly that they had picked some ripened root vegetables from the garden, fed the bruised ones to the pigs, and had prepared the dining room with fresh candles and trenchers.

It was, as Moll knew, far too early in the day for new travelers to have arrived, so the boys had used their time wisely in service to the establishment.

Perhaps, despite their outward dullness, the boys had great promise. She might be able to leave the inn in their hands every Sunday while she attended Mass.

————ᵥᵥ————

The following week, Moll again left the boys alone so she could go to church.

The Fowlers were also there, sitting in their previous pew. This time, Morris Fowler's wife was not pressing a hand to her head.

Afterward, Mrs. Fowler sought Moll out. "Mrs. Dyer, thank you. Your powder truly worked. I've taken it every day and have had no pains for a week. It is truly a miracle." The woman was standing more upright than she had before.

Next to her, Morris Fowler reeked of ale. His wandering eye was moving frantically, as if it were searching for a flask.

"Please, call me Moll, and I'm glad for it."

"You must call me Rebecca. Morris, we will be just a few minutes." Rebecca Fowler tucked her arm into Moll's and led her away from the church. Behind them, her husband grumbled to no one in particular about being abandoned.

"You mustn't pay much attention to my husband," Rebecca said without preamble. "He protects me as best he can from anyone he perceives as a threat. I'm afraid I am not the easiest wife in the world."

"You cannot help your migrams—"

Rebecca nodded and patted Moll's arm. "No, of course not. But I have never been especially well-liked here. Morris has protected my honor more than once."

Moll stopped to look at her new friend. "What do you mean, you are not 'well-liked'? You do not strike me as cruel or sharp-tongued."

Rebecca kept walking, pulling Moll along. "Perhaps not, but many people find me odd. I *am* odd. Look at me."

Once again, the other woman stopped, this time under the giant, leafy oak. Moll wasn't going to pretend that Rebecca was beautiful, but...

"You seem perfectly normal to me. We all have

our imperfections. Like this." Moll untied her cap and lifted one side of it to reveal her hair. "You can't imagine how many people have found me odd because of this."

Rebecca laughed. It made the woman's eyes sparkle and improved her looks immensely.

"Look at this, which I've had from birth." Rebecca pushed up a sleeve to reveal a purple, raised welt on the back of her arm, just above her elbow. It was a strange, meandering shape. Moll could almost make out the shape of two ears and a tail on it.

"I don't suppose you have something that can cure it?" Rebecca smiled weakly. "Others have tried blistering it. I'd not like to endure that again, for certain."

But it was no amusing matter to Moll. She examined the welt, rubbing a finger over it. She imagined that a doctor might have tried a plaster with crushed blister beetles or mustard seed in it.

What ointment did she have might cure Rebecca of this mark? Or at least cause it to fade? "I'm not sure, but I can experiment. Perhaps something with animal fat. I'll bring you a plaster next week."

They returned to where Morris now stood, waiting impatiently. "Time to go. Will take us at least an hour to walk home."

"Have you no transport?" Moll asked. "I would be happy to take you—"

"We'll be fine," Morris said gruffly, taking his wife's arm.

Moll had no idea what she had done to offend the man, but he certainly wasn't the first person to object to Moll's mere presence in the world.

CHAPTER 37

MOLL STEPPED OUTSIDE of her alehouse late one afternoon to throw food scraps to her hogs. One of them was getting large. She'd have to ask Hugh Woodall to slaughter him soon.

With the platter thoroughly scraped with a knife and the pigs grunting themselves into raptures, Moll turned to go back inside.

Emerging from a corner of the building, though, was a young native boy, no more than sixteen or seventeen years by her estimation. He wore a sparse leather covering over his hips that had a fringed flap on the front of it. He also wore beaded moccasins and an ill-fitting shirt that looked like it had come from a settler. Around his neck and dangling in front of him was an elaborately beaded bag.

She knew there were still some Piscataway in St. Mary's County, although most of them had moved to areas north in the colony. Their skin tone resembled that of the men she had seen on the docks at St. Augustine during her ship journey to Maryland.

He approached Moll cautiously. "Rum, please."

"I'm sorry?" she said. "Who are you?"

"Davy, please. Rum, please."

How long had he been lurking on her property? He didn't seem dangerous, but she couldn't be too careful.

"Why don't you enter like all of the patrons and purchase a cup?"

The young man looked at her pleadingly. "No coins."

Moll certainly couldn't afford to hand out cups of rum to any waif that wandered onto her property.

"No coins, no rum," she told him.

Davy's expression was forlorn, but Moll was resolute. If she relented and then he told others that she had given him free drink, what then?

"Powerful spirits come when I drink rum. Must, to see them again."

Moll shook her head. The poor boy was far too young to be so addle-pated from drink. She turned to go back into her alehouse. The sun was lowering in the sky, so it was time to prepare for evening visitors.

But he insisted. "Rum, please," he repeated, following her right into the building.

Moll tossed the scraped plate and knife into a wooden basin she would eventually carry down to a stream for rinsing. "I cannot just give you rum; you must understand that."

Davy removed the beaded bag from around his neck and held it out to Moll, staying a respectful distance away.

She didn't like this. Plenty of men had fallen into their cups at her establishment, but they were all free settlers. What would Davy's tribal elders say if they knew that Moll Dyer was giving him the means to "see powerful spirits"?

But Davy was clearly rooted to his spot, and Moll knew he wasn't going to leave without his heart's desire.

With a sigh, she took the proffered bag, hung it from a nail on the wall, and proceeded to pour him some rum. So many men liked it. Personally, it reminded her of St. Kitts since it was made by fermenting and distilling sugar cane juice or molasses, thus it repulsed her.

Recent ships coming into St. Mary's County frequently carried bottles of rum from St. Kitts, as production plants were now being built there to meet the growing demand in both the colonies and back in England for the spirit.

Was Yaddy still on the island? Had she made it back to Africa?

She cleared her mind of old thoughts that didn't do her any good.

"Just this once," she said, handing it to him. "I cannot give you more. Do you understand?" Davy took the cup and drank greedily from it, downing it in just a few gulps. His expression was already happy as he handed the cup back to Moll and practically bounced out of her back door to places unknown.

Moll shook her head in dismay but thought no more about Davy. He was a curious young man, but harmless and of no concern to her.

CHAPTER 38

MOLL ASKED DANIEL and Jack about Davy a week later as she led them in cleaning all the back working areas of the inn. "Had you seen him here before?"

Jack nodded as he swept back and forth. "Sure. Plenty of times."

Moll rose from where she was on her knees, organizing the interior of a cabinet containing her brewing supplies. Everything got heaped beyond reason when the inn was busy.

"Plenty of times? Was he inside the inn?" As Moll rearranged items, her hand encountered the beaded pouch Davy had given her. She must have tossed it in here to keep it from getting damaged while it dangled on the wall hook. She pulled it out now and placed it around her neck. The beadwork was beautiful, in bright geometric patterns of blues, reds, and yellows.

Jack stopped sweeping to lean against the straw broom. "Naw, he seemed to scairt to come in. He just stood outside and asked for rum."

Moll put a hand to her head, hoping to stave off what threatened to be one of Rebecca's migrams. She spoke carefully. "And did you give him rum?"

Jack shrugged. "A coupla times. He danced around and made me laugh. But then I stopped because he didn't have money. I didn't think you'd like me giving away your spirits."

Moll bit her tongue on a sharp retort as she stood. "Jack," she said as patiently as she could. "That boy cannot be given rum in that manner. I cannot afford it, and I don't want to see him hurt."

Jack shook his head as if he were a wise old man. If she weren't so furious, she would have found it amusing. "Mrs. Dyer, you be a strange one. Always yelling at us. I don't much like being yelled at."

"And I don't much like simpletons who cannot follow plain instructions." Maybe it had *not* been smart to hire these two. Or Jack, anyway.

"What are you wearing?" He pointed to the pouch.

She knew Jack was trying to distract her, but answered the question anyway.

"Davy gave me this." She fingered the beadwork.

"Gave it to you? As a present?"

"No, he gave it to me for…" Moll clamped her lips shut. The little imp had verbally trapped her.

"Sure," he said, nodding.

She should box him about the ears.

Daniel had been wiping out cups and trenchers from a previous meal's leavings. He looked up from what he was doing and, in a rare display of bravery, said, "Jack, don't be rude. Mrs. Dyer pays us promptly each week, and we have a place to live. Don't ruin it for us by being ungrateful." He returned to what he was doing.

Jack was temporarily chastised but perked back up when Daniel got Moll's attention again.

"Mrs. Dyer, I found this. What is it?" Jack held up the carved dragon that Massie had given her when she left St. Kitts.

She hadn't thought about Mrs. Lugg's son in a

long time. After all, she'd left the island six years ago. Why, he would be around Jack's age by now. "A present from a special man," she said, without further elaboration.

But Jack wasn't done being incorrigible. "That looks like a dragon. Is it your familiar? Is the Devil the special man who give it to you?" He laughed heartily at his own joke.

Daniel's expression was stricken.

How dare the imp suggest such a thing? Talk like that was dangerous. Moll lashed out at Jack. "*WHAT?* You are a beast. The only devil in my life is *you*. Go on, the both of you, out to the stables. I'm sure you can keep yourselves occupied with mucking."

Jack dropped his broom, no doubt happy to be done with his task, and scampered out of the room. Daniel followed more solemnly, stopping before Moll. "I'm sorry, maum, that I got Jack all inflamed like that. I didn't mean anything, I swear."

It was a tragedy that they had lost both their mother and father so young. They had no

guidance, and Jack was turning into a very troubled young man.

Moll had pity on Daniel. "I know. But be careful of your brother. He's going to lead you into trouble one day."

Daniel nodded his head dolefully. "Yes, maum, I know."

CHAPTER 39

IN MAY 1685, Moll received a visit from Hugh and Lucy Woodall, along with their eldest son, Lawrence, and his wife, Rose.

They were all headed to Charles County for about a week to see about some advertised property rights there, where Lawrence wished to establish his own farm.

Could they impose upon Moll to take on baby Philip in their absence? Although now two years old, he would be too much to manage on such a long trip.

Moll gladly took him in, creating a makeshift bed for Philip in her chamber. It pleased her that the Woodalls trusted her with the precious babe.

Surprisingly, Daniel adored Philip, playing with him constantly and seeing to his needs.

Jack eyed the child with suspicion. "He's not your responsibility," he said to his brother with a sneer. "You're a dunderhead to care for him."

But Daniel ignored his brother, which pleased Moll even more. The week of caring for Philip passed quickly, and the Woodalls reported that their son had found a prime piece of property to farm.

Moll was already missing Philip as Rose picked him up from his makeshift bed, but Daniel seemed devastated. Soon, though, life returned to normal in a constant stream of customers, cooking, cleaning, brewing, and worrying about money.

She was surprised again by the arrival of Morris and Rebecca Fowler late one afternoon.

"What's tonight's offering?" Morris asked loudly, stroking his considerable beard. A few patrons had already seated themselves and looked up at the noisy intrusion.

"Welcome, welcome," Moll said, escorting them to a table in the corner, hoping Morris would quieten.

"I have some nice perch, fresh from Breton Bay, just this morning. Also, some pickled carrots."

Morris nodded, and Moll quickly found a pitcher of ale. The sooner he consumed some refreshment, the happier he would likely be.

With the boys' help, Moll welcomed more patrons and got everyone served. With that done, she sat down with the Fowlers.

"Moll, your migram cure has been like a holy miracle," Rebecca enthused. "I haven't had pain in weeks. But I am wondering if you can make me more of your powder. We will pay for it this time, of course." She held out an empty vial in her hand.

Taking it, Moll went to her workroom at the rear of the inn to refill the ingredients. She brought it the vial back out to the dining room and handed it back to Rebecca as she sat down once more with the couple.

Jack was at the table, offering Morris a second helping of fish. Moll frowned. Morris would have to be charged for that.

But Jack was frowning, too, as he observed Moll handing the headache remedy vial to Rebecca.

"What's that?" he asked, at the same volume Morris Fowler usually used.

"Just a powder for Mrs. Fowler's migram pains," Moll said, shooing him away.

But Jack wasn't to be moved. "Why do you have migram pain? Is there a demon living in your head? Are you a witch?" he asked Rebecca.

Moll jumped up from her chair. "Jack, begone with you. You'll not speak to our guests in such a rude manner." She pointed toward the back room.

But Jack didn't seem intimidated. In fact, he completely ignored Moll.

It got worse. A patron from across the room spoke up. "Heard there's a witch in Calvert County who's been casting curses on her neighbors."

There were murmurs in the room.

Another man agreed. "Heard that, too. She bewitched some cattle, and they stampeded over their fencing and into the Patuxent River."

This had to be stopped. Moll spoke out. "Stuff and nonsense. Mrs. Fowler isn't even from Calvert. She lives here in Newtowne Hundred."

Jack was back at it. "So, she *is* a witch? Just not the one from Calvert?"

Now all the patrons were whispering and gossiping.

"She does look like one, doesn't she?"

"They say witches can fly about like birds. Maybe she flew here."

Moll fully intended to thrash the boy later. For now, she needed to maintain order in her inn.

"Friends," she said, raising her voice over the chatter. "My young helper is just teasing and doesn't mean what he says. The Fowlers are upstanding members of the community, and Mrs. Fowler is certainly no witch."

All calmed down after that, which told Moll that

her patrons didn't really believe that Rebecca was a witch in the first place.

However, Morris still simmered as Moll escorted the two of them out an hour later.

"How could you have permitted that slimy little worm to have spoken so to my wife?" Morris was balling his fists as the three of them stood outside. Did he intend to strike her?

"Morris, please," Rebecca said, putting out a hand to stay her husband's temper. "You'll get one of my migrams started again."

"Migrams will be the least of our troubles if you get a reputation as a witch." Morris stalked off, leaving Moll and his wife standing near the entrance.

With an apologetic glance followed by a firm hug, Rebecca took off after her husband. Was it Moll's imagination, or was Rebecca starting to hunch over again?

Moll returned inside. Daniel was cowering in a corner near the back room, his face to the wall. What had Jack done now?

"Where is Jack?" Moll said quietly, so as not to upset her customers any more than they had been.

Daniel turned toward her. Even in the shadowy candlelight, she could see that he had a bruise forming along his jawline.

"Did Jack do this?" she whispered.

Daniel stared silently at her.

Muttering several oaths under her breath, she went into the back room, plucked a lantern off the wall, lit a candle stub in the fireplace, placed it in the lantern, and went out the back door to look for Jack.

She headed straight for the stables. A couple of horses huffed at her presence but were otherwise calm. Jack didn't appear to be here.

Returning outside, she picked her way around the property, but it was a futile effort to try to find him in the area surrounding the inn with a single lantern held up in front of her for light. The glow from the dining room was of little assistance.

She quickly gave up as she needed to worry about her customers.

The next morning, she arose as dawn was breaking, determined to find Jack before her guests awakened.

She went outside. All was eerily quiet as she returned to the stables. Daniel poked his head up from his pallet, blinking sleepily. "Sorry, Mrs. Dyer, I didn't mean to oversleep."

"You didn't," she said. "Collect some eggs for me, will you? I'll need to break the guests' fasts soon."

Daniel nodded and yawned.

Jack's pallet was empty.

Now feeling a bit sacrilegious for the curses she was uttering, she left the stables to return to the house. Had the boy completely fled the area?

As she trod back to the rear door, a movement caught her eye. It was her chicken coop. Walking over there, she realized that the reason it had been so quiet when she came outside was because her rooster wasn't crowing, nor were the chickens clucking and flapping as they typically did.

And that was because the gate to her chicken pen stood wide open. There were no animals left, although there were telltale signs of a fox attack. Strewn feathers, trails of blood, and a couple of broken eggs provided Moll with all the evidence she needed.

Her pen was impenetrable by an animal, and Moll was faithful to securing the gate each night. How had this happened?

Feeding her customers sausages and pickled vegetables to satisfy their hunger before continuing their journeys, Moll worked with Daniel on their daily routine tasks in preparation for evening visitors. He offered no explanation for his injury, and Moll chose not to ask again.

By midday, she had the answer to the open chicken pen, for Jack finally returned through the front door, which Moll had forbidden him to do. Only Moll and her guests were to enter through the front; servants were to come through the rear.

She went out to confront him. Jack was with Davy, and they were both obviously inebriated, moving sloppily and laughing together. Jack held a bottle of rum, containing just enough remains to slosh around at the bottom.

Moll was so enraged she could barely speak. When she found her voice, she asked, "Where did you get the money for an entire bottle of rum?"

"Sold a coupla hens to the Red Oak Tavern in exchange for it. Caught up to Davy here in the woods, and I shared it with him." Jack grinned at Moll.

He was brazenly open about what he had done. What did this creature think he was doing? Moll had rescued him from his unfortunate situation, providing him with food, a place for his head, and even a couple of coins each week. In return, he was lazy, slanderous toward her friend, and now, a thief.

"The new law says we can't give liquor to natives anymore." Moll was practically trembling from her anger at his ingratitude, sloth, and troublemaking.

"Eh." Jack shrugged.

Moll couldn't help it. She drew her right arm back and brought her hand forward with all her might, connecting with his left ear. He stumbled briefly but quickly regained his balance.

Based on how badly her hand hurt, the boy's brain must feel like the jumbled eggs she had planned to make that morning, if not for his perfidy.

Jack's demeanor changed instantly. He narrowed his gaze at Moll. "I'm not your slave," he said.

"No," Moll bit out. "For no slave could be as astoundingly stupid as you are. Get out of my sight and do not return. Your brother is worth five of you, and I'll get along better with just him."

"My brother? He's weak. Threatened to tell you I was planning to take the chickens, so I had to make him see reason."

Behind Moll was the sound of Daniel scrambling into the back room. Poor Daniel, so terrified of his vile sibling.

"Come, Davy, let's leave the giant witch to herself. She's plenty of work to do before supper." He was sunny once more, slapping the back of his new friend and whistling as they left together. Through the front door, of course.

CHAPTER 40

September 1685

MOLL HAD AGREED to meet Rebecca and her husband at the King's Grace for supper one evening. Few people noticed Moll entering the inn by herself.

She was a rarity among women. There were so few of them in the colony that it was unusual for her to not be married. It had created consternation at first, for she had refused any suggestions in that direction, but eventually most people simply shrugged at her.

With disease, storms, and unexpected tragedies forever howling at people's doors, there were far more important things to worry about than an unmarried woman.

But because there were so few women in the colony, it was also unusual that she ran her own establishment by herself, with only one boy to help her.

Tonight's offering was crab pie, a flaky crust stuffed with blue crab meat taken from Breton Bay, chopped potatoes and carrots, and laced with a cream sauce.

Perhaps Moll should consider finer meal offerings, although she wasn't that much of a cook.

She and Rebecca had not seen each other in a few months, so it had been a pleasant surprise to have a note delivered to her alehouse, asking her to meet them.

Moll intended to stay the night at the inn, for the journey back was too long to make at night. She'd left Daniel to manage things, praying he wouldn't allow Jack into the inn to create havoc.

Morris Fowler slurped loudly from his cup of ale. He had no manners, but he was devoted to Moll's friend, so she kept her distaste to herself.

She and Rebecca chatted idly together, mostly regarding Rebecca's children, about whom there was no topic too detailed for their mother to dwell on at length, despite the fact that they were all adults and scattered across the northern Massachusetts and New York colonies.

Moll talked about her alehouse—her customers, her future plans, and the ongoing struggles with Jack—which served to dissolve Rebecca in laughter, despite her previous encounter with the boy.

Once their pies were finished, they were served spiced raisin cakes. Mr. Fowler continued drinking ale, while his wife and Moll switched to small beer.

The candle on their table had burned low by the time they were done. Moll looked around and realized there were few patrons left in the tavern.

The front door banged open, causing the remaining customers to jump in unison.

It was Joshua Doyne, the sheriff. "Rebecca Fowler?" he demanded of the room, glancing around before espying Moll's friend.

Moll felt her innards clench. She was transported back to that night when the Roundheads had come and seized Mama. And when Richard had been taken away.

If the law was looking for Rebecca, it could be for no good reason.

"Yes?" Rebecca said innocently before Moll could warn her to remain quiet.

The sheriff came to their table. He was portly as compared to most colonists, making Moll wonder how soft his position must be.

"Mrs. Fowler, I'm here to arrest you." The sheriff's lot in life might be comfortable, but he was also deadly serious.

Rebecca's skin transformed into a pasty gray as her eyes bulged in terror.

"For what reason?" Moll and Morris demanded at the same time.

"She has been accused of witchcraft." The sheriff indicated that Rebecca should stand. When she did so, he tied her wrists together in front of her with rope.

As if such a humiliation were required. Rebecca Fowler was as tame as a lamb and would obey anyone.

But Morris Fowler wasn't quite so obedient. Copious amounts of ale did have a way of making men belligerent. He slammed down his cup. "I demand that you release my wife. She is no more a witch than you are a toad. You are not a toad, are you, Sheriff Doyne?"

For the very first time, Moll had a drop of respect for Rebecca's repugnant husband.

"Mind yerself," the sheriff growled. "I'm just doing my duty here. Judge says several people claim she cast a spell on Francis Sansbury, in addition to other people in Calvert County."

Dear Lord, what had Jack done?

Moll leapt into the argument. "Who accused her? Can anyone in this colony simply make an accusation and have it result in an arrest?"

Sheriff Doyne dismissed her. "This is no concern

of yours, Mrs. Dyer. You've enough trouble of your own keeping order at your alehouse without worrying about the likes of women casting spells on others."

What he was saying was outrageous. "Casting spells? Rebecca Fowler is the most God-fearing, upright—"

Morris pushed away his chair and stood, his face mottled with rage. "I'll be damned if you're taking my wife away, sirrah. I'll put your head on a pike myself before I let you besmirch her fine name."

The other patrons began slipping out of the building, leaving it empty except for the three of them, the sheriff, and the tavern keeper, who stood silently nearby, wringing his hands on a towel.

That drop of respect was spreading fast. Why, Moll's sudden admiration for Morris Fowler might fill a goblet soon.

But Sheriff Doyne had no such esteem for Rebecca's husband. With the speed of a copperhead snake striking its victim, the sheriff lashed out with his fist against Morris's jaw, stunning the man into collapsing back into his seat.

"You can find her at the gaol," the sheriff said, walking off with Rebecca as though she were a prized horse. Or a lamb.

Being led to the slaughter.

CHAPTER 41

THREE DAYS LATER, Moll had made the journey to the gaol in St. Mary's City, where Rebecca was being held while she awaited trial. Moll was granted access with no questions asked. Sometimes it helped to be perceived as a weak, helpless woman.

Morris was huddled with his wife in her damp cell, made of impenetrable stone with a thick oak door on it. A narrow slit up high in the wall was all she had for air and light.

Moisture oozed from the stones in long, green streaks and puddled along the walls. The stink of human waste permeated the air.

How was it even possible that this utterly ridiculous situation had occurred?

Jack Cole.

Along the wall opposite Rebecca's pallet—which had the barest amount of fill in it—was a wooden commode that required three steps to the top of it.

No doubt this was to create a deep well for excrement so that it rarely had to be cleaned out. But in such a confined area with almost no air blowing through, it was practically poisonous.

Rebecca smiled wanly at seeing Moll. "I'm afraid I cannot offer you a place to sit as my lodgings are quite dismal."

Morris said nothing while Moll sat with Rebecca,

talking idly to her friend and even softly singing songs to her. Morris eventually became agitated by Moll's presence, suggesting that she had spent enough time in Rebecca's cell. Moll hugged her friend fiercely before leaving.

On September 30th, Rebecca was brought to trial by the provincial court at St. Mary's, accused of practicing witchcraft at Mount Calvert Hundred and other places in Calvert County.

Rebecca protested that she had never been to those places.

It didn't matter, for it was established that she would have used spells and incantations to travel back and forth.

Rebecca pled not guilty, which also did not matter, for it was well known that witches couldn't help but lie about everything.

Moll stood in the airless room with dozens of other onlookers, trying to control her trembling anger as falsehoods were rapidly spewed about her friend.

"I will testify for my wife," Morris shouted at the court, but a banging gavel refused his demand.

"If she be a witch, then you are under her control," the magistrate said to Rebecca's husband.

A local child had been scratched on the arm by a cat, resulting in gross swelling and eventually the child's death. Rebecca was accused of having told the cat to attack the youngster in revenge against the girl's parents for having slighted Rebecca in town one day.

It was all preposterous.

Moll made her way through the crowd, half of whom sounded intoxicated and acted as though they were enjoying a day at a bearbaiting.

She forced her way to the rail, where she was in touching distance of Rebecca, and shouted out, "I know Mrs. Fowler, and these accusations are as outlandish as they are untrue. Mrs. Fowler is a gentle soul who wouldn't step on a spider, much less harm children or her neighbors."

"You, too, must be under her spell," was the magistrate's response. "Perhaps she uses spiders in addition to cats to attack those she dislikes." Moll's further protests at the magistrate's outrageous statements were drowned out by his gavel.

Rebecca's crone-like appearance surely hadn't helped her, as the case had been developed using sworn testimony from someone whom the judge said wasn't in the courtroom due to his youth.

Jack Cole, Moll thought again.

Inside the noisy courthouse, Rebecca was quickly convicted of using magic to harm Francis Sandsbury and other residents in Calvert, including the child who had died.

The attorney general, Thomas Burford, sentenced her to hanging until death, with the execution to take place ten days hence.

The trial watchers erupted in a blend of cheers and gasps of astonishment as Rebecca was led out of the room to be returned to her cell. Moll left the courthouse, stiff and barely able to lift each foot. There was a buzzing in her ears, disturbing but at least blocking out the sounds of the other onlookers.

Outside, she met Hugh and Lucy Woodall. "Terrible business," Hugh said.

"Yes," Moll said, struggling to hold back tears.

"I heard your attempt to defend Mrs. Fowler," Lucy said, peering into her face. "I had no idea you knew her so well."

Moll nodded, unable to speak.

"Terrible business," Hugh repeated. "Not good for the colony."

Moll fled her old master and mistress, lest she become a burbling mess. For the first time in her life, she felt every one of her fifty-one years. Her back and knees ached, and moving was more painful than it had ever been.

Not that it mattered. Moll had a task to complete.

CHAPTER 42

MOLL VISITED REBECCA again three days later. Fortunately, Morris wasn't there.

Once more, Rebecca expressed joy to see Moll. "You have been such a dear friend. I am so lucky to have you. I suppose that soon I won't have to worry about headaches anymore." She laughed weakly.

"I am so sorry about this, my dear friend. I feel responsible."

"Don't be silly," Rebecca said gently. "Morris holds you to blame, too, you know. Says it all started from the evening we supped at your inn."

Heat crept up Moll's neck. "Yes. I let that stupid boy Jack into my—"

Rebecca put a hand on Moll's arm. Her touch was feeble. "You are not to blame. The blame rests with the man who convicted me. He will have to justify his actions before God."

"But—"

Rebecca shook her head. "I won't hear any more on it."

Moll swallowed the lump in her throat and nodded. "I brought you something to make… the end…easier for you."

She pulled a vial out from her dress pocket.

Rebecca frowned. "Is it poison?"

"No, I'll not give you poison for taking your own life. T'would be an offense before God. This is an elixir that will simply cloud your mind and cause you not to care about what's happening. Take it quickly when they come for you." Moll pressed the vial into Rebecca's hand and wrapped her fingers around it.

Rebecca smiled weakly and nodded.

Moll fiercely embraced her brittle friend before saying goodbye a final time.

CHAPTER 43

ON OCTOBER 9, 1685, a dull, rainy Tuesday, Moll watched from the middle of a crowd as Rebecca—her hands roped behind her back—was brought out from her cell, made to stumble up to a platform, and had a noose tightened around her neck. Poor Rebecca's wild hair was flattened to her face as rivulets of water ran down her head. She gazed dully out at the onlookers, some of whom yelled epithets at her.

A woman threw a tomato at Rebecca, striking her squarely in the shoulder and running down her dress. "Burn in hell, witch!" she shouted.

Rebecca hardly seemed to notice. The potion must have worked. Moll was weak with relief.

The pronouncement against Rebecca was read aloud, and she was asked if she had anything to say. Rebecca didn't respond.

The rain subsided just as the hangman dropped the platform door, sending Rebecca plunging downward. Praise God, there was a loud snap, so Moll knew her friend had died instantly from a broken neck.

To think that that was counted as a blessing in this whole sordid mess.

The sound of Morris Fowler's keening in the distance was so sharp and piercing that several crows roosting in a tree were frightened off, flapping and cawing noisily as they departed.

With the entertainment complete and Morris's howling making for great discomfort, the other watchers started shuffling off in multiple directions.

Moll shivered but stayed rooted to the spot, unwilling to leave until she knew that her friend had been cut down.

"Damn you, Jack," she said aloud. "Damn you and curse you to hell for all that you have done." She found strength in what she was saying. "You spiteful little evil doer. You spawn of the devil."

People were looking at her askance, but she didn't care. "You have brought shame upon yourself and upon me. I'll not allow you to do so again."

Moll was at a loss as to what she could do, given that she had no idea where Jack was, but it was soothing to have verbally denounced him, even if he had no awareness that she had done so.

CHAPTER 44

MOLL RETURNED HOME from Rebecca's hanging with her heart so heavy she found it laborious to trudge up the path to her alehouse.

She had no idea how to smile at her customers this evening.

To her surprise, the Piscataway boy, Davy, was once more lurking at the rear of the alehouse, only this time he was standing in the middle of her herb and vegetable garden.

Moll had never spared another moment thinking about him after he had drunkenly stumbled into her inn with Jack, yet here he was now.

"I care for your garden," he said, sweeping an arm to show her what he had done.

Moll gasped. Her garden was trampled upon as though the hogs had been permitted to run wild through it.

"What did you do?" she shouted.

"Care for your garden," he repeated, although now he sounded unsure of himself.

"By destroying it?" How was Moll to recover from this?

"No. He beckoned her over and bent down to pick up a large basket that Moll typically used for hauling dirty linens down to the stream.

The basket was full of beans, corn stalks, rosemary,

sage, and at least one of everything else she was growing.

Except that everything he had picked had been jostled and scraped and bruised by his rough handling.

What remained in the garden had been flattened under his feet. How could someone who was able to move about so stealthily also be able to smash her garden as though he were a human mill?

"I care for your garden. Rum, please," Davy said. "Must, to see spirits again."

Moll closed her eyes, willing herself to patience.

Not only was she incensed over the destruction, but here he was, asking for liquor when she had told him long ago she would not give it to him again.

Moreover, she would be inviting trouble now to supply him with it.

"I am not permitted to sell nor give you spirits anymore. The council says we are bringing your tribe to ruin."

Davy's expression made it clear that he had no idea what she was saying.

No doubt he had obtained rum from other people, but with the new law in place, he was struggling to find it and was now circling back to Moll.

"You must not drink so much liquor. You've already ruined my garden. You will eventually do something foolish to someone who doesn't care about you and come to great harm."

Davy still just stared at her.

What was she to do with him? She didn't even know where Davy lived. He came and went like a woodland sprite. It was as if he lived everywhere and nowhere.

Moll went into the house with Davy close behind her.

"I will give you one more cup without charge to keep me out of trouble from selling it to you. But I am on the edge of the law. I am risking my livelihood. You must not ever come here again, do you understand?"

Davy nodded solemnly. As before, he quickly drank the rum and scurried out.

CHAPTER 45

August 1689

TIMES HAD BEEN tumultuous. Vague rumblings drifted over from London, which provided more fodder for discussion and argument inside her inn. The childless Charles II had died in 1685, resulting in his brother, James, taking over the throne.

Catholic James had come to antagonistic blows with Parliament, much as his father, Charles I, had. Reluctant this time to execute a monarch, Parliament had simply exiled him. James's daughter, Mary, had come to the throne in April of this year as co-regent with her husband, William of Orange. Parliament was happy as the two were Protestants.

All of it was great gossip for Moll's customers, who had picked apart in great detail Charles II's supposed deathbed conversion to Catholicism, James II's reputed penchant for particularly unattractive mistresses, and poor Queen Mary's inability to have children.

Moll felt a kinship to the queen over that.

All these events paled in the face of the dangerous turmoil that arrived in the form of John Coode. He had fomented a rebellion in Maryland back in 1681, been chased out, but returned in 1689 for more trouble. This time, his timing was right.

More Protestants were moving into Maryland, and these colonists were resentful that many political offices were held by Catholics or close friends of the Calverts.

Additionally, the Maryland government had not yet recognized William and Mary as the rightful monarchs, creating more consternation among the Protestant colonists.

Coode spread a rumor that Catholics had enlisted the help of the native tribes to come in and kill as many Protestants as possible. The idea was laughable, but so high were tensions that it was believed as readily as the Virgin birth.

Leading an army of seven hundred men, he attacked the state house in St. Mary's City, forced the council to surrender to him, and set himself up as "commander in chief" of the colony.

Moll had to admit that it had been masterful, as no blood had been shed in his conquest. However, Catholicism had just been outlawed in Maryland. She would have to worship in secret, just as she had back in England.

At least there was no more talk of witchcraft in the colony.

CHAPTER 46

1690

"WHATEVER DO YOU want?" Moll shouted out the window opening. Someone sounding suspiciously like the sheriff had been hollering and carrying on for several minutes. "It's hardly light out," she said. "Go about your own business."

"You're our business, Mistress Dyer. You need to attend a meeting."

What fool thing was he talking about? "What meeting?"

"They's going to talk about the Indian trouble with spirits. Appears one in particular is getting a good ration of rum from you every day. Come along now."

Moll shut her eyes. Could she not avoid trouble for a single minute?

She followed the sheriff on her own nag, who was still breathing by some miracle. Moll took care not to ride her much these days.

They ended up in a small Piscataway settlement on a field she had never seen before, next to Breton Bay.

Moll dismounted and followed the sheriff into the largest witchott in the settlement.

Inside were what Moll supposed to be tribal elders

gathered in a circle at one end of the long room. She was asked to sit on the ground with them, an excruciating effort for her, although she disguised the pain as best she could.

The "meeting" went poorly. The Piscataway leaders said they had come down from their new home in Charles County to encamp here, specifically to address the liquor problems some of their tribesmen were having.

The sheriff served as an interpreter, since the Piscataway spoke little English, and Moll knew even less of their language.

Moll told them she was aware of a law passed preventing the sale of liquor to the Piscataway.

The leaders were distressed to hear that Moll had been regularly supplying one of their young men with rum.

Moll said she had only done so twice and had not done so for some time. She would never do so again.

The leaders asked if it was true that Moll had been friends with a witch, and what magic could the witch perform?

Moll sighed and told them that she knew no witches.

The sheriff interrupted here, talking with the Piscataway leaders and occasionally pointing at Moll.

Was he taking up their cause against her?

The Piscataway became angry, wanting to know if Moll's friend had used witchcraft against their tribesmen, causing them to see visions when drinking rum.

"No."

Had Moll used a spell on the Piscataway boy that the English called Davy?

"No."

Her hair was a strange color. Did it have powers?

"No."

Did Moll—

"I have committed no crimes," Moll finally replied in exasperation.

The tribal elders seemed to get equally tired of her, for the sheriff announced that the Piscataway had declared themselves dissatisfied and that they no longer wished Moll to be in their presence. However, they made it clear that they expected the sheriff to do something about Moll.

"I will take care of it." The sheriff's grin was disturbing.

A Piscataway woman entered the witchott and handed Moll a basket containing an assortment of berries and nuts, along with a couple of partridges, whose bodies were still warm. Moll supposed that this was to make her feel better for this harsh inquiry.

She left the Piscataway encampment, walking the horse beside her and carrying the basket.

Within a week, the sheriff was at her doorstep.

"You are accused of selling spirits to natives, in direct contradiction to the law." The sheriff's broad smile belied the seriousness of his words.

He was enjoying this.

Just like Rebecca, Moll was arrested, forced onto the sheriff's cart, and carried off to the gaol. The man clearly took pleasure in persecuting women of the colony.

Moll landed in a different cell that was just as miserable as Rebecca's. Except Moll had no visitors as she sat on the damp, cold ground, awaiting whatever was in store.

Two days later, she was hauled before the court, standing exactly where Rebecca had, just five years ago. The sheriff was the main witness against her, although a couple of Piscataway were also permitted to enter testimony against Moll.

It would have been amusing, were it not so unbelievably unjust and frightening. As if this court would have considered a native's testimony in normal circumstances.

Insults and accusations were hurled at Moll, and, despite her firm denial, the gavel rapped its guilty pronouncement.

"You are hereby stripped of all licenses and are forbidden from running any sort of inn, alehouse, or tavern in the colony. Ever again."

Moll refused to react, which would only give the court the satisfaction of seeing her gasp in horror at the sentence, which was effectively one of complete ruination for her. How was she to support herself?

But she knew she was fortunate that she hadn't been accused of being a witch.

CHAPTER 47

1693

MOLL NO LONGER had her inn, which, although not exactly a thriving establishment, had provided her with a bit of income and independence. She dismissed Daniel, then sold off what she could and used the proceeds to purchase a small, decrepit cabin in the woods in Newtowne Hundred, about a quarter mile from her old property.

She walked all her animals over to the cabin and attempted to start anew, but her heart was so sore that it was difficult to muster any enthusiasm for it. She half-heartedly tilled soil, set up an irrigation system, and put up a barrier for her few animals.

She brewed some ale but quickly gave it up. Few people were interested in purchasing ale from a woman who had been stripped of her right to run an alehouse, even if she was offering it for hardly more than it cost her to make.

After all of that, she was too tired to improve her cabin. The roof leaked, just as her parents' cottage had back in Devon. Moll simply moved her chair and table to avoid the drops and placed a bucket under the drip.

Her only nod to caring about her surroundings

was to put Massie's toy dragon in the center of the table. It was the only thing in her life that made her smile. That and periodic trips into town to sell eggs or whatever she had on hand. Others might no longer like her, but it did give her some sense of belonging to listen to others argue, chatter, and laugh in the village square. It was during these trips that she heard news of the colony and of the world at large.

Moll wondered if the Devil was simply determined to have her. Maybe she should let him take her. After all, she could make more of the elixir she had given Rebecca, which would make her numb to everything in the world around her.

But such an action would mean the death of her livestock and the ruination of her crops. No, on she would go, surviving whatever happened.

There was one bright spot, though.

John Coode had finally been removed from power when the new royal governor of Maryland, Nehemiah Blakiston, was appointed in July 1691. Coode would go on to make more trouble in the form of two more uprisings, but his influence was largely gone.

At least that was one point on which Moll could heave a sigh of relief.

As if in delayed mockery of Rebecca's trial and conviction seven years earlier, Salem Village in the Massachusetts Bay colony was rumored to be gripped by a witchcraft frenzy by February 1692. A series of investigations was made into purported witches who were practicing their dark craft there.

By May 1693, thirty people had been found guilty of witchcraft, of whom nineteen were executed.

Moll shook her head. What possessed rational

members of society to be overcome by fear of silly superstitions? It was that irrational fear that had caused her friend to be hanged.

She shivered at the memory of Rebecca's neck snapping as she plunged to her undeserved death.

Praise God, she lived in the Maryland colony, where—despite Rebecca's unfortunate end— witchcraft was not generally deemed a problem. Just improperly serving liquor was.

And, of course, any location was better than St. Kitts, no matter how sad her conditions were now. Another shiver of disgust ran through her.

Moll thought of her brother, William. How was he? Would she ever see him again?

Eight months later, Moll overheard in the village that Blakiston had been removed as governor, as King William and Queen Mary had declared Maryland a royal colony rather than a proprietary province, thus removing all control from the Calvert family.

But what did Moll care of the politics of men? There had been other happenings that occupied her mind.

CHAPTER 48

1697

MOLL HAD RETREATED into a solitary life over the past four years, desiring no companionship, not that anyone desired her company, anyway.

Davy had made a few more appearances, somehow finding her and assuming she still had rum despite her alehouse no longer in existence and her living conditions being sparse. Fortunately, he soon gave up and went away.

She'd never heard another word from Morris Fowler, although she caught a rumor that he had remarried, this time to a Protestant widow, and they had moved to Virginia.

She occasionally heard from Hugh and Lucy Woodall, mostly in the form of a hired boy delivering surplus crops to her, but Moll knew they were far too busy with their own family and farming concerns to be overly involved with what Moll was doing.

Even the deliveries eventually stopped.

She scraped by on her tiny property, selling eggs and vegetables in town for spare change. Most of her livestock was now gone, butchered, and most of the meat sold to sustain her.

Her horse had died, and she hadn't the money to

replace it, so if Moll wished to go anywhere, she walked. Occasionally, a kind traveler would give her a ride, but she became so accustomed to walking to town that she didn't much care whether someone stopped for her or not.

Newtowne Hundred had grown from barely a village into a small town. In fact, the entire colony was growing, which had resulted in changes that were not always welcome.

In 1694, the governor had moved the colony's capital from St. Mary's City to Anne Arundel Towne, then promptly renamed it Annapolis after Princess Anne, sister to Queen Mary.

There had been great consternation locally over St. Mary's City's loss of prestige.

Moll only wished it had happened sooner. If the seat of government had been in Annapolis during her confrontation with the Piscataway, she might never have had to endure a trial and conviction, for who would have bothered to haul her up there for such a trivial thing?

But none of it mattered now.

Having sold off a basket of eggs in town one day, Moll sat in the town square, eating a meat pie she had purchased from a street seller. It reminded her of her days with Dada, walking in towns and enjoying the reward of food from a street cart after having sold well from his medical case.

Except in this town, the smells were not of smoke and decay, but of animals and endeavor.

The sun was warm and pleasant, and, for a moment, Moll could forget how her life had once again been devastated. She even thought she might be prosperous once again, using her medicine chest to provide the ailing with cures. Moll could add some herbs and flowers to her garden, then begin the process of drying, grinding, and mixing them together. Surely someone would be interested in a purchase.

She thought of Dada's formulations for the lovesick and wrinkled her nose. Such chicanery would not work here in the colony. The people here were of plain, hardy stock.

Although some had gotten agitated over the thought of a witch in their midst, hadn't they?

As she contemplated the future, people, horses, and livestock moved about in a haphazard but calm manner, everyone conducting their own business at their own pace.

The pleasantry was intruded upon by the sound of hoofbeats. They were thunderous, meaning the driver was headed in way too fast. She glanced around, trying to figure out where the foolish driver was coming from, when she heard a sickening thud, followed by screams.

Moll raced to the sound of the noise. What lay before her was grotesque and well beyond any healing powders and potions she might have.

A woman lay on the ground, having lost against both a horse trampling her and a cart running over her.

A man, presumably the dead woman's husband, was yelling at the driver and, in fact, climbing up on the cart to reach him, while others were trying to calm him down.

That wasn't of concern to Moll, for what she noticed next was an infant babe, swaddled up in a blanket on the ground nearby and squalling almost as loudly as its father.

The poor mite must have fallen from its mother's arms.

She rushed over to the child, picking it up and checking to be sure there were no injuries.

"Ah, you're a little boy. And a handsome one, too. What might your name be?" she said. She spent time rocking him and singing nonsensical songs to him, creating a pool of calm around the child while confusion reigned everywhere else.

Someone must have fetched the sheriff, for soon his distasteful presence was in the midst. He quickly assessed the situation, determining that both men needed to go to the court in Annapolis, given that the driver could potentially be charged with murder.

Both men began howling, the driver because he claimed it was an accident, the father because of his situation. "My wife! My wife! I must take care of her. And my boy! Wait, where is Ambrose?" He looked around wildly. "My God, I have no one else in the world. My parents dead, my brother in Carolina. What will I do without my boy?"

Moll stepped forward with the child. "Sir, I have him. I live just south of here. I can care for him while you are in Annapolis getting justice—"

The driver spat in her direction, but the globule missed her.

"—for your wife. I will bring little Ambrose back here in one week for you, safe as a chick under a hen, I promise."

"I—" The man seemed confused. Eventually, he must have decided that Moll was trustworthy, for he agreed.

And now Moll had another child in her arms at her advanced age. It being temporary was of no matter. Warmth spread through her.

The next week passed in a blur, as Moll tended to the boy, feeding him cow's milk, goat's milk, and sheep's milk, all of which she was able to procure in town on credit. Since she was known as the woman who was caring for the poor orphan, sellers overlooked her reputation and gladly extended the credit.

She put a drop of ale on her finger and let him suckle it when he wouldn't sleep.

She spent hours washing his linen diaper cloth, wrapping and tearing up her own coverlet to create more for him.

She sang to him, cuddled him, and tried to remember that he wasn't hers to keep.

When Moll arose the seventh and final morning, sunlight was already streaming through the openings in her cabin. How odd that she had overslept. Typically, the restless squawking of her chickens woke her. As of late, Ambrose's cry had also ensured she rose promptly.

She quickly used her chamber pot, then went to check on Ambrose.

The child wasn't awake yet. How strange.

She gently rubbed the infant's belly, but he refused to wake. Dread was creeping up her spine. "Ambrose, it's morning time," she said. "How about a song?"

She reached back into her memory for the song she used to sing when she went to the Friday markets with her mother.

There was a farmer's son,
Kept sheep all on the hill;
And he walk'ed out one May morning
To see what he could kill.
And sing blow away the morning dew
The dew, and the dew.
Blow away the morning dew,
How sweet the winds do blow.

But Ambrose was not moving. Moll rubbed his cheek, his head, his arms. No response.

Holy Mother, the child was dead.

Like poor little Callum. It had been nearly forty years since she'd lost her own child, and seeing the still infant lying before her, rushed back all the memories of her own dead babe.

It was too much for her. Too much. Moll started sobbing over the child's body. The sobbing didn't recede but instead grew into a wailing so loud that the birds in the trees outside became agitated.

Moll didn't care. How was it that God hated her so much that He allowed all this devastation into her life?

Now she would have to hand a dead child over to his father, a man who had just witnessed his own wife being violently killed. How was she to do this?

But she did, calming herself down several hours later and bundling him up in the blanket she had found him in.

It was the longest trudge she had ever made into town. Her mind was frozen over how to explain this to Ambrose's father.

What explanation was there?

Could she make him understand that she, too, had lost her own child as a swaddling infant?

But that would only cast a pall over Moll. Friend of a witch and now two dead children under her care.

She shivered and held the tiny corpse closer to her, murmuring and cooing to him as if he were still able to hear her.

Swallowing her own foreboding, she found the boy's father.

There was little surprise that Ambrose's father

was furious. He was completely resistant to her entreaties and pleas and apologies, and he spread it about to anyone within earshot that Moll Dyer had neglected his child and let him die. "I should have never left him with that old woman," he said.

Someone shouted out that the man should haul Moll into court.

No, please God, not court again. Surely, she would suffer terribly at the hands of "justice."

Moll was shocked that the man declined to prosecute her. "I got no justice for my wife's murder, so why would I get any from my son's death?" the man said bitterly, snatching the unmoving bundle away from her.

"The court found the cart driver's recklessness to be an accident and gave him a mere fine. A *fine*. No justice at all. Now this."

Moll repeatedly tried to explain to Ambrose's father and the other townspeople gathered around that the child had been fine that evening when she laid him down for sleep and had died inexplicably overnight.

No one seemed to believe her.

Distraught beyond all reason, Moll stood in the town's center, once again crying uncontrollably.

Not just crying, but dropping to her face and beating her fists on the ground.

It gave her no solace, yet she seemed unable to cease the wailing and pounding.

"She's a bit tetched, isn't she?" said a female passerby.

"Wasn't she close to that witch, Rebecca Fowler?" said another.

Even the pointed comments had no effect on Moll's grief, which was just an outpouring of over six decades of sadness and troubles.

Eventually, though, she was worn out and exhausted. She managed to stop sobbing and rise from the ground. She dusted off her clothing as best she could, although by now she was filthy.

Head held as high as she could manage, Moll left the town and walked home. No one stopped to offer her a ride.

CHAPTER 49

August 1697

AFTER AMBROSE'S DEATH, most people gave Moll a wide berth upon seeing her in town.

They also stopped buying her goods, thus drying up the tiny bit of income she had. Any thought of selling elixirs in town had vanished.

Further inflaming her problems was the weather.

The summer had proved to be hotter and drier than normal. It was so parched that she found herself gasping after spending any length of time outside. Even hanging laundry on the line was exhausting. Or was it just her age making her infirm?

One day in town, she made the mistake of commenting to a stall vendor, whose meager offerings wouldn't satisfy a dog, that she was harvesting her summer vegetables—some beans, onions, and beets.

That earned Moll a suspicious look. "How do you have so much luck with your crops? I am lucky to pull a few withered ears of corn each day."

Moll scurried away, unwilling to have an argument with any townspeople.

Perhaps she should have explained her irrigation

system, but of what use would it be to others now, when there had been no rain in weeks?

Even the tobacco farmers were rumored to be suffering, despite tobacco thriving in dry warmth. It was simply too arid for anything to grow well.

She wondered if the Woodalls' crops were dying. Maybe that was why she no longer received anything from them.

Moll kept to herself after her encounter in town, tending to her garden and preserving her harvests to ensure she could make it through the next winter.

It did seem as though Moll could no longer do anything right in the eyes of the Newtowne Hundred populace. Everyone had turned against her.

And it had all started fourteen years ago with that little swine, Jack Cole, who had disappeared from any known existence.

Despite Moll's resolve to avoid contact with other people, she became overwhelmed by loneliness and heat. Venturing on a walk toward town, she stopped at what had been her own inn.

Porters Inn and Alehouse
John and Jane Porter, Proprietors

The new owners had hardly changed the name. The exterior looked much the same, although the owners had cleared out more brush than she had, and had appeared to have built both an icehouse and a smokehouse.

It had been seven years since she'd stepped foot inside, and she hesitated briefly at the door. A woman in an apron saw her and welcomed her in. "Mrs. Dyer, isn't it?" she asked. "I remember you. Hope you like what we've done to the place."

Moll nodded her head, suddenly overcome with grief once more over the loss of her business. "Just want some refreshment. Cider, if you please."

Mrs. Porter nodded and went to her back room— Moll's back room—to fulfill Moll's request.

As her eyes adjusted to the darkness of the tavern, Moll noticed that she was the only patron there. That was preferable to having to interact with anyone, whether local or a stranger.

She sipped the cider, which she had to admit was quite good. The interior of the tavern was nearly as stifling as the outdoors, just without the blistering sun, so after an hour, she paid her bill and left. The charges took almost all her spare money. She would have to be much more careful in the future. Winter was coming.

Once outside in the hot sun, she decided to take a walk down to the stream in which she once washed linens and plates. She took a circuitous route so as not to alert the proprietress that she was meandering on the property.

The smell of the tavern's burning hearth carried through the woods. The owners were roasting rabbits, if she wasn't mistaken. It had been a long time since she'd eaten any tasty game.

At the stream, she was startled to find two men down there, seemingly joking with one another. She stopped, unsure whether to proceed, but decided that if she were trespassing, so were they.

It was when she got closer that she realized who was there.

Jack Cole and Davy, the Piscataway.

They were older and taller, but each looked much the same as he had before.

They were not joking with each other, though. Jack was taunting Davy with a bottle of liquor—no doubt rum—demanding that he perform tricks for it. Davy appeared to be willing to do it, hopping like a frog and barking like a dog.

How was it that Davy was still so smitten with liquor?

Moll charged forward to confront Jack. The snapping of twigs and rustling of leaves beneath her feet caught his attention.

His gaze widened at seeing Moll. "Are you still alive?"

What a cretin he continued to be.

"What are you doing to poor Davy? You know that it is illegal to sell liquor to him, and you are treating him worse than any animal."

Jack was unperturbed. "Sell it, sure. But I'm giving it to him. A gift in return for amusing me."

Jack wagged the bottle again. "Walk like a rooster, Davy," he said.

Davy obeyed, strutting and flapping his arms.

It was too much for Moll to watch the native be tortured like this.

"Stop it this instant," she demanded.

"Mind your own concerns," Jack said, scowling. He had grown from a silly brat into a sullen bully in the years since Moll had last seen him.

But Moll had no fear of him. "Leave Davy alone. How did you even find him?"

A shrug. "Davy here showed up at the tavern. I'm working there again. The Porters appreciate me more than you did."

So, Jack Cole had ingratiated himself with the

owners. They surely did not know of his antics with Davy.

Thinking of Jack abusing poor Davy reminded her of something else. "Where is Daniel these days?"

"He took an apprenticeship with a fuller. Nasty work. He was a fool to do it."

Maybe. Moll remembered refusing the work herself. But at least he wasn't spending his time teasing someone who lusted after rum.

"As much a fool as you, torturing this poor Piscataway?" Davy was no longer a boy. He'd grown into a lean, but pitiable, man.

"I don't stink every day. I told Daniel to keep his reeky self away from me until his apprenticeship is over next year."

Jack flicked his free hand in her direction, returning his attention to Davy. "Bet you can't drink the rest of this in one try." Jack was taunting him again. "If you can, I'll buy you more."

Moll was distressed as she watched Davy eagerly take the preferred container and, indeed, downed it all in several successive gulps.

Jack dissolved into laughter.

"This isn't funny. You are going to kill him," Moll said.

"Rum, please," Davy said, looking hopefully at Moll, then at Jack.

In return, Jack walked the few steps to Davy and pushed the Piscataway. "Go on with you, you sot," Jack said derisively.

Davy was full enough of drink that he was unable to maintain his balance and went tumbling to the ground.

Jack found this uproarious.

Moll's fury was such that she could hardly see. It

was as if blood was filling her eyes and blinding her. "You are a—"

But she couldn't finish her sentence, for Jack also pushed hard against Moll, sending her down. She landed hard on her rump. "Ah!" she cried out, closing her eyes and wincing from the pain.

Getting old seemed to mean being unable to withstand falls and bumps.

She opened her eyes. Both Jack and Davy were gone.

Days later, Moll swallowed her pride and walked back to the tavern to see if the owners wanted to purchase any of her vegetables. They didn't, and Mrs. Porter asked her if she'd heard the news.

"A Piscataway man was found drowned on the shores of Breton Bay." Mrs. Porter seemed to relish the news.

"Oh?" Moll said with as little curiosity as she could manage, as dread sluiced through her.

"They say his name was Davy." Mrs. Porter went on with the story, no doubt for the tenth time that day. "I hear tell that a Piscataway named Davy used to frequent this tavern when it was owned by you. Didn't a child recently die in your care? And weren't you associated with the witch, Rebecca Fowler? Isn't it interesting that yet someone else connected to you has died?"

Moll retreated into the solitude of her tiny cabin.

CHAPTER 50

February 1698

MOLL WAS STILL secreted in her cabin and only knew of devastation in the colony because a boy delivered a message to her one day.

"I'm to tell you that Mr. and Mrs. Woodall lost their daughter-in-law, Rose, to an ague last week." The boy's breath was a cloud of frost around him, and he shivered in his threadbare clothing.

Moll gasped at the news. "What other happenings are there in town? I don't get out much anymore."

The boy nodded and proceeded to tell her of the great suffering throughout the colony. "Lots of people dying. Churchyards are getting full."

Apparently, by last fall, not only had most crops failed within the area, but now livestock were dying off at an alarming rate because they lacked food. St. Mary's residents were scrabbling the ground for root vegetables to eat, and much of the wildlife had been killed for meat.

Moll stayed quiet, knowing she had preserved produce in her larder. She must be careful not to use it all up too quickly.

By the time winter had started, people were already weak from hunger. Then disease had come, tearing through St. Mary's County like a furious demon seeking the ruin of souls.

Moll did not have enough money to give the boy even a penny for his trouble. She gave him a jar of pickled beans. He beheld it as though it were a jewel before scampering off, avoiding icy patches along the path leading away from her cabin.

Moll's heart ached for Lawrence Woodall. It was a difficult thing to lose a spouse. Hugh and Lucy were surely suffering, too.

But she didn't have long to dwell upon the Woodalls, for a couple of days later, there came a furious pounding on her door about an hour after darkness had descended for the evening.

"Mrs. Dyer!"

The voice was familiar.

She opened the door, bracing herself against the frosty air. Standing before her was Daniel Cole, holding a lantern. Like Jack, he had grown into a man, only he had a far kinder countenance than his brother. She had no time to comment on Daniel's appearance, for he spoke urgently.

"Mrs. Dyer, quickly, there is a mob headed this way, and they have torches and weapons. You must leave." His breath crystallized into a vapor cloud around him.

Moll shook her head. "A mob? What are you saying? Why would anyone be coming for me, and in this freezing weather, no less?"

She opened the door further to allow him in, but he refused. "There is no time for a visit. They will be here soon, and I am quite certain they mean you bodily harm."

"I am a benign old woman. I—"

Daniel sighed. "You gave Dickie Bowles a container of vegetables, which everyone knows cannot possibly exist. And a seller in town remembered that you had fresh vegetables back in the summer. No one else has fresh vegetables."

"But that's because I irrigated—"

"And there was the baby that died under your care. His father said he was perfectly healthy until you took him away and worked magic to kill him."

Moll was aghast. "I offered to care for Ambrose when his mother was trampled. I cared for him with all my might."

"But he wasn't sick." By the love of the Holy Mother, Daniel was relentless, pummeling her with all these vicious rumors by the townspeople.

"No, but—"

"You were also friends with Rebecca Fowler, who turned out to be a witch—"

"But she wasn't," Moll protested. "She was—"

"—and people remembered you uttering curses at her hanging. Many said it was an ungodly way to speak. So, they think that maybe you are a witch, too."

Moll blanched. "But that is foolish thinking. I would never—"

"I know, Mrs. Dyer. But between the drought in the summer and the harsh winter we are having now, people believe there might be something supernatural at work in the colony. Witchcraft. And when they consider who might be the local witch, well…" Daniel spread his hands helplessly.

Moll put her hands to the sides of her face. Her fingers touched the wrinkles and sagging that now marked her visage. Each line and furrow represented a sorrow in her life. Now, Daniel was here to etch another one into her skin.

"You should know that my brother—" Daniel stopped, as if gathering strength for what he had to say. "Jack has been whipping people up about it all.

He is the one leading everyone to your property. You must leave. *Now.*"

That piece of news was of no surprise. What possessed Jack that he had to spread destruction wherever he went?

If she were truly a witch, she would come up with the worst possible curse for him.

Angry shouts came from the distance. "I believe I am too late," she said. She was simply too tired to continue fighting with people. She would tell the mob that she would leave St. Mary's County in the morning. Where she would go, she had no idea.

"Daniel, you must go. If they find out that you warned me…"

He nodded and melted away into the night. His lantern glow quickly dissipated.

Moll sighed as she shut the door, leaving her in darkness except for a couple of tallow candles that were quickly dwindling down. There was little difference in temperature within her cabin than outside, except that the wind didn't blow as hard inside.

She had no desire to have enemies, yet all of Newtowne Hundred was against her.

The word "witch" had followed her around all her life, from Devon to St. Kitts to now this unforgiving colony. What could she have ever done along the way to have prevented it?

She unlatched the shutter that covered the open window hole located next to the door. The shutter's wood was wormy and warped and did little to keep out either heat or cold, but it did provide a modicum of privacy.

She peered out and was startled by what she saw. There must have been twenty or thirty people out there, their faces contorted in anger in the bright light of their lit torches.

Thump, thump, thump. Someone was beating on the door. Moll closed the shutter.

"Mrs. Dyer, you have visitors!" It was Jack's voice booming out over the rest.

Gathering her courage and swirling it with anger at this miscreant who had caused her no end of trouble, Moll opened the door. The blast of cold was bone-chilling, but she refused to shiver.

Jack stood there, while the others stood back a distance. Except for Jack, they all seemed to be afraid of her. Good, she might use that to her advantage.

"What is it you want?" Moll demanded loudly.

As usual, Jack was brash and overconfident. "There's people in town concerned that you might be a witch. I told them I didn't think so, but that since I know you, I'd talk to you about it. They wanted to come along. In case of a spell or hex or something."

"Hmm." Moll didn't bother protesting as she had with Daniel. This group had made up its mind, no doubt thanks to the man who stood here pretending to be an intercessor.

"I can come in?" Jack said.

She stepped back to let him in. The torches provided light for the small interior of her cabin, and Jack was glancing all around. What did he expect to find? Moll owned practically nothing.

"If you have a message of innocence that I can take to them, I'm happy to do so," Jack said, his hands behind his back as he rocked on his feet.

"Why need you a message from me? You already know that I am no witch."

"I know nothing. People have been talking—"

"*You* have been talking. You must be the most

ungrateful creature that has ever lived. I took you in as an abandoned orphan, and you have done naught but repay me in insults and slander. I should think *you* are the one committing mischief in the colony."

That reeled him back for just a moment, but he quickly recovered. "If you have no explanation for your actions, I cannot be responsible for any punishment that may occur."

Moll crossed her arms. "Are you the sheriff now?"

"No, but the sheriff is also very suspicious of you." Jack continued glancing around. Suddenly, a malicious smile spread across his face.

He walked over to her table, the lone piece of furniture in her cabin except for a rickety chair. He grabbed the dragon that Moll had placed on the center of it. "This proves it," he said, clutching it in his hand and running outside before Moll could protest.

She stood back from the door opening as he held the toy dragon up in triumph before the others. "Look! It's proof! This is her familiar. She brings it to life to help her commit foul deeds."

Jack moved away from the house and went among the others, presumably to show off his find.

There were gasps in the crowd, followed by angry murmurs.

What was Jack talking about? A silly little carved wooden toy was suddenly her attendant? What was happening? How was she the cause of this… malevolence?

She had no more time to contemplate it, for after several incomprehensible shouts from outside, a torch crashed against the shuttered window. Light flared, but the torch did not break through, instead landing with a thud outside.

Moll panted in fear and anger. Jack had taken the

only valuable she still owned and turned it into an instrument of her demise. She ran back to the open doorway. "Listen to me, I am no more a witch than your mothers or your sisters or your wives. You are falsely—"

Another torch landed at her feet, and she jumped back. A third torch made it into the house, landing where she had just been standing. Moll tried to pick it up to throw it back outside, but it had already caught the rush mat that lay at the door. The mat flared quickly.

The men must have considered their work complete, for now they laughed and claimed they could all rest in peace now. The laughter became more distant as the fire licked up higher from the torch.

But Moll was rooted to her spot, for within the flames she saw a shadowy figure. It resembled Alexander Sparrow. At least what she remembered of him.

"Moll," he said. His voice was strong and clear over the crackling of the fire. "Forgive me for leaving you. You were faithful and I was not. I should have brought you with me to share life together. What a wonderful helpmeet you would have been. Instead, I died alone with smallpox."

Was Moll hearing spirits? Was she demented?

The torch's flame seemed to leap to another location.

Within that new flame, old Constance Woodall's face appeared, along with that of a man she did not know. The man asked, "Does my son, Hugh, still keep slaves? So terrible…"

Constance stopped him. "She is being persecuted, Fletcher. Let her be."

They both faded from view.

Moll must be delirious. Perhaps the smoke was affecting her reason.

A new flame rose up along the wall. What was that Moll saw in the fire? She blinked. It was Dada, holding out his medicine case to her. "Remember what I taught you," he said through the flames.

She blinked again. Another flame shot up next to that one. Granda and Mama were visible in it. "You're such a precious little girl," Granda said, smiling.

"Have you used the ale making skills I taught you?" Mama asked. Mama's expression was worried, like it was after her release by the Roundheads.

"I tried, Mama, but I was accused of selling liquor to a native—" Moll stopped. Mama and Granda, too, faded from view.

What was this madness?

Moll whirled around. On the wall behind her table, a flicker of flame had started. Mrs. Lugg's image was in it. Her old mistress reached out a hand. "You were wise not to come to England, Moll. I was part of the Jacobite uprising to restore Catholic James to the throne. King William dealt harshly with us."

"I never wanted to return to England—" Moll started. Surely the apparition was just part of her own mind's ramblings.

Mrs. Lugg was replaced by Yaddy and Sumbar. "We were freed and lived back in Ghana until more slavers came. We were torn apart from each other and our child. But now we are together and happy."

The building was fully on fire now, but the flames were not done torturing her.

Richard appeared, holding Callum in his arms. He smiled as though seeing her as a young woman at the market. "We are waiting for you, sweetheart. Don't be long."

Moll put a hand to her throat in terror, gasping for air and only swallowing smoke.

She put her hands over her ears and began screaming, not knowing whether she was going completely mad at the appearance of all these dead people.

William had not made an appearance in the flames. Did that mean he was still alive?

Moll whirled around again and made her way to the front door, reaching out blindly in the smoke with one hand and holding her dress close to her with the other to avoid popping embers.

She finally found the partially open door, then the door's latch. The latch was fiery hot, but she ignored the searing pain and threw the door completely to one side.

Moll stumbled outside, gasping and coughing, grateful that there was the tiniest bit of air out here.

Oh no. Her skirt hem was on fire. Moll dropped to the icy ground and rolled around, eventually putting out the flames. With effort, she dragged herself up. She had to escape her engulfed cabin.

Where was she to go? Should she head down her drive and to the main road? No, she had no idea where the mob was, but most certainly they had left that way and would not be pleased to see her.

She made her way into the woods. Surely the fire would consume itself when it was done with her cabin, and she could outrun whatever gains it might make.

Moll ran as fast as she could in the frosty air. As she ran, she realized she was barefoot. Dear God, everything beneath her feet hurt, and they quickly became numb.

As her feet froze, each step sent sharp, stabbing pains up her legs. She stopped and looked back. Her cabin was disintegrating, but, ironically, the roaring flames sent out a blanket of warm air. She stayed rooted to the spot for a few moments. She hadn't felt this sort of warmth in months.

But no, she had to escape, lest the flames begin leaping from tree to tree and engulf the woods.

Moll continued to stumble about, darting in one direction then another. Despite the heat from the flames, her feet were still frozen from the bitterly cold ground.

The illumination provided by her burning house wasn't enough to prevent her from tripping over a branch, which sent her sprawling. The pain was excruciating. She reached up an arm to touch her head, which was lying against a rock. No wonder it felt like stars shooting between her ears.

"Mrs. Dyer?" a man's voice called out from a distance.

Moll lifted her head and squinted at a shadowy figure coming through the woods toward her. Who was it?

Why, praise God, it was Daniel. He'd come back to save her. All would be well now.

She dragged herself to her knees, her hand still on the rock as she reached out her other hand to her rescuer. "You've come for me."

Epilogue

WILLIAM DYER AND his wife, Agnes, kicked through the rubble of Moll's cabin, searching for any of her belongings that might have survived what must have been a horrific fire. There was nothing.

William had finally saved enough money after a couple of successive business failures to sail to St. Mary's County on a large ship not likely to be attacked by pirates. Once landed, he and Agnes had been shocked by the flood of rumors about Moll in the colony. Not only had the gossip been overwhelming, it had also been ridiculous.

William's beloved sister could never have committed the acts of which she was accused.

And now she was gone.

A wolf howled in the distance, as if lamenting Moll's death. Next to him, Agnes shivered at the doleful crying.

William and Agnes had traveled north of St. Mary's City and stopped at Porters Inn and Alehouse for a night's stay, then made their way to Moll's cabin.

It was truly a ruin, completely unrecognizable as having ever been a building.

A man had come stomping out of the woods from behind Moll's cabin. "Oh," he said upon seeing them. "Who are you?"

"William and Agnes Dyer. Moll's brother and sister-in-law. Whom might you be?"

The man nodded. "Jack Cole. I was a dear friend of Mrs. Dyer's. Very distressing what happened. I found her, you know."

William took an instant dislike to Mr. Cole. If Agnes's stiffening next to him was any indication, she, too, was suspicious of Cole. There was something glib about the man.

And it wasn't like Moll to have a casual male friend.

"You did?"

"Yes, I went to save her, but she was too injured. Poor thing. Afraid she was put in a pauper's grave."

A wolf howled again, only this time the sound was closer.

William's neck prickled at both the coyote and the man before him. "What's that in your hand?"

Cole held up the object. "This? Oh, it's a rock that Mrs. Dyer was clinging to when I found her. She thought I was Daniel, my brother. He and I look alike, you know. I thought I'd come back for it as a souvenir—er, as a treasured keepsake—of her life."

William narrowed his gaze. "I think not. Put it back where you found it. My sister will not be reduced to a freak show attraction."

Cole had the grace to flush with embarrassment. With a nod, he disappeared back into the woods, the shuffling of leaves just a trail of noise in his wake, but fading the further he retreated into the woods.

William waited patiently. He had many questions to ask the man about his sister.

But he would not get to ask them.

A piercing scream rent the air, followed by angry growls and yips.

"Aaaah! I've been bitten!" Cole yelled. "Damned dogs! Help! Help! I'm dying!"

William picked up two large sticks, handed one to Agnes, then ran to find Cole, who was prone on the ground next to the rock he had dropped. He was bloodied from various wounds on his body. A gash in his neck bled profusely as he thrashed about wildly.

"Wolves must have run away at the sound of his screaming," Agnes said.

William nodded and went to Cole. "Stay calm. We will help stop the bleeding in your neck."

Agnes was at William's side, tearing off fabric from the hem of her dress. "If he will stop moving, I can try to staunch the flow."

But Cole was not listening. Instead, he babbled as he tossed about wildly. "She did this to me. She always hated me. Nasty old witch."

William frowned. "What did you say?"

Cole refused to quit whipping back and forth. "She once told me that the Devil made her hair red so that she could take care of the likes of me. She's doing it now."

What was the man going on about? Was the loss of blood making him mad?

Agnes glanced at William helplessly. "He's not going to allow me to help him."

"Ah, 'tis a fitting punishment for me." Jack Cole convulsed several times, and his breath was a frosty cloud around him. "I bit at Mrs. Dyer too many times to count. It is fitting that I now die of a sharp bite."

"What do you mean by this? How did you bite at my sister?" William didn't like what he was hearing.

Agnes knelt to soothe the man, continuing to encourage him to lie still and be calm so that he could recover. But Cole refused to do. He seemed to be in a delirium.

William tried several more times to get information from Cole, but the man became unresponsive, and soon his breath vapors disappeared.

As if in response to his death, there was silence all around them. Not a leaf crackled. Not a bird cawed. Not a branch snapped.

William was shocked by what had just happened. He was also angry that he had no answers as to what had happened to Moll, who would have been as elderly and harmless as he now was.

William knelt, too, and Agnes joined him as he prayed over the body.

"We shall have to find his kin to take care of him, husband," Agnes said when he was done. "I think he said his brother's name was Daniel."

William nodded absentmindedly. His mind was focused elsewhere.

"Agnes, do you hear laughter?"

His wife's expression was quizzical. "What? No. I hear nothing at all."

William cocked his ear up to the sky.

He distinctly heard laughter. His sister's laughter.

THE END

DID YOU ENJOY this book? If so, reviews are greatly appreciated on your favorite bookseller or social media site.Reviews impact a book's visibility, so you would be performing a wonderful deed for me if you could spend a few minutes giving your thoughts on this story.

Thank you!

Christine

AUTHOR'S NOTE

THE IDEA FOR this book came from the passionate work of my friend, Lynn Buonviri (1946–2024), who was dedicated to unearthing Moll's story.

Moll's life in Devon would have been wracked by poverty, disease, and war. The English Civil War raged in England from 1642 to 1651, and, like most civil wars, destroyed nearly everything in its path. Subjects who only wanted peace found themselves in a delicate dance between Royalists and Roundheads, both of whom were determined to win and neither of whom was willing to give an inch.

The Ulster Rebellion in Ireland, which had many causes that included Ireland's desire to have the Roman Catholic Church restored to its pre-Reformation position, was largely unnecessary. Had King Charles I reconciled with Parliament and given some credence to their complaints about his authoritarian rule, they would not have ended up squabbling about who should be responsible for quashing the insurrection, which might have been handled more diplomatically.

Instead, it became the starting point for a long and bloody civil war.

Lynn postulated in her book that Moll may have been married to a **Richard Northcutt**, but there is little information available, and he quickly disappears from the record. Also, Moll never took his name, suggesting that if they were indeed married, it didn't last long. Lynn theorized that Richard may have gone off to war and died. I took a different approach in my story.

Moll did have six siblings. Little is known about most of them except for William, who married a woman named Agnes and who, like Moll, took an indenture in the Caribbean. William eventually ended up in Dorchester on the Eastern Shore of Maryland, while Moll came to St. Mary's County after possibly going to Dorchester first.

One tiny point: Moll's sister, Dorothy, married Thomas Hawkins in 1655. To better fit the pacing of my story, I had their marriage take place prior to 1648.

Any other errors in the book are mine alone.

At the time of Moll's arrival on St. Kitts to serve **Thomas Lugg**, most sugar plantation workers were indentured servants. I can only imagine how scorching the sun must have been on her skin, as she would have likely been very pale from her life in England. In fact, most indentured servants were unable to survive the climate and tended to die at the same rate as slaves, although they did hold the glimmer of hope of freedom at the end of their indentures. It is a testament to Moll's fortitude that she survived *two* indentures.

Indentured servants were eventually supplanted by slaves from Africa, particularly from West Central and Southeast portions of the continent. Plantation owners reasoned that darker skin was more tolerant of the brutal climate. Whether this was true or not, slavery quickly became the standard for plantation labor.

I find it interesting that Moll was born in February 1634, just a month before the first English colonists landed in Maryland and had their first Mass on St. Clements Island, which was known initially as Blakistone Island.

The Calvert family were instrumental in the formation and success of the Maryland colony. George Calvert was made 1st Baron Baltimore by King James I for his loyalty. George converted to Roman Catholicism at this time.

George died in 1632, five weeks prior to the charter for Maryland being passed. The charter established Maryland as a palatinate, giving Baltimore and his descendants rights nearly equal to an independent state—absolute ownership of the land, both ecclesiastical and civil authority, and the general powers held by the nobility of the Middle Ages.

George's son, Cecil Calvert, 2nd Baron Baltimore, inherited the proprietorship of Maryland. Also Catholic, he continued his father's legacy by promoting religious tolerance in the colony. However, Baltimore never came to Maryland, instead staying behind in England to defend the charter.

He sent his brother, **Leonard Calvert**, in his place, making Leonard the first proprietary governor of Maryland, from 1634 to 1647.

Maryland's state flag today is the banner of the Baltimore coat of arms.

Father Andrew White was a critical figure in the St. Mary's settlement, working relentlessly to not only get the Church established in the colony, but to have a harmonious working relationship with the Piscataway. He was sent back to England in chains when St. Mary's City was invaded in 1645 in the name of Parliament. White would never return to the colony he loved so much.

Newtowne Hundred, today within the limits of the area known as Leonardtown, was the next important settlement after St. Mary's City. **William Breton** received a patent from Cecelius Calvert in 1640 for 750 acres, provided some of the land to the Church, and Jesuit priests soon began missionary activity in the area. Periodic anti-Catholic activities prevented the Jesuits from getting a toehold until Charles II came to the throne, bringing with him religious tolerance.

St. Mary's City, founded in 1634, was Maryland's first capital. Though the initial plans for the city were grand, it was never more than a sprawling mix of wood homes, taverns, docks, and shacks. After Moll's time, the city was abandoned when the capital moved to Annapolis in 1695. The city's buildings were torn down, and the ground returned to farmland. In the 20th century, archaeological excavations began that continue today. Because much of what lay deep beneath the ground was never touched by farmers' plows, reconstructions have been faithfully built atop exact post holes of the original buildings.

St. Mary's City is one of the most important 17th century archaeological sites in the country and is well worth a visit.

Pirates plied their trade throughout the Caribbean and the Chesapeake Bay during the 17th century. **Richard Makeele** was one such pirate who maintained a lair on Watts Island. Makeele appears in the record around 1685, thus he was surely roaming the seas earlier than that and may have been prowling about when Moll sailed to Maryland.

He and his crew plundered ships, towns, and tribal settlements all along the Bay, and he even reportedly attacked some homes along the St. Mary's County shorelines. When the Maryland Council issued a warrant for Makeele, he fled the region for the sounds in North Carolina, another popular hiding place for pirates.

Joshua Doyne was sheriff during part of Moll's time in Maryland.

Other real persons in the story include **William and Elizabeth Dyer**, Moll's parents; and **Thomas Lugg**, Moll's master in St. Kitts.

Minor characters with mentions that are also real include **Samuel Crossman**, the hymn writer; and **William Salter**, William Dyer's master in St. Kitts.

The "seasoning" that Moll undergoes was common for settlers. The humid climate, prevalent diseases, and unfamiliar insects made for a harsh welcome to colonists. Many didn't make it through their first year in Maryland.

What sugar was to the Caribbean, tobacco farming was to Maryland. Tobacco grew well in Maryland soil, and the demand back in England was voracious. For a time, planting tobacco was almost guaranteed money.

It was also labor-intensive, so plantation owners, like their peers in the Caribbean, resorted to slave labor.

I have not always used period-appropriate spellings of people and place names. For example, Maryland was frequently known at the time as Mary Land. But "Maryland" is such a ubiquitous spelling that I left it that way, thinking that the original spelling would be jarring to readers. The same applies to "Charleston," known then as "Charles Towne," as well as various bodies of water. The Patuxent River was called the Pawtuxunt, and Breton Bay was Bretton Bay.

On another note about St. Mary's County, local readers will observe that, although there are coyotes in the area, there are no wolves. However, wolves were plentiful in Maryland until the 1800's, when they became such a nuisance that they were largely eradicated.

Rebecca Fowler was a widow who, according to Lynn's research, was put on trial and executed for witchcraft in 1686.

Although Rebecca lived in Calvert County, she was transported to either Prince George's County or St. Mary's City to stand trial. In either case, she was hanged in St. Mary's City on October 9, 1685. Thus, it is within the realm of possibility that although Moll wouldn't have known her personally, she might have caught glimpses of Rebecca during her notorious trial or may have even witnessed Rebecca's execution. At a minimum, Moll would have heard about the poor woman's fate, with no idea that she would be accused of witchcraft herself just over a decade later.

It is worth noting that, according to Lynn's research, there were only four women and one man accused of witchcraft during Maryland's colonial period. There were also two other women executed for witchcraft aboard ships while en route to Maryland.

Moll's story, although largely lost to history, has reached legendary status in St. Mary's County. In 2021, the mayor of Leonardtown declared February 26th to be Moll Dyer Day, and it is now a weekend-long event celebrated with town festivities each year. We also have a Moll Dyer whiskey, a "Meow" Dyer cat cafe, and many other references to our poor, maligned "witch." Moll was also reportedly the inspiration for the *Blair Witch* franchise's fictional witch, Elly Kedward.

The rock upon which Moll purportedly died now sits on display under plexiglass at the St. Mary's County Historical Society headquarters at Tudor Hall Manor in Leonardtown. It was previously located next to the nearby Old Jail Museum. Lynn Buonviri was instrumental in seeing the rock removed to a more appropriate location with protection against the elements.

Moll is just one of many historical figures who have shaped St. Mary's County into the fascinating place it is today.

ACKNOWLEDGMENT

As MENTIONED, THIS book would not exist without the dogged research of my friend, Lynn Buonviri.

Lynn and I, along with our other friend, Faye Snyder, were all doll collectors. We would meet up for lunch every few months, and I remember Lynn becoming interested in Moll's story years ago. She took it upon herself to undertake the nearly impossible task of researching the reputed witch, trying to determine which "Mary Dyer" or "Margaret Dyer" she might have been, and spending countless hours poring through genealogical records.

Lynn was thorough in that way.

She even portrayed Moll on a few "ghost walks" through Leonardtown, Maryland.

She also managed to pick up a publisher, The History Press, along the way. Her editor thought Moll's story was too brief, and asked Lynn to also research other Maryland witch legends. Lynn's six years of hard work resulted in a book called *Moll Dyer and Other Witch Tales of Southern Maryland*, published in 2019.

I confess that I had no idea that Lynn was ailing so badly, and it was just like her to not let it show. But she had been fighting a tuberculosis–like lung disease for nearly twenty years when she passed in 2024.

Ironically, both Lynn and I served as docents at

the Samuel Mudd home (he of infamy for setting John Wilkes Booth's leg after Booth shot President Lincoln and then fell from the Ford's theater balcony). We had each served as docents decades apart; however, it was just another mark of what we had in common. Lynn would go on to be a docent at the Surratt House Museum, the place where Booth and his co-conspirators cooked up their hare-brained plot.

We both also had careers supporting the U.S. Navy, and we attended the University of Maryland together in pursuit of master's degrees.

With this book, Lynn and I now have one more thing in common, Moll Dyer, about whom there is little known except for what Lynn was able to unearth. I like to think that she would be pleased with my take on Moll's life.

Rest in peace, my friend.

OTHER BOOKS BY CHRISTINE TRENT

HEART OF ST. MARY'S COUNTY
St. Clements Bluff
Three Notch Safari
The Cedar Point Affair

THE ROYAL TRADES SERIES
The Queen's Dollmaker
A Royal Likeness
By the King's Design

THE LADY OF ASHES MYSTERIES
Lady of Ashes
Stolen Remains
A Virtuous Death
The Mourning Bells
Death at the Abbey
A Grave Celebration

FLORENCE NIGHTINGALE MYSTERIES
No Cure for the Dead
A Murderous Malady

SHORT STORIES & ANTHOLOGIES
A Death on the Way to Portsmouth (eBook only)
A Pocketful of Death (The Deadly Hours)
Mrs. Beeton's Sausage Stuffing (Malice Domestic
Presents Murder Most Edible)

About the Author

Christine Trent is the author of the Lady of Ashes historical mystery series, the Royal Trades historical fiction series, the Florence Nightingale Mysteries, and the Heart of St. Mary's County series set in her beloved, history-rich Maryland hometown. The most recent book in the series, The Madness of Moll Dyer, fictionalizes the life of a legendary Maryland witch.

Want to read samples of Christine's work and learn more about her?
Visit *www.ChristineTrent.com.*

Sign up for her newsletter and receive periodic updates about booking signings and upcoming releases..

www.ingramcontent.com/pod-product-compliance
Lightning Source LLC
Chambersburg PA
CBHW051205220726
48293CB00014B/1914